CORRUPTED MEMORY

MEMORY

A TUCKER MYSTERY

RAY DANIEL

MIDNIGHT INK

WOODBURY, MINNESOTA

FIRST EDITION
First Printing, 2015

Book format by Bob Gaul
Cover design by Ellen Lawson
Cover images: iStockphoto.com/4514278/©sorsillo
Editing by Nicole Nugent

Midnight Ink, an imprint of Llewellyn Worldwide Ltd.

This is a work of fiction. Names, characters, places, and incidents are either the product of the author's imagination or are used fictitiously, and any resemblance to actual persons living or dead, business establishments, events, or locales is entirely coincidental.

Library of Congress Cataloging-in-Publication Data
Daniel, Ray, 1962–
  Corrupted memory: a Tucker mystery/Ray Daniel.—First edition.
      pages; cm.—(A Tucker mystery; 2)
  ISBN 978-0-7387-4230-4 (softcover)
  1. Hackers—Fiction. 2. Family secrets—Fiction. 3. Murder—Investigation—Fiction. 4. Domestic fiction. I. Title.
  PS3604.A5255C67 2015
  813'.6—dc23
                              2014050110

Midnight Ink
Llewellyn Worldwide Ltd.
2143 Wooddale Drive
Woodbury, MN 55125-2989
www.midnightinkbooks.com

Printed in the United States of America

ACKNOWLEDGMENTS

Thank you to my wife Karen for supporting my writing career in all ways possible. She's lent me confidence, advice, critique, and editing at the times that I needed each of them. I wouldn't be writing without her. She's also an outstanding copyeditor.

Tom Fitzpatrick lent his outstanding copyediting skills to *Corrupted Memory*, reading an early copy and finding the spots where my meager understanding of comma usage let me down. Thank you, Tom, for taking the time to read and critique the manuscript.

Thank you to my agent, Eric Ruben, for being an early fan of this book and for finding it a home with Midnight Ink.

Speaking of Midnight Ink, thank you to Terri Bichoff for having faith in *Corrupted Memory* and Tucker, and to Nicole Nugent for saving my bacon with her remarkable fact-checking skills.

Thank you to Scott Aron Bloom, Kay Allerdt Helberg, and Tim McIntire for reading early versions of the book and giving me feedback. As always, thank you to Clair Lamb for her outstanding editorial guidance.

Finally, thank you to my friends at Mystery Writers of America and Sisters in Crime who make it so much fun to be part of the mystery-writing community.

AUTHOR'S NOTE

Corrupted Memory is a work of fiction. To be clear, the military aerospace company in the book, Global Defense Systems, is a fictional company. It does not exist and it is *not* a stand-in for any of today's military aerospace companies.

I have had the opportunity to work with many people from the military aerospace industry. I have the upmost respect for the work they do, and I hope they enjoy reading *Corrupted Memory* as much as I enjoyed writing it.

ONE

RED SOX FANS ARE nature's yo-yos. On the way up, we experience an unreasonable exultation that assures us that all is right with the world, that the planets are aligned, and that God loves us. Then we crash, and as we fall we know that life is only suffering, that the world is a cold and malevolent place, and that love and passion are just ruses designed by a vengeful God to crush our spirits and kill our pathetic shoots of springtime hope.

It was a warm September night, and I was on the way up.

The Red Sox were winning. "Sweet Caroline" rang in the bottom of the eighth inning. And the seat next to me, instead of being empty, held a high school biology teacher named Lucy. We were on our third date, having navigated the shoals of introductions, coffee, and dinner to reach the point where I had invited her to a Red Sox game. Better yet, she had just invited me to her apartment to see a baseball autographed by Roger Clemens.

"Bum bum bum!" Lucy sang, pointing her finger at the field to punctuate each *bum*.

The song went on to say that good times had never seemed so good, and I had to agree. My seats are on the first base side of Fenway

Park, up underneath the roof, protected from the rain in the fall and the sun in the summer. We had a clear view of the pitcher and plays at first base. My dad bought the seats in 1987, just after Bill Buckner and the 1986 Red Sox collapsed in the face of the Mets and the forces of history. He was sure that the Sox would be back in the World Series the following year, but he was wrong. The Sox didn't see the World Series again until 2004, when we beat the Yankees four straight and swept the Cardinals.

I was at Game Four when Dave Roberts stole second base and reversed the curse, but my dad wasn't. He had been dead for years, dropped by an aneurysm. I went to that game with my best friend, but I would have given anything for my dad to be standing next to me that day.

Lucy danced until the end of the song, her ponytail bobbing through the back of her pink Red Sox cap. We sat and I draped my arm around Lucy, squeezing her shoulder as she leaned into me. The Orioles bullpen was horrible. The Red Sox drew a walk, hit a single, and then hit a ground ball to the pitcher, who bobbled it, picked it up, looked at third, realized he was too late, spun to first, and realized he was too late again. Bases loaded.

I drank my beer and felt my Droid cell phone vibrate in my pocket. I looked at the screen. It was Bobby Miller, my buddy from the FBI.

Talking on a phone at Fenway was useless, so I texted.

At the ball game. Sox winning. Too loud to talk.

The phone buzzed again.

Need you now. Meet me at your house.

Lucy asked, "What's up?"

"My buddy wants me to go home."

"You're not going, are you?"

I laughed and pointed the phone's camera at her. "Smile."

Lucy gave me a brilliant smile, all white teeth, blue eyes, and tanned September skin. I took the picture and showed it to her. She nodded and I sent it to Bobby's phone with a message.

`Busy tonight. See you tomorrow.`

The Sox were already beating the Orioles 9–2, but the crowd smelled blood and was cheering for a complete drubbing. It looked like they were going to get it. The Sox cleanup hitter stepped to the plate.

My phone buzzed again.

`Get your ducking app down here.`

I showed my phone to Lucy. "He says I should get my ducking app down there."

"Your ducking app? What's a ducking app?"

I program computers for a living. I'm very good at it. I'm especially good at fixing bugs. All bugs look like this one: you have something that makes no sense, and you need to find the key that explains it. The answer usually comes in a flash of insight, like the one that hit me now.

I said, "Autocorrect. His phone thought it was fixing his spelling."

Lucy grabbed my wrist, sending a thrill up my arm, and looked at the phone. "Fucking ass?"

"Bingo."

"He said that you should get your fucking ass down there?"

"Yeah," I said, typing.

`Bite me.`

The Sox grounded into a double play. The crowd moaned and sat. A few idiots started for the exits. Amateurs. You don't sit through a whole baseball game and leave a half inning before it's finished. That's like leaving church in the middle of the closing prayers. Besides, half the fun of winning is listening to "Dirty Water" blare over the loudspeakers at the final out.

My phone buzzed again. I expected another badly spelled expletive, but instead Bobby had sent me a picture. I opened the picture and my stomach climbed through my chest. I put my beer down on my foot. It spilled under the seats. The crowd, the Sox, and even Lucy disappeared as I stared at a picture of a dead guy, lying on a brick sidewalk. The picture was small and grainy, obviously taken with Bobby's camera phone.

It looked like my father.

My brain stuttered and locked up. The guy had my dad's sandy brown hair, his pushed-in nose, his powerful, squat build. I had none of those things. I took after my mother, with her slender northern Italian roots. The guy's eyes were open. Blood pooled on a brick sidewalk. I lived on a street with brick sidewalks.

I texted.

`Is this guy in front of my house?`

`Yes.`

I showed the picture to Lucy and said, "It looks just like my dad."

She said, "But your dad's dead, right?"

"Right."

Another text from Bobby.

`Now get down here.`

Lucy stood. "Let's go."

TWO

WE EMERGED FROM FENWAY'S staircase onto Yawkey Way, where the sausage vendors and T-shirt booths caused blobs of people to block the road. I took Lucy's hand. We dodged down Yawkey toward Boylston. Walking home would take too long. I spotted a kid on a bicycle-powered rickshaw emblazoned with the logo of a local burrito company. I helped Lucy in and gave the kid a twenty. These kids worked for tips and they usually got paid at the end of the ride. By paying him first, I'd made him my buddy.

"Get us to Follen Street in the South End and crank on it."

"You got it, dude!"

He darted the rickshaw out into Boylston Street traffic and headed downtown. Lucy slipped closer to me, our hips touching. We looked at the picture again.

"This can't be my dad," I said. "My dad's dead."

"I can see that it still bothers you," said Lucy.

"It was years ago. I'm over it."

"I guess so," said Lucy. "It's just that your hands are shaking."

I held my hand out, palm down. The fingers bounced of their own accord.

I said, "That's disturbing."

Lucy put her arm around me and gave me a peck on the cheek. "It'll be okay."

A small dart of irritation shot through my stomach. I tensed, and Lucy took her arm back and sat facing forward.

"I shouldn't have come," she said.

"No. I'm glad you're here. I'm sorry. This is just so bizarre."

"Were you close to your dad?"

The kid slipped our rickshaw in front of a cab. The cabbie jammed his brakes and leaned on the horn. We had no seat belts. I imagined us sprawled across Boylston Street, cars bumping over our bodies.

"This was a bad idea," I said.

"I think it's fun," said Lucy. She snuggled back in. I put my arm around her and steadied us in the rocking seat. Her question popped off the stack in my head: *Were you close to your dad?*

"Yeah. I was close to my dad," I said. "I mean, I didn't see him much, and we were very different people, but..."

"Different how?"

I slid into Lucy as the kid turned the rickshaw and drove over the Mass Pike bridge, down Dalton Street. The traffic lightened immediately. Other rickshaw drivers had congregated on the bridge like livery cab horses. The kid rang a little bell at them and they waved. We rode past Bukowski Tavern. I would have given anything to be sitting there instead of rushing to view a corpse. I pointed at the Tavern's red facade. "We should have dinner there sometime."

"Really? It looks like a hole in the wall."

"Exactly. It's my happy place."

"I'd love to see your happy place."

We pedaled past the Tavern. It was all downhill from here. We passed the dark expanse of the Christian Science reflecting pool and careened across Huntington Ave. I'd had enough. I called up to the driver, "You can leave us here."

I helped Lucy out of the rickshaw and handed the kid another ten. "Thanks."

"Sure thing, dude." He pointed down the road to the corner of Follen, where a police car was flashing its lights. "Man, there are a lot of cops over there."

"I know."

I took Lucy's hand. We walked toward the flashing blue lights.

THREE

Confusing the South End with South Boston is viewed as an insult by the residents of both neighborhoods. South Boston considers itself a working-class Irish neighborhood where real men in hard hats drink coffee from the local Dunkin' Donuts in the morning and beer from the local bar at night.

The South End, with its brick streets and houses, is better associated with Starbucks. It has been called artsy, gay, and "full of moonbats." I'd call it diverse. The neighborhood was planned by Charles Bulfinch in the nineteenth century and was built when Boston replaced its swamps with brownstones. I live on the top floor of one of those brownstones—the one with a dead guy on the front stoop.

Lucy and I turned the corner to Follen. Bobby Miller was in a group of people surrounding a mass on the ground. With his bald head, barrel chest, and custom suit, Miller looked like a bowling ball on a job interview. We joined the group and stood next to Bobby. He glanced at me, saw Lucy, grabbed my arm, and pulled me aside. Lucy followed.

"Jesus, Tucker, you brought your date?"

"She's standing right behind you," I said. "Her name is Lucy."

Bobby turned and shook Lucy's hand, "Pleasure to meet you, Lucy. You take a very nice picture." Then he spun back to me. "What the hell are you doing?"

I said, "A gentleman doesn't dump his date in the Fenway Park grandstands."

Bobby said, "A gentleman doesn't bring his date to see his brother's body in the street."

Lucy put her hand to her mouth and looked at the covered body. I said, "I'm sorry. My what?"

Bobby said, "Your brother. I'm sorry, man, I didn't know that when I called you. We just found ID."

"What are you talking about? I don't have a brother." I reached out and put my hand on Lucy's back. She was tearing up. "It's true." I told her. "I don't have a brother."

Bobby said, "You mean, like he's dead to you or something?"

"No, like he never existed. I'm an only child. I always wished I had a brother, but I don't."

Bobby beckoned me back to the body. Lucy followed and looked over my shoulder as he flipped the sheet off the face and shined his flashlight on it. The guy's eyes were unblinking in the beam.

I'd seen pictures of my dad when he was twenty-something. They were taken during the '60s. In a decade where you had to choose between hippie or establishment, he chose establishment. He was an engineer for a defense contractor and wore the crew cut and white shirt that was made famous by the NASA engineers during the space program. He worked for the same company until the day he died.

The guy under the sheet was a young version of my father. He looked just like my dad in those old pictures, except that he was the modern edition. He had a buzz cut instead of a crew cut. He wore a blue button-down shirt instead of a white one. His button-down had a hole in it. His chest had been blown open. The two buttons over his sternum were gone. The pocket remained, with a logo on it. It was the logo for Global Defense Systems: GDS. My dad had worked at GDS.

I pointed to the logo. "So that's why the FBI is interested in this."

Bobby ignored the comment. He asked, "You don't recognize this guy?"

I said, "Of course I recognize him. He looks just like my dad. It's the only reason you got me out of Fenway."

Bobby flopped the sheet back into place. "What does that tell you?"

"That there are people out there who look like my dad."

"Here's his ID. Check out his last name."

Bobby handed me a Massachusetts driver's license in a plastic bag. The license was blue, with a crappy picture of a guy who looked a lot like the one on the bricks. The license had a silver authentication shield across it and a little heart in the corner that told me someone was going to get this guy's kidneys. The address in the center read *Pittsfield, MA*.

I said, "Pittsfield? That's a hundred miles away. What was he doing here?"

Bobby said, "Read the last name."

Lucy read the name from over my shoulder. "Tucker. His name was John Tucker."

I said, "That's my father's name."

Bobby said, "I thought you'd say that."

"It doesn't prove anything. It's a coincidence."

Bobby asked, "If your dad's name was John, why did they name you Aloysius?"

"I was named for my dad's father. He was killed at the Battle of the Bulge, and my dad wanted to honor him."

"Jesus, by naming you *Aloysius*?"

I handed Bobby the license. "Can I take Lucy home now?"

A short Asian guy with a wide face and scraggly hair joined us. He asked Bobby, "Is this the brother?"

I said, "He's not my brother."

Bobby said, "This is Lieutenant Lee. He's investigating your— John Tucker's murder."

"He's investigating it? Then what are you doing here?"

Bobby turned away. "I've got to go." He waved to Lucy. "Nice to meet you."

I said, "Yeah but…"

Bobby said, "He's all yours, Lee."

Lieutenant Lee shook my hand and said, "I am sorry for your loss."

I said, "This is ridiculous."

I broke the handshake and turned to Lucy. "C'mon, let's go get you a cab."

Lee pointed at the body. "Mr. Tucker. I have proof that this man is your brother."

"Really? Why should I believe your proof?"

"Because you wrote it. You need to come with me."

FOUR

I SAT IN A conference room, remembering the soft brush of Lucy's goodnight kiss. That memory plus the buzzing government-issue neon light combined to foment a foul mood that began in my loins and sat in my gut. Lee was pissing me off, and he hadn't said a word. I looked at my watch. Past midnight. The Sox would have finished off the Orioles by now.

Lee bustled into the conference room holding a manila folder. He sat in a chair opposite me, scraping it across the linoleum. The pads had broken off and I could hear the metal chair legs gouging the tiles.

"Mr. Tucker. Your father worked at Global Defense Systems?" asked Lee.

"Yup."

"What did he do?"

"He was an engineer."

"Agent Miller tells me that you are an engineer."

"Really. How did that come up?"

"The victim was also an engineer at GDS. Miller noted that your father had produced two of them."

"My father did not produce two of them. He only produced me."

Lee sighed. "None so blind…"

"What?"

"Nothing. Your father worked on the Paladin missile. Am I correct?"

How would Lee know that? The Paladin missile was probably the most famous piece of disposable military hardware in history. It was a surface-to-air missile that had been designed to shoot down airplanes, and it would have remained an obscure project if it had been used for its original intention. It got famous when the Army used it to shoot down Iraqi missiles.

I said, "Dad didn't talk much about his work."

"Very strange," Lee said, pulling a plastic sheath out of the envelope. "It was probably just so long ago that you don't remember it."

"Don't remember what?"

"Your work on the Paladin."

"Shit, Lee, I didn't work on the Paladin. I was like six."

"In fact, you did work on the Paladin. It was this work that brought your brother to your door."

"I told you, he's not my brother."

"You want me to believe that he just wound up there randomly?"

"Yes."

"With your father's name and your father's nose."

"I guess so."

"Then explain this," Lee said. "John Tucker had it in his hand when he died."

Lee slid the plastic sleeve across the table. Inside was a single sheet of paper. The paper had a smear of blood on it, where John must have clutched it after being shot.

The lower right-hand corner bore the logo *GDS*—Global Defense Systems. This was an engineering document. Across the top were the words *Paladin Air Defense System.*

The rest of the page was taken up by a single drawing that represented the Paladin Air Defense System in action. Bombers streaked across the sky while a cannon fired upon them from the lower left corner. You could tell it was firing because there were slashing lines, in crayon, from the tip of the cannon to the planes. Wherever the lines met a bomber, a flurry of jagged lines obliterated the plane.

Around the lower left-hand corner, stick figures in baseball caps waved their little stick arms in the air and jumped for joy. They had two dots for eyes, and big smiley faces. Some were in profile, with one dot for an eye and an arc for half a smiley. The cannon itself had an American flag drawn on it in pencil. It was a rectangle with five stars in the upper left corner and lines for stripes.

The artist's name was scrawled across the lower right-hand side of the drawing, in the large, double-sized print of someone who had just learned his letters. The *A* was a big teepee with a line across the middle. The *T* looked a like a little cross, and the *R* was a *P* with another line sticking out of it. The signature said *Aloysius Tucker. Grade 1.*

I remembered this drawing. My dad had come home from work one day and I asked him what he was working on. He said they were making a gun that could shoot down enemy airplanes before they could hurt us. That was in 1984, and the threat of nuclear attack permeated life so completely that even a six-year-old knew that we didn't want enemy planes hurting us. I had taken my angst and driven it into that picture. Not one bomber made it past my gun.

Dad told me it was a great picture and asked if he could take it into work. I never saw it again, and now I know why. My dad had turned it into part of a secret drawing, a whimsical cover for his documentation.

I rubbed the plastic sheath between my fingers and looked at a new feature in the document. Someone had written on it in red pen that jumped off the black-and-white page. My name, *Aloysius Tucker,* had been circled, with an arrow pointing to the circle. The other end of the arrow ended in two words: *My Brother.*

I had no idea who this guy was, and I had no idea why he thought he was my brother. But as I looked at the scrawl that defiled my artwork, a question slipped into my mind: *Why did he get the good name?*

FIVE

WAITING FOR LEE, I traced my fingers over the black lines that represented the Paladin missiles. Most ended in black, fiery explosions of crayon. One missed and went shooting off the side of the page. Even at six I'd known that perfection was impossible.

My eye drifted down to the title block in the lower right-hand corner. There was my dad's signature. It consisted of a gigantic *J* and an equally large *T*. The smaller bumps must have been the *h* and the *k*. I traced my fingers over the letters, remembering the time he had written that signature on a credit card statement to buy me a fishing rod. We had gone fishing that weekend, driving to a magical pond where I caught twenty bluegills using cut-up hot dogs as bait.

My dad had saved every bluegill bigger than five inches. We took them home and he showed me how to gut them and scale them and fry them whole with just a little egg and breadcrumbs. Then he showed me how to make tartar ...

"Mr. Tucker." Lee's voice broke though my memory. I looked up at him. Acne scars marred his broad nose. "Do you recognize the drawing?"

I nodded. "I drew it."

"Your brother wrote on it as well."

I slid the drawing back across the table. "He's not my brother. He was confused."

Lee took the drawing and put it back into the envelope. "Perhaps you are confused."

"That's ridiculous. My mother always talked about how happy she was to have only one kid."

"Why would she say that?"

"She said it whenever she got mad. You know, if I couldn't find my shoes or didn't take the garbage out on time." I mimicked my mother's voice with a nasal falsetto: "Tucker, you are so much work. Two of you would just kill me."

"That is a terrible thing to say to a child."

"She didn't mean it. She's a drama queen."

"So your mother is still alive?"

"Oh yeah, and I'm telling you, Lee, there is no brother. I begged my parents to have another kid. My mother would say that it would kill her, and my father said he had enough kids."

Lee ran his hand through his scraggly black hair, took out a handkerchief, and blew wet snot into it. Then he folded the handkerchief and put it back in his pocket.

"Mr. Tucker—"

"Please stop that," I said. "Just call me Tucker."

Another sigh. "Tucker, do you know your Bible?"

"I'm an apathist, Lee. I don't care about religion."

"In the Bible, God promises Abraham that he will be the father of nations. But Abraham's wife, Sarah, can't conceive. So she tells Abraham to sleep with her handmaid, Hagar, and Hagar gave birth to Ishmael."

"Okay."

"Then Sarah did conceive, as God promised, and she bore Isaac."

"Well, good for her."

"When I told this story to my children, they called Ishmael, 'A brother from another mother.'"

It was late. Fatigue clogged my brain. "What are you saying? That my dad was a man-whore?"

"Abraham was not a man-whore."

"That's a Bible story, Lee. In the real world, a married guy who gets another woman pregnant is a man-whore. That's what you're telling me about my father?"

The conference room door opened. Somebody peeked in and Lee nodded and stood. "It's late. Let us give you a ride home."

I stood and extended a hand. "I'm sorry I couldn't help you here."

"Thank you, Tucker. We will be in touch."

He led me out the door, and we started down the hallway. Another couple was coming the other way. It was a cop with a small woman with red-rimmed eyes. She wore a gray UMass sweatshirt, black sweatpants, and no makeup. There wasn't room in the hallway for all of us. I muttered, "Excuse me," and flattened myself against a wall.

The woman said thank you reflexively and looked into my face. Her unfocused gaze coalesced momentarily into recognition. She raised her hand as if to touch my face and took a small breath, about to speak. Then she changed her mind. Her face closed, and she continued down the hallway into a conference room with the other cop.

I asked Lee, "Who was that?"

"That was John Tucker's mother."

I breathed in her perfume, still floating in the hallway. It evoked dim memories of a bedtime story: *Where the Wild Things Are.* Lee blew his nose, and the spell was broken.

SIX

I awoke in the dark and glanced at my clock. A ghostly 5:02 told me that I had slept less than four hours. I burrowed my head into my pillow, willing myself to go back to sleep. It wasn't going to happen. The thinking had started. My debugger brain had been given a problem and had started sifting through it as if it were looking for a lost watch in a pile of leaves. Once my brain started churning like this, sleep was not an option.

Still, I tried for another hour, lying in my bed, suppressing the images and memories that boiled out of my subconscious, trying to connect to each other. I thought about Dad's absences. His business trips. I thought about the strange chill that had wormed its way through our house. Our occasionally tense family dinners. Despite my need to sleep, I kept digging further back into my memory, looking for answers.

It was the perfume. That was the trigger. I knew that perfume; not in an erotic way, but in a comforting way. The perfume smelled like a kiss on a skinned knee, a peanut butter sandwich with the crusts cut off, money for the ice cream truck. It smelled like love. It wasn't my mother's perfume.

I gave up on sleep when I saw predawn light around my window shades. I rolled out of bed and shuffled into the bathroom, then moved to the kitchenette and turned on the lights over the breakfast bar.

My little shotgun apartment was silent. It was an engineer's dream: a line segment, with one point in my living room at the front of the house and the other point in my bedroom. The kitchenette tucked into the side halfway down, with my office across from it. If my mother had lived here, the place would have been full of crap. Perhaps because of that, my apartment was perfectly neat.

I fired up the coffee grinder and started the coffee. Then I made myself an omelet, cleaning as I went, and sat down at the kitchen counter with my roommates. Click and Clack, my hermit crabs, had also started their day. Click scuttled across the pink sand, heading for the feeding sponge, whereas Clack clung to a chunk of driftwood I had picked for him at Revere Beach. I had also gotten them an assortment of shells that hadn't been festooned with paint and sprinkles.

I said, "Sorry to get you up so early, boys. This thing about a brother has got me all agitated."

Clack waved a claw.

"I don't know why it bothers me. It shouldn't. My father was a grown man and he's dead now, so what good can come of stirring the pot?"

Click moved a fraction of an inch on his log.

"You're right. John Tucker should have thought of that too. Even if he was my brother. Can you imagine that? Opening the door to him and having him say, 'Dude, I'm your brother.' It would have been freaky."

Clack stared at me.

"Yeah, I mean it would have been kind of cool. It would beat going to baseball games alone."

Clack had mounted the top of the sponge and was shoveling fish flakes into his mouth.

"Sure I miss going to games with my dad," I said. "It was the only time we talked. You'd think that if I had a brother, he would have mentioned it at a game. What's that, Clack? He *wouldn't* have mentioned it to me?"

Of course, the hermit crab was right. No generation wants to think about another generation having sex, much less talk about it. The night I lost my virginity, I got home late from a party and Dad had waited up for me so he could tell me how irresponsible I was and how much I had worried my mother. While I countered that Ma couldn't be that worried, because she was asleep, I never told him the real news: *Dad, I got laid!* He wouldn't have wanted to hear that. Instead, I told my best friend, Timmy. He slapped me on the back and gave me a high-five.

The same must have been true for Dad. He wouldn't tell me if I had a brother, and certainly he'd never tell my mother, but he'd probably tell his best friend. It was time to visit Uncle Walt.

SEVEN

THE NEXT MORNING SAW me tooling west on a highway that the rest of the country calls Route 90, but that we call the Mass Pike. The Pike runs the 120-mile length of the state connecting Boston to Worcester, Springfield, and, eventually, Pittsfield. Beyond that, you're in New York, heading for Albany.

While John Tucker had worked at the western Global Defense Systems plant in Pittsfield, my father had mostly worked in the eastern plant in the town of Wayland. Wayland, Sudbury, and Framingham made up the northern edge of a region called MetroWest, which lay twenty miles west of Boston.

The three towns had all been centers of Revolutionary fervor back in the day. At that time Wayland was part of Sudbury and had contributed seventy-five troops to the effort of breaking away from England because of taxes. Then, right in the middle of the war, Wayland broke away from Sudbury because of taxes. The people out here really hated taxes—an incongruous fact given that tax money funded Wayland's biggest employer, Global Defense Systems.

Wayland's GDS plant sat on the town's only "main road," Route 20, an old Indian path that had become a mail route (still called Boston Post Road) and had eventually morphed into a two-lane highway.

I arrived at GDS at eleven o'clock, which meant that the parking lot was full. I parked a quarter mile from the entrance, peered into the distance to find the lobby, then walked for five minutes through a vast asphalt desert.

Uncle Walt's car, on the other hand, sat next to the front door. GDS employees who had been with the company for forty years got a parking row right up front. It was a perk of longevity, and perhaps an admission from GDS that their forty-year employees might not survive the trek from the back row. My dad would have had one of these spots if he had lived long enough.

Dad had met Uncle Walt in this very parking lot. Neither believed in rising early enough to get good parking. Both believed a morning walk would make them stronger. So, every morning, they'd arrive in the back row at the same time and hike to the lobby together. My father, the engineer, and Walt, the janitor, had formed an unlikely friendship out of their daily battle against the New England elements.

Uncle Walt was not really my uncle. He was a pseudo-uncle, and we were connected by pseudo-blood. His uncleness derived from my parents' discomfort with me calling him either "Walt" (too informal) or "Mr. Adams" (too formal). Thus my dad's best friend, Walter Adams, became "Uncle Walt."

Uncle Walt leaned against his pickup truck waiting for me, his ropy arms crossed in front of his small runner's body, his bald head acting as a navigational beacon in the sunlight. He watched me navigate the last few rows of cars. We shook hands and hugged, Walt's strong, bony frame jabbing me in the shoulders. I gripped his bicep.

"Jesus, Uncle Walt, you are in great shape," I said. "Life's good?"

"Hell, Tucker, I got a truck, a motorcycle, and a mobile home. Couldn't be better! Let's go inside and get a cup of coffee."

We approached the security desk. A plump woman with black hair and crow's feet smiled up at us. "Walt, who is this young man?"

Walt clapped his hand on my shoulder. "Agnes, this is my buddy, Tucker. He's John Tucker's boy."

Agnes's smile dimmed, then brightened. "Oh, you mean *our* John Tucker." She patted my hand. "Your father was a wonderful man."

I said, "Thank you. What do you mean, *your* John Tucker?"

"We had a security briefing this morning and—well. I really can't get into it."

Uncle Walt said, "I'd like to sign Tucker in and get him some coffee."

"Certainly," said Agnes. "Sign in here. Do you have a phone with a camera on it?"

I said, "Who doesn't have a phone with a camera on it?"

"I know, it's just terrible. You'll need to leave your phone here with me."

GDS, like all defense companies and some commercial ones, staged elaborate scenes of security theater. These little dramas demonstrated that the security department had done all it could to prevent bad guys from stealing information, though they rarely did anything that would actually keep a bad guy from stealing information.

The problem with security theater is that it relies upon the bad guy to be honest. You ask me if I have a phone with a camera on it, and I hand over a phone. But if I'm a bad guy, I keep a camera in my back pocket.

I handed over my Droid, silencing it so that its ghostly Droid voice wouldn't scare anybody.

Agnes took my driver's license and put it into a machine that printed a temporary badge with an indecipherable little black-and-white copy of my license picture. She put the badge into a plastic holder with a clip on it.

"You need to wear this on your shirt front," she said. "Be sure to return it before you go. Have a nice visit!"

Uncle Walt and I entered the GDS labyrinth. I slipped back to a time when my dad had walked me through these same halls. I had just started at MIT and had enrolled in computer science. Dad was upset. He told me that I was smart enough to be a "real" engineer, and he had taken me on a tour of GDS to show me what "real" engineers could accomplish.

The place hadn't changed in all these years. The long hallways were painted a generic gray, a color that complemented the thin maroon carpet. Murals adorned the walls, successors to my first-grade drawing. They showed planes, ships, and tanks communicating within a web of network lines.

We reached an intersection where a large photograph showed a soldier in full battle gear. It was mounted under a sign that said, *Serving those who protect us. Quality is Job 1!* Next to the picture was a wall of military headshots. They were the adult children of GDS employees, a reminder of who would die if GDS's products didn't work.

The quasi-shrine made me feel as inadequate today as it had when my dad pointed it out years ago. While I was messing around with viruses and security software, real engineers like my dad and, apparently, John Tucker had been designing real hardware with a real purpose. We walked past the shrine without comment.

We bought coffee and sat against a window in the empty cafeteria. Breakfast was over, and the lunch rush was an hour away.

Uncle Walt said, "You know, your dad and I used to get coffee here every day. He'd sit right in that chair. It's nice here. Private."

"You guys talk about much that needed privacy?"

"Hell, Tucker, every man needs some privacy. Speaking of which, what's on your mind? I haven't see you in years."

I looked out at the trees. The leaves were a dark, tired green. It was almost time for them to turn orange and die. "Remember when Agnes called my father 'our John Tucker'?"

"Yeah. That was strange."

"Well, last night I saw the other John Tucker."

"Who is he?"

"He *was* a GDS employee who got murdered in front of my house last night."

"Holy crap. You mean he was mugged?"

"I don't think so. He was holding a drawing from the Paladin. The cover art."

"You mean that picture you drew for your dad when you were a kid?"

"My dad showed you that?"

"Yeah, before he used it on the Paladin. After that it was classified."

"This guy, John Tucker, had a copy of it. He had circled my name on the picture and written 'My brother' next to it. So the police think this guy was my brother."

"This guy was named John Tucker?"

"Yeah, from Pittsfield. You've never heard of him?"

"I never get out to Pittsfield. It's a hundred miles away. Your dad got to drive back and forth, but I was stuck here. Janitors don't travel."

I looked around at the little nook. Walt and I were wedged in the corner of the cafeteria, far away from everyone. It was time to ask the question.

"You were Dad's best friend. He'd have told you if he'd had another son. So I'm asking you. Do I have a brother?"

"No."

"My dad is dead now. You don't need to protect him."

Walt drank his coffee despite its burnt flavor. Maybe he liked it. I had given up on mine after smelling it.

He said, "It's not like your father didn't want to give you a brother—or a sister. Your mother put the kibosh on that. You don't have a brother, as far as I know."

"As far as you know."

Walt spread his hands. "What more can I say? There were lots of things your dad wouldn't tell me. The man worked at GDS. He knew how to keep a secret."

"Yeah, that's true," I said. "It was weird, though. I bumped into John Tucker's mother at the police station. She was really familiar. Maybe I should ask her."

Walt stood. I followed him back toward the front desk. "Doesn't make sense to me. If your dad was screwing around, he wouldn't have brought the girl around the house. If your mother got a whiff of anything, she'd have given that girl concrete galoshes."

"Come on, Walt. That's silly."

"Silly? Your mother and all those Rizzos are nuts. I'll tell you this, I told your Dad to stay away from your mother." He pointed two fingers toward his face and waggled them. "She had the crazy eyes."

I was silent.

Walt stopped walking. He put his hand on my shoulder and said, "I'm sorry, Tucker. I shouldn't have talked that way about her. She's your mother. I apologize."

"That's okay, Walt."

"How's she doing?"

"Fine, I guess."

We started walking again. "You should go see her. She's right around the corner."

Guilt shot through me and I frowned. "Yeah. I should."

Walt raised his hands. "None of my business. I shouldn't have brought it up."

We were silent until I reached the front desk and Agnes handed me my phone. I'd missed a call. I'd check it later.

I said to Walt, "You know, you're right. I should go visit my mother, and I shouldn't let this thing with her keep me from reconnecting with my cousins in the city."

Walt shook my hand. "Reconnect all you want, but I wouldn't mention this thing about John Tucker to your cousin Sal, or to any of the Rizzos. They scare the shit out of me." Walt put a finger aside his nose. *La Cosa Nostra.* He turned and walked back into GDS.

I shook my head. Walt came from an older generation who believed that all Italians were in the Mafia and all Irishmen were drunks. My generation was full of mutts like me. We didn't buy the generalities. People were people.

I headed back to my car, fiddling with my Droid. The missed call came from a 413 area code.

Pittsfield.

EIGHT

Bostonians have a simple view of the world. Looking west from Boston Harbor there's Downtown Crossing, Fenway Park, Route 128, some indiscriminate wasteland, then California. Pittsfield was part of the indiscriminate wasteland. I didn't know anyone in Pittsfield.

Or maybe I did.

I touched the 413 number on my Droid. Across the state, a phone rang. One simulated ringing sound, two simulated ringing sounds, three simulated ringing sounds. A woman's voice.

"Hello?" The voice was tentative, trailing up at the end, converting the greeting to a question.

I was stuck in that awkward moment when you blindly return a call. Mavens of etiquette frown upon "Who is this?" as a greeting.

I said, "Hi, this is Tucker. You called my cell, and I'm calling you back."

"Oh," said a quiet voice. "I'm sorry. That was a mistake."

"A wrong number?"

"A bad idea."

The pieces fell into place.

I said. "I'm sorry for your loss."

Silence.

"Are you still there?" I asked, testing the connection.

"How did you know it was me?" she asked.

"Technically, I don't know that it's you because I don't know your name."

"I'm Cathy Byrd," she said. "John Tucker's mother. But you knew that part."

"How did you get my number?"

"Lieutenant Lee gave it to me. He said we should talk."

I had no idea what to say next. There are no guidelines for this kind of conversation, no appropriate questions. The only question worth asking hung between us like my father's ghost.

It was Cathy's turn to test the line. "Are you there?" she asked.

I asked the question. "Is he my brother?"

"He isn't anyone's brother. He's dead."

"*Was* he my brother?"

A second of silence, and then a sob. I felt like a jerk.

Cathy spoke through her tears. "Why did you call me?"

"I'm sorry. I just have to know."

I heard the receiver clatter to the table. A landline. Then, faintly, the sound of Cathy blowing her nose, and a skittering sound as she returned to the call. "This is a terrible idea. You shouldn't have called. I don't want to talk to you."

"Then why did you answer?"

"I thought you were the funeral parlor."

I had forgotten her generation didn't use caller ID.

"I'm sorry," I repeated.

"I suppose I should invite you to the funeral."

Talk about bad ideas.

"I don't think that's appropriate," I said. "I didn't know him."

"Still, it's only right, ironic even. He'd always wanted to meet you, ever since—"

"Ever since what?"

"I can't do this over the phone. Please come to my house tomorrow. Noon, for lunch. I'll explain then."

What could I do? "Okay, I'll be there," I said.

Cathy gave me her address and hung up before I could back out.

NINE

I DROPPED MY ZIPCAR in the Hilton's parking garage and wandered onto Dalton Street. Took a right and headed down Dalton for my house. I didn't make it. The rippled waters of the Christian Science Church reflecting pool caught my eye and drew me in. I sat on a bench and watched the reflection of the First Church shimmer on the water.

The church's dome arched into a light blue September sky. Cumulus clouds drifted behind the church. A pigeon with a clubfoot clomped about with its mates, pecking at the ground for nonexistent food.

I'd had a brother, and the only thing we'd possibly do together was attend his funeral.

I pulled out my Droid and took a picture of the First Church with the brilliant blue sky behind it. Tweeted the picture:

`A good spot for contemplating life's sense of humor.`

It was becoming pointless to resist the notion that John Tucker had been my brother, regardless of what Uncle Walt had said. Still, I grasped at alternative explanations. Cathy had refused to answer a simple question: Was he my brother? Maybe he was a distant cousin.

The Droid was heavy in my hand. I futzed with it and dialed.

"*Buenos dias*, Señor Tucker," said Lucy.

"*Buenos dias*, yourself," I said. "I see the police got you home okay."

"They were great. They even dropped me off around the corner so my parents wouldn't see me getting out of a police car."

"I still can't get over the idea that you live with your parents."

"I don't live with my parents. They live in the downstairs apartment and I live upstairs. Still, they keep an eye out for me."

"Is it nice? Being watched over?"

"Tucker, what's wrong? Was that guy your brother?"

"Who knows. I've been invited to lunch with his mother tomorrow."

"And you're going?"

"Sure. Why not? It seems like the only way I'm going to know the truth."

"Do you really need that? The truth?"

Clubby the pigeon launched himself and flew away with his flock, heading for a little kid with an overflowing bag of popcorn. The kid saw the incoming swarm of birds and fled back to his father. He stood under his father's legs and peeked out at the flock. The dad took a handful of popcorn and tossed it into the mass of birds. The kid got the idea and tossed some, laughing as the birds pecked around their feet. Did I ever do that with my dad? Who else would remember him?

"Actually, I had another reason for calling," I said. "I feel bad that last night got screwed up. I'd like to make it up to you. Would you like to come over to my house for dinner tonight? I'll make us ratatouille with some fresh vegetables from Haymarket."

"Just the two of us at your house. Sounds like fun. Do you think my virtue would be safe with you?"

"Your virtue? What about *my* virtue?" I said. "I've heard that women today can be quite aggressive."

"I'll be good," said Lucy. "I promise."

"Me too," I said. "Let's have dinner at six and be done by eight. I wouldn't want your parents to worry."

"Okay. Dinner at six."

We broke the connection. I followed the reflecting pool to Mass Ave and crossed the street to Symphony Hall station. The train would take me to Haymarket, right by the North End of Boston.

I made a call before I descended into the tunnel. The phone got picked up on the first ring.

"Yeah?"

"Hey, Sal, it's your cousin Tucker."

"What the fuck do you want?"

That's some good family bonding right there.

TEN

PEOPLE SAY THAT BOSTON was planned by cows, whose random tracks were paved to make streets. This is grossly unfair, as much of the city is laid out in a logical Cartesian grid with alphabetical street names (Boston's planners having more imagination than those of certain other grid-like cities, who numbered their streets).

However, the cow-path theory of urban planning holds when it comes to the North End. The North End has been here from the beginning, its streets a warren of tight paths better suited to horses than automobiles. The neighborhood fills a rough semicircle that stretches along the waterfront from Christopher Columbus Park to the Charlestown Bridge. The straight border of the semicircle is a green park that was once an elevated highway. Hanover Street cuts through the neighborhood from the waterfront to the park, and Prince Street cuts the other way.

My mother was raised here, in a *Honeymooners*-style apartment on Prince Street with the rest of her Italian family: the Rizzos. I grew up visiting the North End to see my grandmother, celebrate holidays, and gorge on fried dough and quahogs at the feasts—annual street parties that celebrate the patron saints of Italian towns.

There was no feast on Hanover Street today, just the usual jostling of a busy community. It was three o'clock and even though it wasn't yet dinnertime, tourists blocked the sidewalks meandering down the Freedom Trail. They'd swing over to North Street to see Paul Revere's house, then past his statue, and on to the Old North Church. I dodged around them until I reached Cafe Vittoria, the self-proclaimed "Oldest Cafe in the North End."

The narrow cafe had a granite entryway, a raised white floor, and small chrome tables. A cappuccino bar ran along the one side, and tables ran down the other. One of the tables was tucked up against the window next to the entryway.

Sitting in the window, sipping coffee from a tiny cup, was my cousin Sal. He was alone and had a cashmere greatcoat draped over a chrome chair next to him. Sal saw me, frowned, and beckoned me inside.

Sal dressed like a classy undertaker, in a black suit with a blue striped shirt and a paisley tie. He was big in the way that a silverback gorilla is big—exhibiting an innate largeness that said *keep your distance.* He had always been bigger than me. He was the firstborn of my generation, sixteen by the time I arrived. He's been an adult for as long as I can remember.

Sal said nothing. He gestured for me to join him and then motioned to the barista, holding up two fingers and pointing at his biscotti as I pulled up a chair. He watched me sit and said, "I should kick your ass. You move back to the city and you go to the fucking South End with the fucking hippies, instead of to the North End where you got family. How come you never come around here?"

I never come around here because I don't want to be harangued about how I never come around here.

I said, "And how are things with you?"

"They're the fucking same."

"How is Auntie Rosa?"

Sal raised his hand shook his head, "Don't get me started. She's like all old people. She's got nothing to do till she dies except make everybody miserable. How's your ma?"

"Fine, I guess."

"You *guess*? When was the last time you saw her?"

I didn't want to talk about my mother. I hadn't seen her in six months, and I didn't want to get an earful from Sal. I was saved by the barista, who had gotten the message and brought us espresso and biscotti. I bit into a cookie rather than answer the question.

Sal drank his espresso and looked out the window at his world. Two guys in Bruins jackets walked past the window and nodded their hellos to Sal. He nodded back. I wasn't sure what Sal did for a living. He never talked about his work, and I never asked. But a lot of people treated him with respect.

I said, "There was a dead guy outside my house last night."

Sal said, "No shit. I guess the South End isn't as great as you think."

"I mean *right* outside my house. On my front stoop."

"You know the guy?"

"No. But his name was John Tucker. The police think he was my brother."

Sal grimaced and took a bite of his biscotti, slurped his espresso and said, "That's bullshit. Did you tell them that your ma had one kid and that was enough for her?"

"Yeah."

"And what did they say?"

"They said my dad might have been screwing around."

Sal shook his head. "Right to your fucking face? The cops got no respect."

I looked out the window and drank my espresso. We were silent for a moment, until I said, "You're right. Lee disrespected my dad. I never thought of it that way."

"Nobody thinks that way anymore. Respect. Family. Doing the right fucking thing. Nobody cares about that shit. Speaking of family, did you think I forgot my question? When was the last time you saw your ma?"

"Six months ago. On her birthday."

Sal pointed at me with his biscotti. "That's a fucking sin, you know? You gotta see your ma."

"It's complicated."

"It's not fucking complicated. You go. You see her. You bring her some candy and give her a kiss. What's so fucking complicated?"

The candy box would have been complicated, but I didn't say anything.

Sal continued. "You know, she could be dead tomorrow. Then what? Then you spend the rest of your life saying you should have seen her more. You never know when it's gonna happen. You of all people should know that. Your dad, your wife, even that fucking guy they shot in front of your house. None of them knew it was coming."

I finished my espresso, noting the brown smear of coffee grounds across the bottom of the cup as I considered the sudden losses in my life. Dad died of an aneurysm and my wife died in a home invasion. Sal was right: neither of them saw it coming, and I always regretted that I wasn't better to them.

Then this John Tucker got shot…

I looked at Sal. He had finished his espresso as well and was leaning forward to get up to leave. I put my hand out and touched his forearm. I said, "I never said the guy was shot. How did you know he was shot?"

Sal pulled his arm away and stood. He said, "I hear things."

I remained sitting and said, "And you didn't mention to me that you heard about this? What else did you hear? This guy was my brother, wasn't he?"

Sal took a step and loomed over me, pointing a finger into my face. He whispered at me in quiet fury. "What did I tell you? You don't have a fucking brother. If you had a brother, then someone would have introduced you and said, 'Hey Tucker, this is your fucking brother.' You would have bought each other birthday presents and seen each other at Christmas and maybe went to hockey games. But none of that happened, because you don't have a fucking brother."

I crossed my arms and said, "Well, we'll see what his mother says."

Sal put on his overcoat and said, "Who?"

"Cathy Byrd. John Tucker's mother. I'm going to see her tomorrow."

"Yeah, well there's something you gotta know about Cathy Byrd," said Sal.

"You know her?"

"Yeah," said Sal, walking to the door. He opened it and said, "She's a fucking whore." He walked out the door and took a left, heading toward the Paul Revere Statue and away from the South End.

ELEVEN

I PROBABLY SHOULD HAVE charged out into the street, chased Sal down, and made him explain himself about Cathy Byrd's whoredom. Instead, I stayed rooted in my seat. My older cousin scared me. Whenever I saw him, I reverted to being a six-year-old kid at holiday dinners, with Sal at the adult table and me at the little table with the plastic dishes.

I asked the barista, "What do we owe you?"

He said, "Don't worry about it, Sal has a tab."

I dug two dollars out of my wallet and put it on the table as a tip. Then I left the cafe and turned right toward Cross Street. I worked my way down Cross, over Salem, and into the produce store. I had a buddy there who got me the best produce.

"Tucker!" said Ralph. "What are we cooking tonight?"

"Ratatouille," I said.

"Dinner for one?" asked Ralph as he picked among the eggplants.

"Nope. Two this time. I've got a date."

"Good for you!" He hefted an eggplant. "Then this is a good size."

Ralph rooted among his vegetables, choosing green peppers, tomatoes, and the other ingredients of the dish and placing them into a paper bag.

"I was just visiting with my cousin," I said.

"Yeah? Who's your cousin?"

"His name is Sal Rizzo. Do you know him?"

Ralph placed the paper bag on the counter and said, "What do you mean 'Do I know him?' Of course I know him. I didn't know you were Sal's cousin. I'll have to start treating you with more respect."

"What are you taking about, Ralph? You treat me with plenty of respect."

"Yeah, well, you know. There's respect and then there's respect, *capisce*?"

I took the bag. "I guess. How much do I owe you?"

"Don't worry about it, it's on the house."

"No, seriously, Ralph, how much?"

Ralph waved me off, both hands in the air. "No. No. It's my gift to you. For your date tonight." He turned and started helping another customer.

The bag of vegetables rested heavy in my arms as I left the store and ducked into Maria's Pastry next store. I bought two cannoli and put them in the bag with the vegetables. I didn't say a word, didn't mention that my cousin was Sal Rizzo. I hustled out of the store, across the park that was once the Big Dig, and into Government Center.

It was time to visit the FBI.

TWELVE

City planners created Government Center in the belief that they could free the world of vice by bulldozing vice-infested buildings. They destroyed Scollay Square, the old red-light district, and replaced it with a brick plaza surrounding an inverted pyramid of a building. Apparently the planners had missed the irony of replacing a whorehouse with City Hall.

The whorehouses had moved over to Washington Street to create a new neighborhood of debauchery. This new neighborhood, the Combat Zone, did a flourishing business in porn and prostitution until it was finally destroyed by DVDs and the Internet. Today all that's left of the Combat Zone is Centerfolds—a men's club where, I'm told, they have ladies who dance with no clothes on.

After crossing Government Center, I saw a break in the traffic on Cambridge Street and jogged across, a perfectly legal move in Boston where pedestrians run wild and free. Bobby's office building followed the curve of Cambridge Street. I entered and took the elevator up to the FBI lobby, a plain, carpeted room that showcased large gold FBI letters along the back wall.

The receptionist was a prim woman with small reading glasses. Her short hair exposed dangly earrings made of colored glass. I smiled and told her, "My name's Tucker. I'm here to see Bobby Miller."

"What's the nature of your business with Agent Miller?" she asked.

I raised the bag of groceries and took out the eggplant. "I'm here for his therapy session."

She cocked an eyebrow. "Eggplant therapy?"

"Oh yeah, it's all the rage. We're hoping to have his hair all grown back in six months."

"What do you do with the eggplant?"

"Well, that's a matter of patient/doctor confidentiality."

"I see."

"Let's just say that the eggplant doesn't survive the procedure."

She picked up the phone and dialed. "Agent Miller, a Mr. Tucker is here with your eggplant … No sir, he's standing right in front of me. I think you should tell him to do that yourself. I'll bring him in."

The receptionist brought me to Bobby's door. I waggled the eggplant at him and asked it, "Did you miss your daddy?"

Bobby said, "Did Monique tell you to shove the eggplant up your ass?"

Monique giggled and walked away.

"No," I said. "She's obviously too much of a lady."

"Well, shove the eggplant up your ass."

"I've got other vegetables, you know."

"Why do you even have vegetables?"

I walked into Bobby's office and said, "I'm making dinner for Lucy. The girl from the ballgame."

Bobby sat in an unadorned box of an office behind an aluminum and Formica desk. His sad and abused work chair squeaked whenever he moved. Bobby motioned me to sit and asked, "So, is John Tucker your brother?"

"I have no idea. My dad's best friend says that I don't have a brother."

Bobby poised his pen over a legal pad. "Who's that?"

"Walt Adams. He worked with my dad at GDS and said that my dad didn't screw around."

Bobby said, "Hmmph."

"Then I talked to Cathy Byrd, John Tucker's mother."

"Yeah? What did she tell you?"

"Nothing. I'm going out to Pittsfield to have lunch with her tomorrow. When my cousin Sal heard, he got all pissed off and called her a whore. Something's up."

"What's Sal's last name?" asked Bobby, pen poised.

"Rizzo. He's Sal Rizzo."

"Your cousin is Sal Rizzo? North End Sal Rizzo?"

"Yeah, I guess. He lives in the North End."

"Is there any reason you never told me you were connected?"

"Connected? Connected to what?"

Bobby rolled his eyes. "Connected to the Mafia. You're telling me that you don't know that Sal Rizzo runs the Mafia in the North End?"

"Cousin Sal? That's ridiculous."

"I'm sorry. I'm just an FBI special agent who investigates organized crime. I guess I should just go back into the war room and tear down that whole fucking org chart with Sal Rizzo at the top of it."

I crossed my arms. "This is bullshit."

"Shit, Tucker. You got a dead brother you never heard of and a cousin you didn't know was in the Mafia. That is one screwed-up family life. What do you do on the holidays?"

"I hadn't thought about it, actually." It would be my first holiday season since I lost my wife.

"Thanksgiving is coming."

"I guess I'll watch some football games."

"You're welcome to come to my place."

"I'm fine. I don't need to come to your house for Thanksgiving."

"At least have coffee with me tomorrow in Pittsfield. You could even be useful."

"Why are *you* going to Pittsfield?"

"I'm talking to some people about your non-brother's work. I could bounce some ideas off you."

"I thought Lee was investigating John Tucker's murder. What's your angle?"

"I'm working on a different problem."

"What problem?"

"I really shouldn't tell you about it."

"But you will anyway."

"I think John Tucker was a spy."

"Holy shit. This just gets better and better."

"That information is between us."

"That's why you were in front of my house last night."

"Will you help me?"

I gathered my vegetables and stood. "See you in Pittsfield."

THIRTEEN

"THE MAFIA?" LUCY ASKED as she drank her Lagavulin on the rocks.

We sat on the couch after a dinner of ratatouille and a dessert of cannoli. My family room ran the width of my narrow condo, with windows facing the street. I had divided that space into a living room and dining room by placing a couch across the center. The space in front of the couch was the living room, the space behind the couch was the dining room. We had moved from the dining room to the living room.

Lucy had arrived a few minutes late and had brought a bottle of red wine. She was wearing a gray sweater dress with a high collar, black leggings, and black leather boots that reached almost to her knee. The sweater hugged her breasts and hips, and the boots exposed a small bit of leg. The outfit covered her body while showing it off. I managed to give her a peck on the cheek to say hello, take the bottle of wine, and get back into the kitchenette without drooling, tripping, or lighting myself on fire. It was a triumph of focus.

Lucy sat on a barstool at the kitchenette counter and looked at the terrarium.

"Who are these guys?" she asked.

"They're my roommates, Click and Clack. They're hermit crabs," I said before I remembered that Lucy was a biology teacher. She obviously recognized hermit crabs. I expected Lucy to bust me for not giving her credit for her knowledge of crustaceans, but she let the remark go. *A keeper?*

I asked, "So, how was your day?"

Lucy told me about her school day. Apparently she had had a dustup with a parent over one of her kids' grades. The kid had no interest in biology, no willingness to learn it, and no inclination to study. He failed his midterm test, and the parent came to complain . . .

I had learned years ago that if I asked a woman a simple open-ended question and listened to her answer, she would carry 95 percent of the communication load and consider me to be a sparkling conversationalist. The approach also kept me from having to answer such questions as whether I had a job (I didn't), what I did for a living (very little), and why I was single (long story).

This approach didn't work with Lucy. She finished her story about the helicopter parents, looked at me, and said, "So who is John Tucker? Is he your brother?"

This, too, was a long story, and I told it as I transferred the ratatouille to a serving plate, poured us some wine, and served the meal. Lucy was a probing conversationalist, and apparently she had learned the same trick as I had. Her blue eyes watched me intently. She asked compelling follow-up questions, kept me talking about myself.

Lucy ate some ratatouille. "This is delicious."

"Thanks." I ate some myself. She was right.

"So you still don't know if the guy in front of your house was your brother?"

"Not for sure. I'll find out tomorrow."

I told Lucy about Cathy Byrd, John's mother. I left out the part where Sal had called Cathy a whore. We made small talk about the drive to Pittsfield, which Zipcar I would take, what it would cost, the length of the drive.

For my part, I found myself thinking less about my "brother" and more about the curves under Lucy's sweater dress. I got up from the table and brought out the cannoli I had bought at Maria's. Lucy gave a happy moan as she tasted chocolate dusted on the creme filling. The sound transported me to the bedroom, where I imagined sliding my hands along Lucy's black leggings, feeling the muscles of her thigh. Lucy suggested that we move to the couch. I thought things were moving in the right direction, then she brought up the topic of Sal again.

"Yes, apparently I'm connected," I said, and kissed Lucy.

She closed her eyes and returned the soft kiss, her mouth tasting of Scotch and chocolate. My breath quickened and I brushed my thumb across Lucy's breast. She arched her breast into my hand and pulled me closer for another kiss.

Then she opened her eyes and asked, "So why *did* you move to the South End?"

I blinked. "What?"

"The South End. You told me that you have relatives in the North End and that Sal was mad at you. So why did you move to the South End? Was there a schism in the family?"

My brain, jammed with lust, had lost all functionality. I said, "Ahh—well—err—I guess it never occurred to me. I moved here right after my wife died last year."

Lucy sat back on the couch. She said, "You're a widower?"

"Yeah."

"But you're so young."

48

"Yeah."

"How did it happen?"

"She was murdered in a home invasion. I moved to Boston right after that. I didn't want to stay in the house. Sal and my cousins weren't even part of the equation. I was pretty wrapped up in myself."

"It was shitty of Sal to give you a hard time about it."

"No. He's right. I should make more of an effort. Even if I don't live there, I can at least visit."

Lucy reached forward and leaned in on me, giving me a hug. She said into my ear, "I'm so sorry I brought it up."

I settled into the hug and said, "That's okay." I could feel her making her next move. Her body tensed as she was about to stand.

Lucy said, "You know what, Tucker?"

"What?"

"You are a really good guy."

"Why, thank you."

"I like you."

Uh oh.

Lucy stood and said, "I need to be getting home. It's a school night."

Naturally.

FOURTEEN

GRAY SEPTEMBER CLOUDS SCUDDED across the sky as I drove west on the Mass Pike toward Pittsfield. The road had shifted from being broad and straight into more of a mountain pass. The Pike's builders had blasted their way through mountains, leaving gouges in the rock alongside their two-lane road.

A brown sign told me that I had reached the Pike's highest elevation at 1,724 feet—highest at least until Route 90 got a bit higher in Oacoma, South Dakota, at 1,729 feet. I imagined the Pike stretching through New York, skirting the Great Lakes, plunging through Chicago, and shooting across the plains and mountains until it reached Seattle.

I passed under the Appalachian Trail footbridge and toyed with the idea of staying on this road, ignoring the exit, and driving on to a new beginning in the West. I would ensconce myself in the Seattle high-tech scene, visit the Sox when they came to town, and get far away from unwanted family entanglements. I'd be free.

I fiddled with Pandora on my Droid, setting up a Soundgarden channel and wondering what it would be like to live in the city that produced this music. Settlers founded Seattle at the time when

Boston was planting the Public Garden and launching the Swan Boats. It was literally a new place. I'd trade the Public Garden for the Space Needle and the Red Sox for the Mariners.

With that, the fantasy of running away broke up. I'd never leave. After driving for two hours, I hit Exit 2, pulled off the Pike, and started north on Route 20—the same Route 20 that went past the Global Defense Systems plant where Dad had often worked.

The stretch of road that wends its way from the Mass Pike through Lenox and up into Pittsfield cuts through a swath of terrain called the Berkshires. The Berkshires are the place where people from the Hamptons go for summer vacation. The New York rich spend their summers hiking, antiquing, eating at expensive restaurants, and listening to the Boston Symphony Orchestra at Tanglewood.

Driving through Lenox to meet John Tucker's mother, I didn't see the allure. Lenox looked like a long stretch of two-lane highway that had never developed the economic density to support a strip mall. Car dealers, motels, and fast food restaurants peppered the road in stretches where small third-growth trees hadn't reclaimed the soil. The vacationer's paradise must have been hidden from me, which was fine because I wasn't vacationing.

I entered downtown Pittsfield and wondered how often my dad had made this drive. He worked at the Pittsfield plant two or three days a week for years. I drove past the Colonial Theater, with its three stone arches and iconic columns built into the façade. Had he attended cultural events? Had he visited the Berkshire Museum and marveled at the model stegosaurus on the front lawn, or had all of this just been backdrop for a commute from a motel to the GDS plant?

I approached the center of town. The GPS lady in my Droid told me to take a right at what remained of the town green. It was now a long paramecium of a traffic circle. Even so, Pittsfield's stately grace suggested that it had been dropped through a wormhole from the '50s. It had a bank that looked like a bank instead of a McDonald's, its yellow stone and detailed architecture suggesting security instead of convenience. It had a stone church alongside the green, instead of the white wooden church that was traditional for New England.

The GPS lady took me to Copley Terrace, Cathy's street. I followed her directions and stopped my car as Cathy's big purple Victorian house came into view.

Two cars were parked in front of the house—one in the driveway and one on the street. The screen door on the porch swung closed, and I realized that someone had just driven up in the second car. Perhaps it was some sort of sick interventionistic ambush. Was Cathy gathering a circle of unknown relations who would sit me down and spring a new family tree on me? My heart accelerated as my stomach twisted. I didn't need more family surprises.

I parked five houses away from the Victorian. I had imagined that this would be an unpleasantly intense lunch around a kitchen table. We would eat tuna fish sandwiches on white bread toast and Cathy would tell me the story of John Tucker, perhaps including the tale of how she'd met my father. Perhaps not. It would be a one-on-one revelation. But now someone else was invited to the party, and the scene got darker in my mind.

I saw two of them looming over me as I sat in a darkened living room on a soft couch. They were explaining some twisted fact of my birth that threw my identity into crisis, which perhaps included a genetic history of wasting diseases to boot. My heart started to thunk in my chest as I imagined the scene.

My hand grabbed the key in the ignition. I could either twist the key and run, or put the key in my pocket and face the truth. It lingered and I watched it, fascinated, as my hand decided that the key would go in my pocket. I would face the truth of my existence.

I got out of the car, locked it with a *beep* of the fob, and walked down the tree-lined street past white Victorian houses in various states of repair, toward the bright purple nexus of my history.

The car in front of the house, a Ford Taurus, clicked as it cooled. Its interior displayed the generic cleanliness of a rental. Who would rent a car to come visit Cathy? Did they even rent cars at Pittsfield's airport? I turned up the walkway, past the autumn remnants of the black-eyed Susans lining the path. The stairs creaked under my weight. I stood on the porch, gazing at the doorbell in its golden metal dome on purple paint. I pulled open the screen door, and the large glass window in the pink front door shattered as gunfire blasted my eardrums.

I stumbled back on the porch, slammed my kidney into the banister post, and spun down the steps, sprawling through the flowerbed and across the lawn. Gunfire flashed and blasted away inside the house.

I lay on the grass, my brain vapor-locked into inaction. I was between whoever had that gun and the car parked in front of the house. I was an unarmed obstacle to escape. Two shots rang out from the back yard.

The shooter had already tried to kill me. I needed to move. Turning and running down the street seemed like a good way to get shot in the back. Lying on the lawn looked like a good way to get shot in the chest. I got my feet under me and scrambled to the side of the house away from the driveway, pushing and clambering my way through dense rhododendrons. I crept toward the back of the house and peeked around the corner into the back yard. A crumpled pile of clothes, hair, and blood lay on the grass.

A car started at the front of the house. I turned and pushed my way through the bushes to get a look at the shooter, but the rhododendrons defeated me. By the time I reached the front lawn, the Taurus was far down the street and making a turn on to Route 9. I hadn't even gotten the license plate.

I crossed in front of the house, stepping through the flowerbeds on both sides of the path. I crunched up the gravel driveway, past an ancient Toyota Corolla, and into the back yard.

Cathy Byrd lay on the grass, two bullet holes in her back, blood seeping from her chest into the lawn. She had been running but hadn't made it out of the yard. I knelt and leaned close, hoping to hear a breath from her parted lips. There was none. Her hair shifted in the breeze as her dead eyes stared at a beetle climbing a blade of cut grass.

FIFTEEN

THE PICTURES WERE INCONTROVERTIBLE. They stood along the fireplace mantel, adorned the furniture, and hung from wall above the stairs that led to the second floor. Bobby Miller stood next to me as I struggled to comprehend them, to fit them into the life story I thought I had known.

Bobby pointed at a picture and said, "Here's another one."

It was a graduation picture. A younger version of John Tucker stood wearing a high school graduation gown. My dad stood next to him with his arm wrapped around John's shoulder as his stubby fingers gripped the boy and pulled him in for a hug. John, for his part, held a diploma in his own stubby fingers and made a face that said that he had taken too many pictures that day. They were obviously father and son. No wonder they called the son JT. It avoided confusion.

I turned away from the picture but found no relief. There were more pictures. Dozens of pictures crammed onto every surface, covering every wall. My dad stood next to JT in a white communion suit. My dad and JT held a Pinewood Derby car and a trophy. My dad and JT cooked lobsters, my dad and JT launched a rocket, my dad and JT with a ham radio. My dad held an infant JT. The date stamped in the corner agreed with the date that had been on JT's license. He had been almost three years younger than I. Still was, I suppose, though he wasn't getting any older.

I worked my way around the house. Here were pictures of Cathy. Cathy in an apron, Cathy on Dad's lap at a picnic, Cathy with JT in a swimming pool. Cathy, JT, and Dad laughing in surprise as they rode a fake log down a roller coaster. I had never seen so many informal pictures. All five pictures in my home had been formally posed and had rested in frames on an end table. We rarely had cameras at my family events. Each event came and went unrecorded.

I walked up the staircase, eyes flitting from picture to picture, my breath coming in shorter and shorter rasps, until I saw a picture that caused the whole story to fall together in my engineer's mind. I remembered Cathy. It was a dim memory, and I wasn't certain how much of it I was constructing on the fly from the picture in front of me, but I knew who Cathy was and why I remembered her perfume.

This wasn't a picture of JT. It was a picture of me at my second birthday party, probably taken by an aunt or uncle. I was sitting at the head of the table, ready to blow out the candles. My father was on my right, supplying advice and encouragement. My mother was sitting at the table halfway down, ignoring me, a frown on her face as she righted an empty paper cup that had tipped over.

Cathy Byrd, my babysitter, was hunkered down on my left, mirroring my father. Her eyes were wide and smiling and her mouth formed the exaggerated *O* that we make when we teach our children how to blow out candles. Her hand was on the back of my chair as she coached me. My father's hand was on hers.

John Tucker was born ten months later.

SIXTEEN

I FLED DOWN THE staircase and out the front door. Bobby followed. He caught up as I made my car *beep* with the key fob.

"Hey! You okay?" Bobby asked.

My breathing was a little ragged, but I managed, "Yeah. I'm fine."

I opened the car door and started to slide onto the safety-inspected leather of the Volvo interior. Bobby grabbed my arm and said, "You don't look fine. What was in that picture?"

"You know what was in that picture."

"The whole house is full of pictures. How should I know?"

"It was full of pictures of my dad sharing happy memories with John Tucker. They were all pictures of him."

"Yeah, but you were staring at the one on the stairs. What was going on in that picture?"

I gazed through the windshield and thought back to the picture, back to the paper party hat cone I had been wearing. It had R2D2 on it. How did I get a Star Wars party hat? I don't remember any birthdays with any party hats. My mother thought those kinds of things were ridiculous.

"That picture was the proof."

"Proof that John Tucker was your brother?"

"That's the least of it."

There are two kinds of software bugs: easy ones and hard ones. In the easy ones, you have all the data and you know how the software works. They are no more difficult than fixing a Sudoku puzzle with two 5s in the same row. You start at the bad number and work your way back to the source of the problem.

The hard ones hide their information. They present a bewildering series of seemingly random events, tied together by some common cause. You can't step back through them, so the solution has to come to you in a flash. Then everything makes sense.

The picture on that wall was ostensibly a picture of me, blowing out candles and wishing for some two-year-old's idea of Heaven. An ice cream cone, perhaps. But that wasn't why Cathy Byrd had put the picture on her wall. All her pictures captured happy family turning points: a graduation, a football championship, an amusement park ride. Nestled among them was the moment when my father reached out and touched her hand. While my mother was fussing over a cup and I was blowing air at two candles, Cathy Byrd and my father were taking the first step toward creating my father's second family. Someone had captured that moment. Cathy Byrd had framed it.

Bobby leaned on the Volvo. We looked at the big purple house that had once held a small family of three. Cathy, the mother; John, the son; and John, the father who often went back to Wellesley to visit his other family. His other son.

My father had walked up those steps after a short commute from the Pittsfield GDS and called out, "Honey, I'm home!" Did Cathy come to greet him at the door wearing a little apron, her hands wet from cooking? Did she kiss my father softly on the lips just before their son JT tore down the stairs and jumped into his arms? Did JT ask, "What did you bring me?" and did my father produce some small wonder he had picked up near *my* house in Wellesley? Did they go into the dining room and have a pleasant family dinner while Cathy told my dad about her day and made JT eat his carrots?

It was pretty to think of all this happening in the big purple house, because it never happened in mine, where my stomach would knot at the sound of my father's car door. He'd open the door, hang his coat in the hallway, and hunch his shoulders at my mother's first nagging recrimination about some forgotten household chore. The ritual fight would start five minutes later, every time, and I would hide in my bedroom sitting next to my imagined brother, a stuffed bear named Mr. Lumpy.

My lip trembled as a familiar burn took hold of my throat.

Bobby called out to a Pittsfield cop, "Hey! I'm taking Tucker out for a cup of coffee. We'll be back in an hour or so."

The cop nodded. I had already given them my statement four times and had even been fingerprinted so they could screen out my prints. Not that I'd touched anything in the house.

Bobby said, "C'mon, Tucker."

My trance broke. I sniffled and said, "I don't know where there's a coffee shop out here."

Bobby pointed at my Droid and said, "Are you kidding? That phone of yours must be able to find a Starbucks."

We climbed into Bobby's car and my Droid found a Starbucks about ten minutes away.

We never reached it.

SEVENTEEN

BOBBY DROVE TO THE end of Cathy's street. The Droid told us to take a right onto Route 9, away from the center of Pittsfield. A city center without a Starbucks? I knew there was a reason I'd never been to Pittsfield. Route 9 turned down a hill and presented a broad vista with a large industrial plant across the road. Train tracks ran alongside the road then behind a mammoth office building that featured a big black and red sign. The sign said GLOBAL DEFENSE SYSTEMS, with the *G, D,* and *S* forming the GDS logo.

Bobby said, "That's where I've got a meeting."

"With who?"

"Whom."

"Thank you, Dr. Grammatico. With whom are you meeting?"

"John Tucker's boss."

"Want me to come?"

"You up to it?"

"Sure."

"You know, you might be useful for catching bullshit. You're an engineer like John Tucker."

"No, I'm not an engineer like John Tucker, or like my father for that matter. The stuff they designed flew through the air and blew shit up. My stuff just gives your computer a virus. If my dad were here, he'd explain the difference very clearly."

"He didn't approve of your life choice?"

"No. It almost ruined Thanksgiving. I said, 'Dad, I'm going to be a software engineer,' and all hell broke loose. You'd think I'd told him I was joining the Hare Krishnas. He called me an ingrate and a loafer. Said I was wasting an MIT education."

"What did your mother say?"

"What she always said. 'You should listen to your father.' She was useless." I looked at the smokestacks that marred the blue sky. "Thanks for bringing it up."

Bobby pulled into the GDS driveway. "You sure you're up for this? We can get coffee after."

"I'll be fine."

Bobby stopped the car in front of a traffic barrier that lay across the driveway. The guard heaved himself out of the guard shack and approached the car.

"I'm here to see Paul Waters," said Bobby. Security theater raised its head again as Bobby gave the guard his driver's license. The guard looked at Bobby, looked at the license, handed it back, and opened the guard gate. We rolled through.

"What the hell was that about?" I asked.

"Security. You can never be too careful."

"Security? He looked at your license and saw that it matched your face. What does that accomplish?"

"It gets him to open the gate," said Bobby.

"But it didn't do anything for security."

"Not my problem."

Bobby parked the car and we entered the lobby, asked for Paul Waters, and did the rigamarole with the front desk. Soon we were wearing unintelligible photocopies of our driver's license pictures and standing in Paul Waters's office.

Paul Waters sat among towers of paper that spoke to a career that had stalled in the 1990s. It was clear that he had rocketed up the org chart for all of one rung, gotten stuck due to a lack of either will, smarts, or political savvy, and remained firmly in place. His office was an archeological treasure. *IEEE Spectrum* electrical engineering magazines were piled three feet high against the wall. One of the bottom editions had slipped out of the pile. The ancient headline read *Ballistic Missile Defense. It's back!* My dad might have read that article.

Waters had the paunchy body of a man whose muscles had atrophied to the point where they could only support his minimal daily activities: sitting, walking to meetings, sitting, and drinking coffee. He had eschewed one flight of stairs for the elevator. I suspected strenuous activity, such as heading outside for a fire drill, would kill him.

His desk held model missiles, family photographs, and a white coffee mug, stained to an indelible brown. The mug said PALADIN MISSILE SYSTEM. I remembered my dad drinking coffee from a mug just like it.

Waters peered at me. "You said your name is Tucker? Is that your last name?"

"Yup."

"JT and his dad, John Tucker, both worked for me. Are you any relation?"

My face turned hot, flushing red with unexpected shame. I considered the simple lie of denying any connection but couldn't see how it would help solve this puzzle.

"Yes. John Tucker was my father. JT was my half brother."

My shoulders relaxed. There it was. Spoken out loud. It was easier than I had imagined. It had not killed me. I sank against the vinyl of Waters's guest chair, adjusting as the truth seeped through me.

Waters said, "Oh yes, you're the son from John's previous marriage."

A gasp slipped past my lips at this new layer of my father's lies, this one designed to inoculate the people of Pittsfield if they should ever meet me—the other Tucker boy.

Waters continued, "I'm sorry for your loss. It's a terrible thing, to lose a brother."

My reality tilted. Here was a world that had existed alongside my own for more than thirty years, a world in which Cathy Byrd was my father's wife and my father's son was named John Tucker Jr. A world in which Aloysius Tucker was the "son from a previous marriage," a guy these people might treat with respect, but who was the unfortunate result of my father placing his seed in the wrong vessel, the spawn of an ill-considered and ill-fated matrimony.

Somewhere outside my head, Bobby Miller was telling Paul Waters that Cathy Byrd was dead and Waters was covering his mouth in surprise and Bobby was asking him if he knew of anything that could explain the two murders and Waters was saying that he knew of nothing. Their words slipped through my ears and over my brain. They didn't stick. They couldn't stick. I was a ghost, a fly on the wall, a man who phased out of this reality and into his own. This wasn't my world, this wasn't my reality. I couldn't be here. I needed to be somewhere where my history still mattered, where my reality was the only reality, a reality where John Tucker Jr. didn't have football trophies or graduation gowns. A world in which my babysitter was just the distant memory of a young woman who took care of me when my mother ran errands. A world in which there wasn't a house full of photographs of my father standing alongside his young clone, and the young clone wasn't happily sharing moments of triumph with his buddy—a wisp of a kid who had appeared over and over, always standing next to JT. Who was that kid?

My trance broke as Bobby nudged my arm. "Tucker, we're done here. You got any questions?"

I blinked and looked from Bobby to Waters, who regarded me with pale eyes set under soft lids.

Waters said, "Are you okay?"

I thought about the wisp of a kid in all those pictures and asked, "Who was JT's best friend?"

Waters looked down at his desk and nudged a model of a missile so that it was square with the desk. "Oh, him. Yeah. Between JT getting murdered and him quitting, I'm stuck. I've got no one to pick up the pieces for the Paladin."

Bobby said, "Who?"

"Dave Patterson. JT's best friend. He almost got fired, but he quit first."

Bobby asked, "What do you mean he almost got fired?"

"Well, I really can't go into that. It's against company policy."

Bobby leaned his forearms on Waters's desk and folded his hands. "Paul, the FBI is investigating some serious security issues with the Paladin. So I need you to tell me what you meant."

"I can't. It's confidential."

Bobby asked, "Security confidential or human resources confidential?"

"Human resources confidential."

"Fine. So spill it. Why did they fire Dave Patterson?"

"It's confidential."

Bobby nodded. "So when I leave here and meet with your boss and ask him the same question, do you think he'll give me the same answer? Let's say he does. Let's say he backs you. What do you think will happen when I go through channels and notify the Department of Defense that there are serious concerns regarding the security of the Paladin project?"

"What concerns?"

"Serious concerns. Do you think that the information you're keeping from me will remain secret when the Department of Defense starts its investigation?"

"Well—"

"Let me give you a clue. It won't. What will become clear to your boss and his boss is that a shit storm got started because Paul Waters didn't share important information with an FBI agent. Because, believe me, everybody will know that I asked you."

Waters nudged the model back into square. "I could get into trouble if I tell you."

Bobby said, "No, Paul, you won't. Because if you tell me now, nobody will know it came from you. It will be our secret. Right, Tucker?"

I nodded. *What the hell. What's another secret?*

Waters sighed and said, "They were going to fire Dave Patterson because of security violations. He shared his password with another engineer. He just did it to save time, but he got caught doing it twice and they were going to fire him."

"So he quit first?"

"I told him to quit. If he got fired for a security violation, he'd never work in defense again. There's only one other company in town that does defense work, and they wouldn't have touched him with a ten-foot pole."

"Who's that?"

"General Dynamics. He started there last week."

"How about the guy who got Dave's password? Does he still work here?"

"No. That was JT."

"Figures," said Bobby.

EIGHTEEN

GENERAL DYNAMICS SITS ON Plastics Ave. The name is a legacy from the time that a brash young chemical engineer named Jack Welch took the advice that Mr. McGuire gave to Benjamin Braddock in *The Graduate*: he got into plastics on the ground floor.

Unlike Benjamin, whose hormones had been addled by Mrs. Robinson, Welch rode that plastic elevator straight to the top of General Electric. Once Welch reached the top, he looked back at his roots in Pittsfield's GE facility and promptly dismantled it. Most of its jobs were sent away and the remaining company was sold, to the delight of GE stockholders and the chagrin of the people of Pittsfield. Today, Plastics Ave is a reminder of that history.

We drove past the long, low brick building that housed General Dynamics. Large white signs with plain black lettering declared that General Dynamics made naval ordnances and that they had instituted the ISO 9000 quality practices, a marketing pitch that left me cold but that probably worked on naval procurement officers. All the visitor spaces were full, so Bobby parked at the end of the row of cars under a No PARKING sign.

We walked along the building, past another of the big white marketing signs, and up the front steps, where we requested entry into a naval ordnance design center by pressing a little doorbell in the doorjamb. *Bing bong!* The door buzzed and we entered the lobby. It looked like a doctor's office, with large comfortable chairs, a plasma TV showing Fox News on the wall, and a nifty one-cup-at-a-time coffee maker tucked into the corner.

At a low security desk, Bobby flashed his badge and asked to speak to Dave Patterson. While he did that, I checked out the coffee maker, taking one of its little flavor packets and following the instructions on the screen to get the thing to kick out a cup of okay coffee. Bobby moved to the machine and went through the process.

I said, "Does this count as the cup of coffee you were going to buy me?"

"We'll see," said Bobby. "If you're good, I might still take you to Starbucks for a cookie and some juice."

"Mmmm, cookies," I said. I drank my coffee, looked around the lobby, and listened to some hot woman on Fox read news of Israel and its Iron Dome missile defense system. The system was shooting down missiles fired from the Gaza Strip.

Bobby said, "Those Israelis are clever bastards. They can shoot down missiles. How come we never made something like that?"

I said, "We did. It's called Paladin."

The hot news babe backed me up, sharing that Israel was buying the US-made Paladin system to contend with missiles from Iran. Fox went on to say that this was another example of American innovation. It would have been a proud moment for my dad. And apparently for JT as well.

I changed the subject. "Thanks for getting me out of that house."

"I figured it was getting a little rough for you in there," said Bobby.

"All those pictures," I said. I drank my coffee, the paper cup clicking against my teeth. "They just seemed so happy. I don't think I ever saw my dad smile so much."

"You guys didn't have pictures?"

"We didn't have—Here's our man," I said. A little guy wearing a flannel shirt and jeans entered the lobby and talked to the guard at the front desk. The guard pointed at us. I gave him a wave.

Bobby murmured into my ear, "Don't tell him you're JT's brother. We'll save that for later."

Dave Patterson was hunger-strike thin. Limp black hair hung over his ears in wisps. A thin caterpillar of a mustache crawled across his lip.

Bobby showed his ID and said, "I'm Special Agent Miller." He pointed at me and said, "This is Mr. Bologna."

"Like the town in Italy?" Patterson asked.

"Like the luncheon meat," I said.

"That's a tough name to grow up with."

"You learn to fight and avoid sandwich shops."

Patterson looked at his watch and said, "What's this about? I'm on the clock. My time with you guys is getting charged to overhead. My manager hates overhead. He wants all my time charged to a project."

"What project did you work on when you were at GDS?" I asked.

"The Paladin."

"Really," I said. "Did you know John Tucker?"

Patterson gave us a long look. "You guys know he's dead, right?"

"Yes," said Bobby. "We're sorry."

Patterson shook his head and said, "He got shot two nights ago in Boston. He probably went to visit that crook half brother of his."

Crook?

Bobby asked, "Who was his half brother?"

"Some stupid name like Alphonse or something. It was a big secret. Not even JT knew until his dad died."

I started to speak, but Bobby interrupted me. "What happened when John Tucker died?"

"Well, JT's mom wouldn't go to the wake or the funeral. She said that she didn't want to be humiliated. It turns out that Mr. Tucker had another family. He was married to a woman in Boston. That woman was doing the wake and the funeral, and she didn't even invite Ms. Byrd or JT."

I said, "Maybe she didn't know about them."

Patterson grimaced. "That's bullshit. How could she not know? Mr. Tucker was out here all the time."

"And what makes this half brother a crook?" I asked.

"The guy is some sort of Mafia hacker," said Patterson.

"What the hell are you talking about?"

"That's what JT told me. That's why he was in Boston. He was going to get this Alphonse—"

"Aloysius."

"Yeah, whatever. Aloysius was supposed to help him with something."

Bobby asked, "To help him with what?"

Patterson rubbed his neck, his face blank. "I don't know."

"Really," said Bobby. "You don't know. Are you shitting me?"

"I swear, I don't know. I mean, JT's dead now. What does it matter?"

"JT's mother, Cathy Byrd, was murdered earlier this afternoon."

Patterson blinked and whispered, "But why would they kill *her*?"

Bobby said, "*They*? *They* who?"

Patterson slumped into one of the overstuffed chairs. He put his elbows on his knees and cradled his face in his hands.

Bobby repeated, "Who?"

Patterson looked up at Bobby and asked, "Where did you say you're from?"

"The fucking FBI," said Bobby. Bobby's professional veneer was cracking. He loomed over Patterson, who shrank back in his chair. The security guy stood up.

Bobby repeated, "Who killed Cathy Byrd?"

"I don't know," said Patterson. "How should I know? I don't know. If I knew, I'd tell you."

"You said, 'Why would they kill her?' Who is *they*?"

Patterson looked around the room, made eye contact with the security guy, and then looked back at Bobby. He said, "They. They. You know, like in, 'They stole my bike' or 'They stole that road sign.'"

The security guy edged around the desk. He tapped Bobby's shoulder and said, "Sir."

Bobby wheeled on him. "You go sit down or, I swear, I'll get your clearance junked so fast that you'll be arrested for trespassing at your own fucking desk."

The security guy looked at me. I said, "I'd listen to him. He'll do it. He's crazy."

It was fun being the good cop.

The guy left and we looked at Dave Patterson, who was sitting up straighter and had composed himself.

Bobby asked, "Who killed Cathy Byrd?"

Patterson said, "I don't know."

"What was Tucker supposed to do for JT?"

"The brother? *I don't know.* I don't. You've got to believe me."

"I don't have to believe you. I swear to Christ, I will put your life through a wood chipper. Don't fucking hold out on me."

Patterson shrunk back into himself, looking even more skeletal in the giant chair.

Bobby reached into his shirt pocket and pulled out a business card. Flipped it onto the chair next to Patterson. "You think of anything, you call me." He wheeled and headed for the front door.

As he passed the security desk, he made eye contact with the guard. He pointed into his own eyes with two fingers and then toward the guard. *I'm watching you.* The guard ignored him with impressive intensity, staring hard into a video monitor. We exited the building and trotted down the front steps.

Bobby said, "So, Alphonse, what work are you doing for the Mafia?"

I said, "What? You're going to start in on me now?"

"You didn't answer the question."

"I'm not doing any work for the Mafia. You're the one who told me I was connected. I didn't know that."

"So why did JT think he could get your help?"

"I have no idea."

We reached the car and stood on either side of it. Bobby leaned on the roof. "If you get an idea, would you let me know?"

Bobby dropped into the driver's seat, and I sat in the passenger seat next to him. I stared at the No Parking sign. "Why does Patterson think I'm a Mafia asshole crook?"

"JT told him you were."

"Why would JT say that?"

Bobby started the car. "Welcome to the wonderful world of family."

NINETEEN

I INSPECTED YET ANOTHER picture of Dad, one of many hanging on a wall of memories. He was smiling, his hand on JT's football-padded shoulder.

I remembered my football pads. I had done four weeks of hard time in high school football, sentenced by my dad for the purposes of "toughening me up." My pads fit so poorly. They chafed my collarbones and gave me bruises on my neck. Running in them was a nightmare. Getting hit in them was worse.

The coaches seemed hell-bent on teaching me that collisions were fun. The drills exhausted me, bruised me, and humiliated me. After four weeks of drilling, we played our first game. I looked into the stands and saw that Dad had found the time to come see me play. It was the first time I had seen him at a school event. For a moment, football held out the promise that it would bring us together. I spent the whole game standing on the sidelines, forgotten by the coaches.

After the game, I threw the pads onto the equipment pile and walked away from football. Dad gave me a speech about how winners never quit and quitters never win. I told him that brain-damaged idiots didn't find work and that I was too busy for football. He shook his head and walked away.

The picture on the wall showed that Dad had not given up on his dream of siring a football player. JT stood with his parents, holding a gigantic trophy. My dad stood between JT and Cathy, one arm around JT's shoulder and his other hand resting on Cathy's hip. His fingers on her hip curled down, their tips resting inside the pocket of her jeans.

The son, the father, the mother; they were all gone now. Someone had erased Dad's second legacy. Nothing was left but these pictures in this house.

Sadly, I had never gotten my Starbucks coffee. I didn't even get juice or a cookie. Lieutenant Lee had driven out from Boston and we had come back to the house to meet him. Lee was done talking to Bobby and turned to me.

"You're sure that you never knew about any of this?"

"You think this would have slipped my mind? Of course I didn't know about any of this."

Bobby said, "Tucker, Lee's just doing his job."

I turned on Bobby. "Well he sucks at it."

Lee said, "You never saw strange people at family events? Perhaps people you didn't know."

"I *always* saw strange people at family events. My mother's family is huge. It's like a family bush. I had all these second cousins, or half-aunts, or nieces once removed, or whatever the hell. She had the whole damn thing memorized, but I couldn't follow it. Shit, Bobby had to tell me that my cousin was in the Mafia. I didn't know that."

Bobby said, "Tucker's cousin is Sal Rizzo."

Lee said, "Your cousin is Sal Rizzo? You could have mentioned this. Why didn't you mention it?"

"Which part of 'I didn't know' didn't you understand? Look, this is bullshit. I don't even know if you guys are telling me the truth about Sal. I don't really know anything about him. I have no fucking clue. And if I don't have a clue about my first cousin Sal, why would I have any clue about a family that my father was hiding from me?"

Lee said, "It seems impossible to me that he kept you completely separate. What about his funeral? In Genesis, Abraham died and it says 'his sons Isaac and Ishmael buried him.' You and your brother didn't see each other at his funeral?"

I turned away from Lee and wandered through the house. There was so much here. The place was a tribute to a full and happy family life. I stopped in front of a picture of my dad with a young JT in a Cub Scout uniform. They held another trophy and a Pinewood Derby car. The car was low and sleek. Clearly it had been sanded, painted, shellacked, and, judging by the trophy, tuned to win by an adult.

I didn't remember my dad being very interested in the Pinewood Derby. I'd made my car myself. It looked like a Kleenex box on wheels. I had painted it blue with red flames on the side. My dad had come home from Pittsfield to watch the race. I proved that aerodynamics was less important to Pinewood Derby cars than you would think. I came in seventh out of thirty. No pictures were taken.

I looked across the wall of photos like a hobo peering through a restaurant window. The family life that I hadn't known was possible had been here all along, hidden from me in Pittsfield.

Bobby gripped my shoulder and squeezed. "Here," he said, handing me a handkerchief.

My face was wet. I wiped my eyes and blew my nose. "I need to get out of here."

Bobby said, "I know. I'll finish up with Lee."

"I need to see my mother."

TWENTY

I WAS FINE UNTIL I saw the sign. Then my palms began to sweat. My stomach became a living thing, churning and flipping, threatening to reach up my esophagus and strangle me from within. Adrenaline spurted into my bloodstream. My hands trembled. The sign said:

EXIT 12

FRAMINGHAM

1 MILE

My mother lived in Framingham, a bedroom suburb thirty miles west of Boston and seventy miles east of Pittsfield. She had moved from our big house in Wellesley to a small cookie-cutter ranch about a year after Dad died. I was studying at MIT when she called and told me that my childhood home had been sold to a very nice proctologist and that I needed to come home that weekend to clean out my stuff.

I exited the highway and drove down Route 9, past an unremitting collection of auto malls and restaurants, until I turned off the road at Framingham State University. FSU had once been Framingham State College, but it apparently had received a promotion. I turned down Edgell Road, past the spot where Henry Knox had dragged the cannons he had swiped from the British at Fort Ticonderoga, then I swung onto Central and navigated a maze of ranch-filled roads. My stomach clenched at each turn. A small voice in my mind said, *It's not too late. You can still run.* I would have lost my nerve, but I had called my mother in advance. She was expecting me. The call forced me to go through with the visit.

I parked in front of my mother's Campanelli ranch house. The Campanelli ranches had been dropped all over Framingham by a 1950s builder named, oddly enough, Campanelli. It was as if he had gotten hold of the SimCity house-building tool and had indiscriminately drawn great swaths of identical houses, some flipped in mirror-image fashion for variety.

My mother's small house lay low at the top of a lawn. Its façade featured a picture window from the living room and two bedroom windows. The house blocked the setting sun, casting a long shadow across the lawn. A curtain covered the picture window and pressed against the glass as if a couch had pinched it there, but I knew there was no couch in that room.

I took a deep breath, steeled myself. I got out of the Volvo and climbed the driveway, past my mother's car, which had long ago been expelled from the garage. I approached the front door and rang the bell. A simple chime announced my presence. A faint rustling sound whispered through the door, but the door remained locked.

I knocked and called out, "Are you okay?"

My mother's voice said, "Just a *minute!*"

I heard more shuffling and scraping from beyond the door. The lock cycled. The door creaked partially open. I pressed on it, but it couldn't open any farther. The smell hit me, as it always did—a musty library smell. A shiver ran down my spine.

My mother called from behind the door, "Well, get in here. It's cold out."

I stepped in. The door closed behind me, trapping me in hoarding hell.

After my dad died, my mother had decided to save all his papers. She felt it was his legacy. She collected each scrap that he had written and more scraps about him from the newspaper. Obituaries had run in the local paper, in the *Boston Globe*, in the *Boston Herald*, and on the Internet. She'd gotten sympathy cards and insurance forms and his old wallet and bank statements and cancelled checks with his signature on them. There were books that he had read and books that he had intended to read, books that he had bought for me and books that he had bought for her. There was the newspaper that came out the day after his funeral, the first paper that was printed in a world without him, and then a second paper printed in a world without him—three papers, actually, the *Globe*, the *Herald*, and the *New York Times*. For a while, my mother would go through the newspapers looking for mentions of Global Defense Systems and cutting them out to put in scrapbooks. When she ran out of time to do that, she started storing the newspapers, saying that she would "get to them later."

When my mother moved, she had the movers put all the papers into the living room until she could find a place for them. She never did. Instead, she discovered free circulars. She saw opportunities in little boxes on every street corner. She'd open the door to the little box and take out that week's *Real Estate News*, or *Writing Workshop Newsletter*, or coupon book for local stores. These went into the house. She gathered take-out menus. These went into the house. Framingham had a free newspaper called the *Tab*. It went into the house. The *Middlesex News*? That went into the house. Junk mail went into the house.

Receipts went into the house. Magazine subscriptions to the *Reader's Digest* went into the house. *Money, Runner's World, Real Simple,* and AARP newsletters all went into the house. Everything my mother could touch or see or read went into that house.

Nothing came out.

Towers of paper as tall as me crowded every corner of the living room. My mother would stack paper in one place until she couldn't reach the top, and then she'd start a new pile. Fortunately, she was only five feet tall. The house was dark, since every window had been blocked by stacks of paper. She was unable to stack paper in the kitchen sink, so that window alone remained uncovered.

A sliver of setting sun slipped through the window and traced an orange rectangle across the ceiling. The dying light made the room look gloomier.

My mother had been standing on the small pile of papers that she had moved to open the door. She climbed off the pile and stood in front of me on the goat path that wound between stacks of newsprint. Her body had adopted an untended plumpness. She wore a faded housedress, no shoes, and a tired expression. Every time I looked at her, I felt guilty for not visiting more often. Then I'd look around the house and feel disgusted for having visited at all.

My mother said, "Well, give me a kiss," and she raised her cheek so I could kiss it.

I kissed her cheek and said, "Hi, Ma."

She said, "I'm sorry that I couldn't get to the door faster. I was straightening up before you came over."

I looked around the room. "Straightening up" meant that my mother had picked up some of the scraps of paper and moved them to other piles. She caught my glance and said, "Come on, let's go to your room before you get all snippy and start judging my housekeeping."

She led the way down the goat path. I was slightly wider than her, and paper brushed against my legs. At the fireplace, the goat path split. One branch went into the kitchen. My mother hadn't given up cooking. This forced some spots to be clear of paper: a counter, the range top, and a spot on the kitchen table. There was a TV room off the kitchen. I knew she kept a spot clear in there as well so she could sit and watch her shows. The TV was playing the six o'clock news. I could hear the anchor's breathless description of the latest tragedy. Apparently, a house had caught fire somewhere.

We took the goat path that led down the bedroom hallway. We walked past the bathroom. The door was jammed open by a stack of paper. Across from the bathroom was another bedroom. This one contained a new wrinkle in my mother's hoarding: a growing pile of dolls and stuffed animals. They were crammed together, the gloom washing out their color, their lifeless eyes staring into the darkness as if they were awaiting mass burial.

My mother's bedroom was at the end of the hallway. She grunted as she moved a pile of paper from in front of my door to in front of her door. I'd learned long ago not to offer to help. She got upset if I touched anything. She indicated the padlock on the door and said, "Go ahead."

My mother and I had fought constantly for a full year after she had moved her hoard into this smaller house. I had just started my own life, with a new job and my own apartment. Each time I visited my mother, I'd be shocked by the growing piles and start moving things around and asking, "Do you need this? Do you need this?" My mother would wring her hands and tell me to put things into new piles. I couldn't get her to throw anything away and our fights got worse. Finally, we struck a deal. My mother would give me one room to keep clean, and I would stop complaining about the mess.

She gave me the bedroom next to hers. We cleaned it out and furnished it with a couple of recliners and a television. The deal lasted until my first visit, when I found my room full of growing piles. I cleaned the piles out as my mother fretted and shouted. Then I put a padlock on the door and told her that I'd only visit if the room remained locked.

I worked the combination on the padlock, and we entered a clean, airy space. The two recliners, a big one for me and a smaller one for my mother, faced a small HDTV that tapped into my mother's cable. We sat in our chairs and my breath came easily for the first time since I had left the highway. I sighed and rested.

My mother asked, "So, what's new?"

I said, "Not much. I met a new girl. Lucy."

"The poor thing. I suppose she'll last as long as the others."

The relaxation fled. I said, "Yeah. The poor thing. You know, my wife, Carol, lasted quite a while."

"You and Carol fought all the time at the end. Just before she died."

"I'm just saying—"

The silence hung between us. I struggled to remember why I had made this visit. I thought about the house in Pittsfield, full of light and air and pictures of my father being happy. I hadn't seen any pictures of our family for a long time.

I asked, "Do you have any pictures from when I was little?"

My mother gestured out of my room and said, "They must be out there somewhere. Why do you ask?"

"I just realized that I don't have many pictures of our family."

"Well, film was expensive."

"I guess."

Silence. Then my mother said, "I saw on the news that a man was killed in the South End."

"Yes." I didn't mention that it was in front my house.

"His name was John Tucker. The same name as your father."

"I know. Isn't that strange?"

The elephant had entered the room, but I wasn't going to acknowledge him. People talk about the elephant in the room as if he's a large, benign pet, who would be much happier if we stopped ignoring him.

That's bullshit.

The elephant in the room is a raging rogue that stomps the shit out of anyone foolish enough to address him. I was not going to talk about JT, Pittsfield, or my father screwing the babysitter.

My mother said, "Why this sudden interest in pictures? You never cared about your childhood."

I said, "I don't know. Midlife crisis? I want to understand Dad better."

"There is not much to understand. Your father was a very simple man. He worked hard and was a good provider. Our house was paid for by the time he died. We never wanted for anything. He was fond of you."

Fond of me.

"He traveled a lot," I said.

"Yes. He was always in Pittsfield, working all those hours. That's all there was to do in Pittsfield. There's nothing there."

Nothing but his other family.

I said, "Do you have any of his old project papers?"

My mother stiffened. "What do you mean?"

"You know, diagrams, engineering books, things from his work."

"Why do you ask?"

"I'm just curious. I've been feeling a need to connect with him."

"Well, I'm sure they're somewhere, but I don't have the time to find them."

"I could look."

"No. I don't want things disturbed. I know where everything is."

"Then you can point out his papers?"

"Why are you suddenly so goddamn nosy? Did you come to see me, or did you just come out here to poke through my things?"

I said, "I came to see you."

My mother said, "Turn on the TV. I want to watch the news."

I turned on the TV. The twenty-four-hour news came on. Iran was being an international douchebag. Israel was intercepting missiles. The world was on the brink of collapse.

Situation normal.

My mother and I sat in the deepening gloom. The blue light of the TV washed over us as we settled into our visit.

Then the doorbell rang.

TWENTY-ONE

My mother glared at me, asked, "Did you invite somebody here?"

I pictured the piles and piles of papers, the lifeless dolls, the dark, cavelike living room. Disgust flashed across my face as I said, "No!"

"You don't need to be nasty about it."

My mother pulled herself to her feet. She opened the bedroom door and stepped into the goat path on the other side. I turned off the TV and the lights and followed her into the path. I locked the door. If I didn't keep the door locked, my room would be flooded with crap inside of a week.

The doorbell rang again. My mother padded to the front door and said, "Yes?"

A male voice said, "Mrs. Tucker, my name is Lieutenant Lee. I'm with the Boston Police Department. May I have a word with you?"

I said, "Lieutenant Lee?"

My mother said, "Do you know him?"

I tried to answer, but my mind locked as I realized that the story of John Tucker was about to crash down upon me. My mother was going to kill me. I should have been the one to tell her about my father's affair, but I hadn't had the guts. Now she would hear it from a stranger. My mind darted and jumped, gnawing at the bars of this problem like a caged rat thrown into a river. The water rose and my inevitable fate became clear.

Lee called through the door, "Mrs. Tucker. May we speak?"

My mother opened the door a crack and said, "What do you want?"

I could hear Lee through the crack. "May I come in?"

"No," said my mother.

"No?" Lee had pushed his badge up against the opening in the doorway. Now he was peeking around it. I doubted he could see the dark room. He said, "This is police business."

I said, "You heard the lady. No."

Lee said, "Tucker, are you in there?"

My mother looked at me and said, "I thought you didn't know him."

"I didn't say that. I said I didn't invite him."

"This is ridiculous." My mother squeezed out through the door into the front yard. Lee backed up to make room. I followed.

We moved into the front yard. The sun was gone. Gloomy light spilled over us from a purple sky. The lawn sloped away, ending at a street without a sidewalk, a sure sign of being in the deepest, darkest suburbs. We followed Lee to the edge of the grass, stood next to his car, and formed an isosceles triangle, my mother and I standing next to each other at the base facing Lee at the apex.

Don't do it, Lee. Please don't do it.

Lee said, "I'm investigating the murder of John Tucker."

My mother said, "You mean the one from the news? What does he have to do with me?"

Here it comes.

Lee looked at me. He said, "You haven't told her?"

I said, "No."

"When you said you needed to visit her, I thought you were going to tell her."

My mother said, "Aloysius, what is he talking about?"

I hate my first name for many reasons. For one, it's dorky. For another, it's impossible to spell. But the biggest reason is that whenever my parents used it, I knew that things were about to go very badly for me.

I crossed my arms, said nothing. I wasn't taking the fall for this.

Lee plunged in. "Mrs. Tucker, your husband was the father of another child."

My mother gasped.

Lee continued, "The child's name was John Tucker, apparently named after him. The mother's name was Cathy Byrd. She had lived with the child in Pittsfield and was mu—"

"The babysitter?" my mother interrupted.

Here it comes.

"Yes, ah, apparently."

"That bastard was sleeping with the *babysitter*?" My mother's voice rose. I was very sorry that we were standing in the street.

"Yes. She lived in a house in Pittsfield and—"

My mother turned to me. "And *you*. Did you know about this?"

I raised my hands, "No, Ma, I didn't. I swear. Not until today."

"You knew about this *today?*"

I could see no way out. My cage was underwater.

"Yes, but—"

"And you didn't think to tell me when you *came into my house*? You let me stand out here in the street like a *fool* and hear about it from this man?"

I was silent. There was nothing to do but wait for this storm to pass.

"Did you think I wouldn't find out? What are you? Retarded? Did my retarded boy think that I wouldn't find out about his son of a bitch of a father?"

I said, "I'm not retarded."

Lee interjected, "Mrs. Tucker, I'm sorry you had to learn about your husband this way."

My mother turned on him and said, "Where is she?"

"Ma'am?"

"Where is the little whore?"

Cathy Byrd is a whore. Sal had said that.

"She's dead."

"Dead? How could she be dead? She must only be in her fifties."

Lee said, "She was murdered this morning. That's why I've come to talk to you."

"Murdered?" My mother turned to me. "Did you have something to do with this?"

I said, "No, Ma, I—"

Lee said, "Tucker was a witness this morning."

My mother slapped me, her hand flashing out of nowhere and catching me across the cheek. Her fingers burned across my skin, leaving red trails of maternal hatred.

My mother screeched, "Does the whole world know about this? Do they all know that your father made a fool of me? How long have you known?" The screeching went up an octave as my mother lost control. "How *long?*"

"I just said—"

Lieutenant Lee said, "Mrs. Tucker, if we could just step inside."

My mother turned on him and switched to deadly politeness. "I want to thank you, officer, for bringing this to my attention."

Lee said, "Yes, but I need—"

My mother turned to me. I was cradling my face. She said, "Go home. Go back into your little hole."

Lee said, "Just a few more—"

My mother said, "Goodbye, Lieutenant Lee." She turned and stalked up the lawn into her dark house, leaving Lieutenant Lee and me in the street. The suburban night was silent, though I could see curtains rustling in the front windows of the other Campanelli ranches. We had created quite a spectacle.

The crazy we grow up with is like a pair of dirty underwear that lies unnoticed in the bathroom until we realize that a guest has seen them. Then we see our shabby world through their eyes, and feel the shame that we probably should have felt all along. My humiliated blush hid my mother's red fingermarks on my cheek.

Lee walked me to my car and stood over me as I levered myself into the Volvo. I looked up at him and said, "I'm sorry you had to see that."

Lee said, "I've seen worse."

"Not from where I sit."

"I know. I'm sorry."

I closed the door, started the engine, and rolled down the window. "Why did you come here?"

"Isn't it obvious?"

"No. I must be missing something."

"I came to see if your mother has an alibi."

TWENTY-TWO

I STOOD ON MY front stoop and imagined the contents of my refrigerator: eggs, milk, almond butter, orange juice, and a Pyrex bowl of leftover ratatouille. I was starving, disoriented, and depressed. Ratatouille was not going to help. The only solution for this combination of ailments was Bukowski Tavern on Dalton Street, where I could find an endless supply of beer and comfort food.

Bukowski Tavern is a long, low bar, built into the side of the Hilton's parking garage. The red façade juts out of the concrete walls, like a brilliant ruby set in a steel pinky ring. A bar runs down one side of the space, across from small round windows that overlook the Mass Pike. I'd had enough of the Pike for one day, and sat at the bar.

Mikey the bartender greeted me. "Dude!"

"Hi, Mikey. You still got that Dogfish 90?"

Mikey shot me with his finger, cracked open a bottle of the IPA, and poured it into a tall glass. I took the glass and downed two-thirds of it in one gulp.

"God, I needed that," I said.

Mikey looked concerned. "Dude?"

"What a shitty day, Mikey. I got shot at, I found out that my dad screwed my babysitter and had a kid with her, and my mother slapped me in the face." I pointed to the handprint.

Mikey wagged his head and looked down at the bar. "Dude."

"Exactly," I said. "I need a Barfly Burger and some sweet potato fries."

Mikey snapped his finger and pointed at me, nodding. "Dude!"

I downed my ale, relishing its hoppy goodness. "And another one of these."

Mikey brought me my beer. I reveled in solitude and played Angry Birds. Angry Birds is a game that simulates the eternal struggle between mechanical engineers, who build weapons, and civil engineers, who build targets. In the game, I launched various weaponized songbirds at rickety structures erected by hapless pigs. The swine were doomed. The game rewarded me for wreaking the most havoc possible with the fewest number of birds. It was an engineering problem I couldn't resist. I forgot about my crazy mother, her disgusting house, and my unremitting guilt and unleashed hell upon the pigs.

I sensed someone standing over my shoulder. I turned to look into the eyes of a small, bald, dark-skinned man sporting a graying goatee beard and a rumpled brown suit. He indicated the seat next to me. "May I sit?"

I said, "Sure," and went back to destroying the pig homeland.

He said, "I need to speak to you, Mr. Tucker."

"Mr. Tucker is my father. You can just call me Tucker." I pressed a button on my Droid and the Angry Birds disappeared. "How do you know my name?"

The guy ignored my question and said, "I am Talevi."

I drank my beer, waiting to see where this would go.

Talevi continued, "What do you plan to do about the death of your brother?"

My mother was right. Everybody knew this secret but us.

I said, "I plan to avenge him, raining fire and sweet death upon the dogs that took him from this Earth."

Talevi's eyes widened. He said, "Really?"

"No, not really," I said, "I have no idea what to do about my brother. I didn't even know I had a brother until today."

"Then why were you in Pittsfield?"

"How did you know I was in Pittsfield?"

"The same way that I knew to find you here," Talevi said. "I have sources."

"And what do your sources think I should do about my brother?"

"Nothing," said Talevi. "Nothing at all. They, and I, would like you to stay away from this sorry business."

Mikey brought my burger. He looked from Talevi to me, pointed his chin at Talevi, and said, "Dude?"

"Don't worry about him, Mikey. He was just leaving. Could you bring me another Dogfish?"

Mikey turned to get the beer. I took a fry from my burger plate and ate it slowly. I downed the rest of my beer, and took a bite from my burger.

Talevi said, "So?"

"So what?"

Talevi moved his hand and put it on his hip. The hand caught under his suit jacket and pulled it back to reveal a gun, in a holster, under his arm. I ignored the gun. Depression takes the edge off existential threats.

Talevi said, "Do not worry about your brother. He was a very bad man, you know. You should not risk your safety over him."

"A bad man, you say. What did he do?"

"This is none of your business."

"Hey, you brought it up."

"He got what he deserved. There is nothing more to be done about it."

"And Cathy Byrd?"

"What about her?"

"Did she get what she deserved?"

"I cannot say."

"Because I'm figuring that she got royally screwed in this."

Talevi leaned close. "If you do not become involved, this will end. Are we agreed?"

I said, "You know what, Talevi? There's nothing I'd like better than to say yes. I'd love to tell you that I'm going to ignore my dead half brother, and my dead babysitter, my dead cheating father, and my crazy mother. I'd like to do nothing more than go back to the life that I had two days ago."

"This is good."

"But my mother is being investigated for murder. So even if I told you now that I was going to ignore this mess, I probably wouldn't do it."

Talevi shook his head. "Very disappointing."

"Yeah, well, that's life."

Talevi stood. "Ignore this thing, Mr. Tucker. Go back to the life you had two days ago." He turned and I watched him wind his way out of the narrow tavern.

Two days ago I'd been a guy at a ballgame with a pretty girl. I was worried about the Red Sox bullpen, the lifespan of hermit crabs, and how I was going to spend the impending holiday season. It was my first autumn living in my new place, and my first Thanksgiving alone since my wife, Carol, had died.

I didn't know what to do about the holidays. Carol and I used to spend Thanksgiving with her family. In December, we'd take my mother out to a restaurant for a holiday dinner, then fly to Barbados for a couple of weeks of warm weather. Christmas in Barbados doesn't get captured on greeting cards, but it doesn't suck.

That life was gone. There was no Carol, no need to visit her folks, no pattern or order to the holidays. I was staring down the barrel of a Thanksgiving spent alone in my condo, watching football, talking to crustaceans, and cooking a turkey for one.

Shit. I had become a character in "Eleanor Rigby."

Of course, I did have family. Sal was clear about that. I guess my mother would go to Auntie Rosa's for Thanksgiving. Perhaps I could wangle an invitation. There could be Christmas with the Mafia. I'd show up outside Sal's house in the North End, holding a bottle of wine and getting my picture taken by an FBI guy sitting in a car across the street. I'd have to make sure that Bobby got my good side.

I had finished my burger and downed my third beer. The combination of grease, starch, and alcohol had improved my mood and reduced my inhibitions. If I was going to have Thanksgiving at Sal's house, I needed to know some things.

I dialed my Droid.

Sal answered, "I'm busy. What do you want?"

I said, "We need to talk."

TWENTY-THREE

"You are a fucking idiot," said Sal.

We sat on a bench in Christopher Columbus Park. The morning sun sparkled off the dirty Boston Harbor water as boats rocked at their moorings under a blue-white cloudless sky. A thick, black iron chain stretched between imposing black mooring posts. The chain acted as a fence, but it wouldn't keep Sal from pitching me into the ocean if the notion struck him.

"I'm not an idiot," I said. *Snappy comeback*. Words failed me around Sal.

"Why would you ask me that? Use your fucking big MIT brain and tell me how I'm supposed to answer that question."

"I think yes or no should be good enough."

"Yeah? What if I say 'No, I'm not in the Mafia'? Would you fucking believe me?"

Nobody could hear us, yet Sal whispered with furious intensity. I thought about his question. He was right. I wouldn't believe him if he denied being in the Mafia.

Sal wasn't going to let it drop. "Well? Would you believe me?"

I said, "Yeah, I would."

"Don't you fucking lie to me. I can see when you're lying."

I crossed my arms and didn't answer.

Sal went on, "And if I didn't say no, then you'd be some sort of witness. Fuck. Are you wearing a wire?" He reached over and began to paw at me. He opened my Sox jacket and ran his hands down my chest and back. He patted my thighs and reached up my crotch. It was like airport security.

"That's not a microphone," I said.

Sal said, "Fuck you."

I pushed his hands away. "I'm not wearing a wire. What do you think I am?"

Sal said, "I don't know what you are."

"Well, I'll tell you this. I'm not a liar."

"What's that supposed to mean?"

"You told me that I didn't have a brother, and it turned out that I did. You lied to me."

Sal stood and took a step toward home. Then he turned, stuck his finger in my face. "Of course I lied to you. It was none of your fucking business."

I stood, not wanting to be loomed over, and got in Sal's face. "My half brother was none of my business?"

"No. He wasn't."

"That's ridiculous. And I suppose Cathy Byrd wasn't—"

"She's a whore," said Sal.

"You shouldn't talk that way about the dead."

"Dead? What the fuck are you talking about?"

"She's dead. Somebody shot her yesterday, and the Boston Police suspect my mother." I sat.

Sal sat back down too. "They think Auntie Angelina did it? Idiots."

Sal's breath formed small puffs in the morning air. With his greatcoat and suit, he looked like he could either head over to the financial district or back to the North End. He had an early-morning five o'clock shadow, and there was a nick high on his sideburn. The blood had crusted, forming a scab. I tried to fathom how this guy was related to me and what that meant.

Sal said, "She didn't know about Cathy Byrd."

"Then how did you know about her?"

"I just knew that my mother said that Auntie Angelina's baby-sitter was a whore," said Sal.

"Why would Auntie Rosa say that?"

"Because your father asked my father for money."

"Money? Money for what?"

Sal was silent.

Money? I turned the information over in my head. It was another data point in the puzzle. The mystery was like a tough game of Tetris. I twisted the new data, trying to get it to fit in with the other blocks of information and generate a flash of insight. Sal had started to rise when the information about the money snugged into a slot in the puzzle. The blocks disappeared and I knew why Dad had wanted the money.

I put my hand on Sal's arm to keep him seated. I said, "The house. He wanted the money so he could buy Cathy Byrd a house."

Sal glared at me. Then he said, "Yeah."

"He wanted to borrow money from your father."

"Yeah. It was stupid. We couldn't lend money to Auntie Angelina's husband. It would be bad business. My dad offered to give him the money."

"So your dad bought Cathy Byrd's house?"

"No. Your father didn't want a handout. He wouldn't take the money."

"So where did he get it?"

"I don't know."

We stared across the harbor as a 757 lumbered its way into the air, rising from Logan into the blue sky. Somehow, my dad had bought a house and my mother never saw a hint of the cash.

I said, "Maybe he got the money from Uncle Walt."

Sal barked a laugh. "That deadbeat? I'll tell you this: if that son of a bitch has any money, he had better use it to pay his debts."

"You lent money to my Uncle Walt?"

Sal rose and said, "Tucker, keep your fucking nose out of this. It doesn't matter anymore. Everyone's dead. You keep poking around this shit, you're gonna get hurt."

I stood. "That's what Talevi said."

Sal said, "Talevi? What do you have to do with Talevi?"

"He found me at Bukowski Tavern yesterday and told me the same thing you did. He said I should stay out of this."

Sal gripped my upper arm in his beefy hand and looked me square in the face. "Do not fuck with Talevi. That guy is a dangerous little shit."

"Yeah. He threatened to kill me."

"You fuck with him, you'll be lucky if he kills you. Last guy who fucked with Talevi got his hands shoved into a wood chipper."

"I'll be careful," I said.

Sal let go of my arm and pointed at my face. "You get out of this fucking thing and go home to the South End."

"I'll think about it."

"You do more than think about it. And another thing: don't you fucking ever tell Talevi that you know me. You got that? *Capisce*?"

"Yeah. I *capisce*."

"Now forget this shit."

Sal walked down Atlantic Avenue toward the North End, leaving me standing next to a black iron piling. I pulled out my Droid and fired up the Zipcar app. A car was ready over on India Street, so I started walking.

I was heading back to the suburbs to invite Uncle Walt out for lunch.

TWENTY-FOUR

WITH ITS PEAKED ROOF, demure gray exterior, beige trim, and carefully manicured landscaping, the building on Route 20 in Sudbury could have been a bank, a doctor's office, a small museum, or a McMansion. Instead, it was a Chinese restaurant called Lotus Blossom. The restaurant had tossed away any attempt at looking Chinese and had, instead, fit itself into the suburban homogeneity that surrounded it. Uncle Walt insisted upon eating here.

Uncle Walt wanted to sample Lotus Blossom's lunch buffet. I had gone with the white rice, buffet sushi, stir-fried vegetables, pot stickers, and my guilty pleasure, a piece of General Gau's chicken. Walt had loaded up on egg rolls, chicken wings, fried wontons, and crab rangoon. If it was fried, gooey, or crispy, it was on Walt's plate.

Uncle Walt stuck his fork into a crab rangoon, squirting white goo onto the dish. He held up the fried pocket, dripping ooze.

"You gotta try this!" said Uncle Walt.

"No. I'm good," I said.

"You're missing out."

"You want any sushi?"

"Is it cooked?" asked Walt.

"No. It's sushi."

"Get back to me when it's cooked." He popped the rangoon into his mouth and went after an egg roll.

"How do you stay so thin, eating like that?"

"I only eat this stuff on special occasions, like when you call me twice in the same week. We haven't talked in years and suddenly you're out here all the time. What's up?"

"Cathy Byrd was murdered yesterday, and they think my mother did it." I watched Walt for any reaction to her name. There was none.

Walt said, "Who?"

"Cathy Byrd. JT's mother and my father's second wife."

"Second wife? What the hell are you talking about?"

I told Walt about the house, the murder, and the pictures—all the pictures of my father enjoying a happy life with his other family.

Walt said, "Holy shit."

"Yeah."

"He never told me about any of this."

"Are you sure?" I asked.

"What's that supposed to mean? Of course I'm sure. Do you think I'd forget him shacking up with some hot little number out in Pittsfield? Do you think I'd forget about a second kid? As far as I knew, you were John's only kid, and he was kind of stuck with your mother."

"Stuck with my mother? What does that mean?"

"Come on, Tucker. I mean, you lived with them. Could you call that a happy marriage?"

"How would I have known?"

"I mean, with all due respect to your mother, she had problems. She was unstable. He was always tiptoeing around, trying not to set off the land mines."

The food on my plate looked like a pile of dead fish on white rice. I wasn't eating that. I poked at a piece of salmon with my chopstick.

"If things were so bad, why didn't Dad divorce her?"

"He just didn't believe in it. He figured that he had made his bed and that he could lie in it. Plus, I think he was afraid of the Rizzos."

"Well, that can't be true," I said.

"Why not?"

"Because he asked my uncle to lend him the money to buy the house for Cathy."

Walt bit into the egg roll in his hand. Flecks of shredded vegetable fell out of the egg roll onto his plate. He chewed and then washed the fried mass down with a chug of his Budweiser. "He asked Frank Rizzo for a loan? Was he crazy?"

"Why would he be crazy?"

"Because the Rizzos are in the Mafia, Tucker. Didn't you know that?"

I pushed my plate away. "No. Apparently, I was the only one who didn't know it."

"That's because you never paid attention to your family. The Rizzos are crazy bastards."

It was time for my gambit. "Then why did you borrow from them?"

Walt reddened. "What did you say?"

"Sal said that you owe him money," I said.

Walt pushed his plate aside and pointed his fork at me. "That's bullshit. I don't owe Sal anything."

"That's not what he says."

"Tucker, I love you like a nephew, but we're done here. This is all none of your business. Just back off."

"I can't back off. They think my mother killed Cathy Byrd."

"She probably did. Your mother is a lunatic."

I was standing and our beers had tipped across the table. My fist was balled. I pointed at Uncle Walt.

"You shut up!"

"Will you sit down, for Christ's sake? You're making a scene," said Walt.

I leaned on the table. "You fucking take that back."

"Sit down!"

The restaurant was silent. Even the buffet line had stopped moving. The lunchtime crowd stared at me. I stared back. A guy in a business suit broke eye contact with me. Two women who had been talking went back to their conversation. A serving spoon clinked at the buffet table. I sat and the restaurant slipped back into motion.

Walt said, "Look. I'm sorry. I shouldn't have said that about your mother."

I drank my water. "So you don't owe Sal money."

"I don't want to talk about it. It's none of your business. You mind telling me what you're trying to accomplish?"

"I'm trying to figure out what's going on."

"Why?"

"Because I know my mother didn't kill Cathy Byrd, and I'm going to prove it."

That was what I said, but as I paid for lunch and Walt and I walked to our cars, I reflected upon the real reason. Two days ago I'd had a clear picture of how the world worked and who I was. I was Aloysius Tucker, the only son of John and Angelina Tucker. I had family in the North End—loud and Italian, but just a normal family. I was a widower, but I was getting on with my life. I was inching toward having a girlfriend.

Suddenly, all that was gone. I was Aloysius Tucker, the older son of John Tucker, who had another family with another wife and another son. A wife and a son he seemed to prefer to my mother and me.

These new people, these other people, had been murdered, and my mother and I had been dragged into it. My father had set wheels in motion that threatened to crush us. He had set up a mythical world that had shattered and left me without a foundation. I couldn't live without a foundation. I wouldn't stop digging until I knew exactly where I stood and what I was standing upon. I refused to live the rest of my life as a puzzle piece looking for a place to fit.

TWENTY-FIVE

My Droid uttered its name in its spooky robotic voice as soon as I pulled out of Lotus Blossom's parking lot. Lucy. A little happy flutter skipped through my stomach. I believed it was time for her to have a unique ringtone.

I stuck my Bluetooth headset into my ear and continued down Route 20 in Borg-like comfort.

Lucy said, "I'm calling you with a question of etiquette."

"Good. You've come to the right place. I'm all about politeness."

"If a girl were to go to a man's house, let him cook her a delicious meal, neck with him a little on the couch, and then leave abruptly, would it be okay if that girl called the man for a follow-up date?"

"If the girl wants to be known as a brazen hussy and part of the general moral decay that will soon be the death of our beloved country, then yes. It would be fine."

"Good. Would you like to go out on a date tonight?"

"Absolutely. What did you have in mind?"

"I thought we'd be tourists."

We agreed to meet at six o'clock at the Samuel Adams statue in front of Faneuil Hall, and I continued driving down the old Indian trail that was Route 20. Colonists had widened it to create the Boston Post Road. The road took you from Boston, through Springfield, and down to Hartford, Connecticut. I imagined what the road would have looked like before all the trees had been cut down for fuel and farming. New trees grew along the road, but they were much younger than the path I followed.

Your mother is a lunatic.

I had told Walt to take it back, but that didn't make it wrong. The slide into hoarding, the temper flare-ups, the slapping—I had grown up with all these things, integrated them into my life, into what I called *normal*.

I opened that corner of my mind where I had shoved my motherhood baggage and was overwhelmed with its crushing weight. My vision narrowed to the car in front of me, the sunny day eclipsed by my mother's shadow. Could she have killed Cathy Byrd? Did the Rizzos have some genetic flaw that had turned my uncle and cousin into Mafiosos and my mother into a killer?

I couldn't see it. The woman couldn't even buy a cell phone. How would she get a gun? Of course, my mother's sister Auntie Rosa was married to the mob, so my mother was connected. But why now?

The shadow cleared and I was driving on a sunny September day. I wasn't on Route 20 anymore, I was on the Mass Pike, heading into the city. I had navigated Route 128 and the exchange without conscious thought. My Bluetooth headphone dangled from my ear. I thought about Pittsfield. Dialed Information, called General Dynamics, and asked for a name, then got connected through.

"Patterson," said a voice.

"Dave Patterson, this is—Mr. Bologna, from yesterday's meeting."

"Oh," said Patterson.

"Dave, I have a confession to make," I said.

"Really? What's that?"

"My last name isn't Bologna. It's Tucker."

"Tucker?"

"I'm Aloysius Tucker, JT's half brother."

"Oh, shit. Jesus, I didn't mean to say all those things about you yesterday."

"You seemed sincere."

Silence.

"Dave? Are you still there?" I asked. Cell reception is usually perfect on the Pike.

"Yeah," said Patterson. "Why did you lie to me?"

"That was Bobby's idea. He was investigating something and didn't want to distract you."

"What do you want?"

"I wanted to tell you that I never heard of JT or his mother until JT was murdered in front of my house. Since then, things have gone off the rails. JT's mother was killed and a guy named Talevi threatened me. Also, I found out—Well, never mind. I saw you in those pictures in JT's house. You're his best friend. Do you have any idea what's going on?"

Silence.

"Dave?" I prompted.

Patterson said, "Look, Aloysius—"

"Please call me Tucker. Everyone calls me Tucker."

"Okay, Tucker. I wish I could help you. I really do. But I can't."

"Do you have any idea why JT was coming to see me at my house? Why was he carrying the cover of the Paladin spec?"

A pause, then, "I don't know why he would have done that. He hated you."

I said, "Hated me? Why would he hate me?"

"Because you got to sit in the front row at his father's funeral and he had to sit in the back."

"I didn't—"

"I was there. It was fucking horrible. Everybody was comforting you and your mother. They ignored JT."

"Yeah, but nobody knew."

"That made it even worse. Mr. Tucker never told JT about his other family. He let JT think that he was married to Ms. Byrd. We never knew why JT's mom wouldn't take the name Tucker. We thought it was some women's lib thing. Turns out they weren't married at all. JT was never the same after that funeral."

"So who killed him? Was it Talevi?"

"He wouldn't—I don't know. How would I know? Look, I gotta go. Give me your cell. I'll call you if I think of anything."

I recited my Droid's number and the line went dead. I told my Droid to dial Bobby Miller.

Bobby Miller answered, "What's up, Tucker?"

"We need to talk."

TWENTY-SIX

"Great. Just fucking great," said Bobby Miller. We were sitting kitty-corner at the bar of the Millennium Bostonian Hotel, next to Faneuil Hall, drinking Oban 14-year-old Scotch whisky. The bar's cold marble top contrasted with the warm maple paneling and complemented the array of liquor bottles displayed along the wall. Bobby's head reflected the light from one of the glowing incandescent tubes that hung from the ceiling. Big windows behind him showed traffic oozing along North Street like rush-hour sludge. Bobby had just learned about my confession to Patterson.

"I'm sorry," I said and swallowed some Scotch.

"You made me look like a fucking idiot."

"I thought I might learn more if he knew who I was."

"And did you learn anything?"

I looked into my Scotch; it was gone. "I learned that my father was an asshole."

Bobby said, "Welcome to the club. We all learn that eventually. Shit, our kids are gonna learn it too."

"No," I said, "I mean a real asshole. He never told JT about me or about my mother, just like he never told us about them."

"Why would he?"

"It would have been the decent thing to do."

"It would have been a stupid thing to do. You saw those pictures in his old house. That was one happy motherfucker right there. Why would he screw that up?"

"He couldn't be happy with me? With my mother?"

Bobby waved the bartender over to reload us. "Don't be so hard on him, dude. Only two people know what goes on in a marriage. Judging them won't help."

The Scotch was having the desired self-medicating effect, easing me into a Zen-like state where I focused on how my body moved and what was happening in the moment. My father's indiscretions and my mother's lunacy were fading into the background.

"How about my Uncle Walt? Can I judge him?" I asked.

"What did he do?"

"He owes Sal money."

"Did he tell you that?"

"No. Sal did."

Bobby said nothing. He looked into his Scotch, looked up at the ceiling, got up from his chair, and headed out to the bathroom. The Millennium bathrooms were through the lobby and down the hall. Bobby would be gone for a while. I puzzled about his departure, took out my Droid, checked the time. Quarter to six. Opened Angry Birds and got three stars on a particularly tough pig fortification.

Bobby returned. He stood next to me, shot down his Scotch, and then grabbed me by the back of the neck, looking into my eyes.

I said, "Hey!" and resisted his grip, but he wouldn't relent.

Bobby said, "I was in the men's room when you said something, to yourself, about Sal Rizzo's business. I never heard it, because if I had heard it, then I'm sure it would have made you into a material witness."

I swallowed.

"Never," said Bobby, "never, never, never, tell me anything Sal says. You got that?"

"Yeah, but—"

Bobby's grip tightened. "Fucking *never*."

"Okay. Okay."

Bobby released my neck, patted my shoulder, and sat back down. "It's for your own good. It would be a terrible thing to have to testify against your own family."

I rubbed my neck. "I guess."

"Family's the thing, my friend. You can't choose them, but you gotta love them."

"So was JT part of my family?"

"Whether you wanted him or not, he's definitely part of your family. Hell, he's making trouble for you and he's dead. Imagine if he were alive."

I drank Scotch and thought about the trouble JT had created. I said, "Bobby, what am I going to do about my mother?"

"Did she kill Cathy Byrd?"

"No, she didn't kill Cathy Byrd."

"Then don't sweat it, leave it alone."

"That's what Talevi said."

Bobby said, "Holy fuck, you are just full of surprises today. How do you know Talevi?"

"He came to visit me at Bukowski yesterday. He told me to leave this thing with my mother alone or he'd kill me. How do *you* know Talevi?"

"He works for the Pakistani embassy. We think he's a spy, but he's got immunity and we haven't been able to prove it. I'll tell you this, he's a mean fucker."

"That's what Sal said."

"What did I just tell you about Sal?"

I raised my hands in surrender. "I know. I know. I'm sorry."

"But now that you brought it up... How does Sal know him?"

I finished my Scotch and waved off the bartender. Threw cash onto the bar. "Don't ask me."

Bobby said, "Now you're getting the hang of it."

I said, "No. Seriously. I have no idea what's going on. All I know is that Talevi told me to drop it."

Bobby finished his own Scotch and threw his cash on the bar. He said, "If it were anyone but you, I'd tell them to drop it. Let Lieutenant Lee and me handle it."

"But you're not going to say that to me?"

"It's a waste of breath with you. I'll tell you this, though."

"What?"

"If your uncle lives out west and owes money, then he owes it to Hugh Graxton, not Sal."

"Who's that?"

"He's the guy who runs all the action between Newton and Worcester."

"Why are you telling me this?"

"Because you're not related to Graxton, and I'd love to nail that bastard. Let me know if you learn anything else about him."

"Sounds like you don't like the guy."

"If you ever meet him, you won't like him either. He's a mouthy asshole."

"What's wrong with being a mouthy asshole?"

"Good point. You two might get along fine."

"Okay. I gotta go. Lucy's going to be waiting for me."

"You have fun."

"Will do."

"And be careful."

"Sure, Bobby. Whatever."

TWENTY-SEVEN

SAMUEL ADAMS STOOD ON his pedestal, his face stern, his right foot tapping the ground, and his arms crossed with a newspaper rolled up in his left hand. The sculptor Anne Whitney had either caught him in the act of demanding that British troops leave Boston or scolding his dog for pooping on the rug. It was hard to tell.

The statue stood in the middle of the broad stone plaza that fronted Faneuil Hall. Peter Faneuil had built the structure in 1742 and donated it to Boston so that the city might have a central marketplace. The Boston Town Meeting had voted to accept the gift by a close vote of 367–360, honoring a long tradition in New England of regarding anything that is new or free with profound suspicion.

Whether it was due to my forays into the suburbs, my dustup with my mother, or my introduction to a dead brother, Boston seemed especially alive tonight. The crowd breathed life into the place, lifting my spirits and showing me the bright side of life.

It was a warm September evening. Breakdancers twirled and leapt while their friends worked the crowd, collecting money in a Red Sox hat with an oversized logo splashed across its side. Mayor Kevin White's gigantic statue strode into the tourist attraction he created, his jacket thrown over his shoulder, his free hand gesturing to an invisible conversationalist.

I scooted through the gap between the statue and the breakdancer crowd. Faneuil Hall lay in front of me. Commuters charged through the plaza on their way to the Government Center train station, dog walkers led their charges, and shoppers rushed home with their loot.

Lucy crouched at the base of Sam Adams's statue, petting a cocker spaniel. The dog's owner, an older woman wearing a business suit, smiled at the attention and then gave the dog a little tug to continue its walk. Lucy stood and looked around the plaza. When our eyes met, she smiled her brilliant smile. It was a smile that said *I'm so happy to see you!* It was just what I needed.

I said, "I'd be careful of cocker spaniels. I hear they're a love 'em and leave 'em breed."

Lucy said, "I'll be sure not to get my hopes up. Besides, I don't think he had a job."

Lucy threw her arms over my shoulders and pulled me close for a kiss. I responded. The kiss went on for a beat longer than I expected. It was a nice surprise. She pulled back and said, "Somebody's been drinking."

"Yeah—Bobby Miller. He was definitely drinking."

"I see."

"Let's get some supper."

Lucy took my arm as we walked around Faneuil Hall toward Quincy Market. We rounded the corner of the building and winced at the loud drumming of a guy who had inverted a series of buckets and was rapping out a staccato bucket solo. Lucy pulled herself closer to me in response to the auditory assault. Her breast pressed against my arm and thoughts of Sal, JT, and my mother were banished. Lucy and I ran past the bucketeer and into the market, where we were immediately rewarded with one of the best smells in Boston.

Quincy Market houses a long line of exotic food court eateries. We walked into the market and past a brightly colored collection of curries, a raw bar serving clams on the half shell, a submarine sandwich shop, a Regina Pizzeria, and a Mediterranean place that served gyros and falafel. There were cookies, chocolates, beers, wines, roast beef, and boiled lobster. There was a Japanese place that gave free samples, and there was, of course, a Starbucks.

Lucy said, "I don't know where to start."

I said, "I think this situation requires a complete reconnaissance before we can make an informed decision."

We wandered down one side of the food court and back up the other, comparing options and taking note of the especially yummy. We stopped for a beer, then retraced our steps through the market and bought food at the winning eateries. We bought a lobster roll, chicken curry, hummus and pita bread, and an Italian sausage with peppers and onions. For dessert we chose a chunk of fudge and two coffees. Then we walked back to the center of the market and into the great hall.

The rotunda of Quincy Market is like the hub of a propeller. It's a large, circular, domed room with tables and chairs set up for wandering diners. Staircases swept up the corners to the second level. We climbed the stairs and found a circular eatery, where we sat at a butcher-block table against the railing that overlooked the lower level. The market's gleaming dome arched above us.

Lucy cut the lobster roll in half and we shared it as we talked.

Lucy bit into her piece of the roll and said, "You haven't mentioned your brother."

I said, "I'm trying to forget my brother."

"Really?"

"Since he showed up, things have gone from good to bad and then bad to worse. Bobby yelled at me, my cousin called me an idiot, some guy named Talevi threatened me with a gun, and my mother slapped me in the face."

"Oh my God! She did?"

"Yeah. It happens sometimes."

"Are you okay?"

"She's a little bit crazy, so I need to cut her some slack."

"There's cutting people slack and then there's allowing yourself to be assaulted."

"Well, I really can't call an open-handed smack from a five-foot-tall Italian woman an assault."

"You can if it's from your mother."

I was annoyed. This wasn't how tonight was supposed to go. I dipped some pita bread into the hummus, ate it, and changed the subject to something lighter.

"Personally, I'm more worried about the guy with the gun," I said.

"Talevi?"

I said, "Yeah. Bobby says he's a spy. My cousin Sal seems to know him too, but I can't see how."

"Is Talevi Italian?" said Lucy.

"No. He works for the Pakistani embassy."

"His name ends in an *i*. Could be Iranian."

"You think the Mafia's letting Iranians in?"

Lucy said something, but my brain had gone for a holiday, trying to fit an Iranian spy into an Italian loan-sharking operation. The piece not only didn't fit in, but it was the wrong size and color. It was like having a puzzle piece with a little skull on it when you were trying to make a puzzle of a kitten hanging onto a rope.

I came back into the conversation and heard the tail end of Lucy saying, "—Pittsfield?"

"Huh?" I said.

"I asked how things went in Pittsfield."

"Pittsfield was bad," I said. Then I told her just how bad it was. I ended with the story about my mother being a murder suspect and the slap. When I was done, she was silent.

I said, "I'm a hell of a fun guy, aren't I?"

Lucy put her hand on mine. "Tucker, you are a great guy and a good man. None of this is your fault. I'm sorry I keep bringing it up."

"It's kind of like slowing down to look at a car accident, isn't it?"

Lucy smiled. "Yeah. A little. Let's forget about it. Deal?"

"Deal."

I prepared another bite of lobster roll and asked Lucy about her day at school. She took over and told me about how her high school students were splicing glowing genes into E. coli to make a new form of glowing life. We had never done *that* in high school.

"I don't know," I said. "It seems that there are things that man was not meant to know."

"Well, my kids had better know it," said Lucy.

I munched my food and nodded while she spoke. It was pleasant. Comfortable. We finished up our food and threw away the refuse. As we walked down the staircase, I said, "Let's go shopping."

Buying a present was supposed to be the capstone to a beautiful evening. It wasn't.

TWENTY-EIGHT

TRADITIONS DIE HARD IN Boston. Quincy Market was built as a place for pushcart vendors to hawk their wares and, by God, Bostonians were going to maintain that tradition for as long as there were vendors and wares. As a result, pushcarts adorn the outer edge of Quincy Market, protected by a glass lean-to that keeps shoppers warm and dry in the winter and cool and dry in the summer.

I was never one for shopping at the pushcarts. Not that anything was wrong with them, but they specialized in the kinds of trinkets and doodads that tourists buy. I didn't need a sign that read No PAHKING.

Lucy, on the other hand, reveled in the pushcarts. She pulled me from cart to cart, showing me Christmas ornaments, little men made out of corncobs, jewelry fashioned out of beads, and finally a scarf with a long zipper.

The guy at the cart demonstrated. "It starts out as a tube." He tugged on a zipper that wound around the tube, unrolling it like an apple peel. "Then it unzips to become a scarf."

Lucy said, "You should like this, Tucker. You're an engineer."

At the word *engineer,* my critical side slipped out. "It's a zipper."

"It's a very clever zipper."

I wasn't going to let my evening get derailed over this guy and his zipper, so I stifled the comment that it was still just a zipper and went with, "It's like a knitted Transformer."

The guy selling the thing gave me a look. *A Transformer?* But Lucy was happy to run with the idea.

"Exactly! It's a Transformer. It transforms from a hood to a scarf." She wrapped it around her neck and let the tail of it trail over her breast. The scarf was a deep sky blue.

I said, "It matches your eyes."

"Really?"

"Yes, I think it's very pretty. May I buy it for you?"

Lucy blushed and said, "Why, thank you."

I paid for the zipscarf, and Lucy and I walked back down among the carts. We were passing a cart full of sports pictures when the beer and coffee caught up with me.

I said, "Excuse me, m'lady. I need to pee."

Lucy pointed at the restroom sign in the middle of the building and said, "Pee away, m'lord. I'll be right here tchotchke shopping."

I said, "You go, girl," and headed to the bathroom sign.

The bathrooms in Quincy Market are in the catacombs under the building. A hallway stretches from one side to the other. So you can leave one set of pushcarts, walk through the restroom hallway, and come up among more pushcarts. The hallway has white tile, and signs hang above the men's room and the women's room.

The men's room starts as a twisty passage that ensures privacy without the need for a door. There is more white tile, and a gizmo that will weigh you for a quarter—perhaps for guys who want to do a before-and-after analysis. Once through the twisty passage, the bathroom opens into a long low rectangle with stalls and sinks to one side and urinals tucked away into a dead end on the other.

The bathroom was empty. Man Law dictated that I walk down into the dead end and take the urinal farthest from the door. This allows other men to use the urinals without having to stand next to you. You only stood next to another guy when there was no other option, and then you kept conversation to a minimum.

I approached the last urinal, unzipped, and started my business. Another guy came into the men's room. I glanced at him peripherally but kept my eyes on the work in front of me. A cigarette in the urinal beckoned for destruction.

The other guy walked into the urinal cave and said, "Hey, Tucker!"

I looked up and got a glimpse of a narrow bald head. Then my world exploded. A loud cracking sound reverberated through my skull. My head whipped back around from the blow and smacked into the wall tiles.

The guy kicked my knee out from behind, the kneecap hitting the urinal as I folded backward onto the floor. He grabbed me by the shirt front, and I smelt the stink of cigarettes on him. I raised my arms to shield my face, but he hit me again on the side of the head with something hard. His boot caught me in the solar plexus. My eyes crossed. My stomach twisted. Nausea and dizziness overwhelmed me.

The guy grabbed my shirt and pulled my face close. He had yellow teeth, his breath stinking of beer. A black tattoo teardrop bled from the corner of one eye. Teardrop said, "Mind your own fucking business!" Then he dropped my head on the floor, disappearing as I puked across the tiles.

TWENTY-NINE

STITCHES SCRAPED ALONG THE pillow, making a grating sound that drove me from a dreamless sleep. Pain pulsed in my temple, reminding me of my beating. Just before I opened my eyes, I recalled an image of a brass-knuckled fist bearing down on me.

I opened my eyes and lay in my bed, not moving, assessing the damage. My head hurt. My side hurt. I wiggled my toes and flexed my fingers. My right hand hurt. My stomach twitched, but the rest of me was okay. I sat up and looked around the room.

It turned out to be my bedroom. A large framed picture of Fenway Park hung on the wall across from me. A small window faced out over the parking lot behind my building. The trees across the road swayed in the late summer sun. I swung my feet over the edge of the bed, resting them on the warm floor, and reconstructed how I had gotten here. My memories were a swirl of police, EMTs, emergency rooms, and Lucy looking horrified as they wheeled me out of the men's room. Still, she stuck with me. She and Bobby had brought me home and dropped me into bed.

A mug clunked onto the counter in my kitchen. I opened the door, expecting to see Lucy. Instead I saw Jael Navas.

There are all sorts of friends: happy friends, sad friends, childhood friends, interesting friends, sports friends, work friends, and boring friends. In Jael Navas, I was lucky enough to have a deadly friend.

Bobby had hooked me up with Jael back when the Russian Mafia was threatening my life. He knew her from some murky international entanglements and her work for Mossad. Jael had given up that life and become a PI in Boston.

If Jael was sitting in my house, then Bobby thought that things had gotten dangerous.

Jael looked up from her newspaper and said, "You look worse than I had expected."

"Good morning to you too."

"Agent Miller told me that you had been beaten. But I had not expected stitches."

"Do they look bad?"

Jael got up from the bar chair to inspect my stitches. At five-ten, she looked me straight in the eye. She had short black hair and wore black jeans with a gray top that came up to her neck. The top's tight fabric revealed hints of the muscles in her back and arms. Her steady and surprisingly gentle fingers probed my stitches.

"The cut is near the hairline. The scar should be small and easy to hide."

"Where's Lucy?"

"Agent Miller drove her home after I arrived." Jael's nose twitched. "You should take a shower."

I went into the bathroom and looked in the mirror. Jael was right about the stitches. There was a crescent cut on the side of my brow up near the hair about a half-inch long. My cheek had a purple bruise, and there was a bump on the back of my head. My ribs hurt where they had been kicked.

I showered and dressed. Ground some Bitches Brew coffee from Wired Puppy, brewed, and poured it. I made us wheat toast and almond butter sandwiches. While we ate, Jael examined Click and Clack, the hermit crabs.

She said, "I assume these are not food."

"No," I said. "They're pets. I doubt they're kosher."

Jael, who was an observant Jew, said, "No. They are definitely *trayf*. I wonder if they should be kept in a kitchen."

"Even if they have their own silverware?"

Jael watched Clack harvest food bits from his sponge and asked, "Why were you beaten?"

"Bobby didn't tell you?"

"Agent Miller didn't know."

I told Jael the whole story up to yesterday when I had my drink with Bobby. It didn't get easier in the retelling. In fact, it got worse. I had a dead brother I didn't know about. My father had a family I didn't know about. My cousin had an occupation I didn't know about. My pseudo-uncle had loans I didn't know about. Yet, despite everything I didn't know, somebody was worried that I knew too much.

Jael said, "It would be smart to stop asking questions about this."

I said, "You too?"

"What do you mean?"

"Are you also going to tell me to quit?"

"No. I do not understand how you could consider quitting after a man has beaten you."

Jael was right. Some guy had beaten me up. He had shown me that I was unable to keep myself safe, that my face was his plaything. He had snuck up on me while my dick was in my hand and assaulted me. I'd never forget him—his dark skin and teardrop tattoo, his smell, the rough feeling of the skin on his hands as I feebly batted at them and tried to get away. If I found him right now, I'd kill him.

I hated him.

I drank my coffee with a shaking hand and said, "I am bullshit."

Jael said, "Bullshit? This is not bullshit. This is serious."

"No. I *am* bullshit. I'm angry."

"When Bobby Miller told me that you had been beaten, I knew your enemies had made a mistake."

"Enemies? I've got enemies?"

"People with no enemies rarely get beaten in a toilet."

"What mistake did they make?"

"They punched the bear."

"You mean they poked the bear."

"Yes. They poked the bear."

"So now what do I do?"

Jael smiled. "Poke them back."

THIRTY

"IT IS LIKELY THAT Hugh Graxton will recognize you. He is very smart," said Jael. We were driving west on Route 9 in her Acura MDX. Jael drove with smooth, athletic economy. Her eyes flicked constantly across the road and between her mirrors.

"How do you know him?" I asked.

"We have had dealings."

"Friendly dealings?"

Jael glanced at me. "Graxton is an attractive and charming man." This was news to me. I had never heard Jael venture any opinion of any man. "He is also dangerous. He cannot be trusted. He makes much of his money from loans."

"You haven't told me about your dealings."

"They were professional."

"I see."

Jael drove on. "I do not like your plan," she said.

"Why not?"

"It is pointless."

"I'm tired of people lying to me. I want to get an edge. I want to know some information before I start asking questions."

Jael said nothing and we continued west to Chestnut Hill.

Chestnut Hill is an affluent chunk of neighborhoods that overlie Boston, Newton, and Brookline. It doesn't exist as a city, but as a place name embedded in the minds of Bostonians. It is home to high-end malls and high-end people, one of the most affluent places on the East Coast.

While my cousin Sal likes to sit in the Cafe Vittoria on Hanover Street, Jael had told me that Graxton liked to sit in a Starbucks in Chestnut Hill near the Longfellow Cricket Club (where they play tennis).

"What does he do in there?" I asked.

"He drinks coffee, surfs the Web, and talks to people."

"So, he's like a consultant."

"Yes. The untrained person will think that he is a businessman."

I said, "You know, I like to drink coffee and surf the Web." Then I had told Jael my plan and convinced her to drive me to Chestnut Hill. She pulled into the parking lot, backed into a space, and turned off the car.

"Graxton knows me," Jael said. "I cannot accompany you."

"I'll be fine. He won't shoot me in a Starbucks."

"What if he sees what you are doing?"

"He won't."

"I will stay here," Jael said. "Call me if you need help."

"Will do." I grabbed my laptop and headed for the Starbucks.

The Chestnut Hill Starbucks is a low rectangular box with a barista station in one corner. I entered and scanned the place. I saw the usual assortment of blond wooden tables, merchandise racks filled with dozens of ways to make or drink coffee, and tall metallic bags of the stuff itself. It was eleven o'clock in the morning. We were between the first-cup rush of the day and the afternoon pick-me-up crowd. Five people were sitting in the Starbucks. Four of them had Macs, one had a PC.

The guy with the PC was a human boulder. He pecked at the thing with thick fingers, his lips moving. He sat at the last table in the Starbucks. Boulderman sat next to another guy with a brand-new MacBook Air. From Jael's description, the guy with the new Mac was Hugh Graxton.

Graxton looked as if he frequented the cricket club. He was fit, craggy, and handsome. His short salt-and-pepper hair gripped his scalp; it would not, *could not*, be mussed. He was wearing a white shirt, open at the throat, and a gray checked sports jacket. Graxton made eye contact with me as I entered and broke it immediately.

I got myself a coffee and a chocolate biscotti. While they poured my coffee, I texted Lucy. She was teaching class, so it was pointless to call.

Thanks for the help last night. Call you later.

I ensconced myself far away from Graxton and his pet rock. Then I opened my computer and launched Firefox. Time to do some Facebook hacking.

THIRTY-ONE

SAY THE NAME "ERIC Butler" to anyone in computer security, and you'll get one of three responses: an eye roll, as in *Oh jeez, that guy is a tool*; red-faced indignation—*Son of a bitch!*; or a thoughtful pause—*Well, I wouldn't have done it, but he has a point.* I fall into the third camp.

Eric Butler took a vexing computer security problem that was being ignored by Facebook, Twitter, and other sites, and turned it into a public security problem that would cause either panic in the streets or improved computer security. Butler wrote Firesheep, a hacking tool so fiendishly easy to use that your grandmother could sit in a Starbucks and spy on your Facebook account.

Whenever someone logs into Facebook, the site checks their username and password and then puts a little file on their computer called a cookie. The cookie is their key into Facebook. Normally Facebook doesn't encrypt these cookies, so Firesheep steals them and presents them to you as a neat list of hackable people. You just double click on the picture of the person who interests you and *voilà*, Facebook thinks you are that person. I was going to use Firesheep to learn more about Hugh Graxton.

I started up Firesheep. It presented the profile pictures of the three hackable people in the Starbucks. I looked around and matched them up.

A fat guy named Wallace Jones was sitting in an easy chair across the room. His blubber filled the chair the way pudding fills a bowl. His computer rested on his immense stomach, a gut-top. His profile picture was an unsightly closeup. He looked like Jabba the Hut wearing hipster glasses.

The next profile belonged to a voluptuous nurse named Nancy McCarthy. She wore stretchy tights as pants and a long cable-knit sweater as she sat at a table and pecked away on her iPhone. I figured she was a nurse because her profile picture showed her in scrubs. I flirted briefly with the possibility of using Firesheep to pick up women. *Nancy! How are you doing? It's me, Tucker! You remember me, right?*

I reminded myself that I must only use my powers for Good.

Hugh Graxton was not on the list. Graxton had to assume that the FBI would follow all his WiFi traffic. He was probably using hidemyass.com to make himself invisible on the WiFi network. But Hugh Graxton was not my target.

My target was the boulder sitting next to Graxton. I had guessed that he was less likely to be computer savvy, and more likely to be stupid about his online presence. I was right. His Facebook account said his name was Oscar Sagese.

Oscar had a profile picture of himself with a shot glass in his hand and a blonde on his lap. I clicked on the picture and logged into Facebook as Oscar. I jumped to his info page. It told me that he was Catholic, interested in women, and lived in Watertown. I took a screenshot of his contact page in case I wanted to use his cell phone number or email address later. Then I got to work.

Social network users are the barnyard animals of the server farms. They feast happily on the free offerings of Farmer Facebook, Farmer Twitter, or Old Man Google, but they never stop to consider why they are being given free room and board in the barn. They complain about every change to the service, every moment of downtime, and every lapse in privacy as if they were the customers of social network companies, never realizing that they are not the customers. They are the products.

In exchange for letting Oscar Sagese post a picture of himself groping a blonde and drinking a shot, Facebook gathers and sells information about where Oscar shops, what Oscar likes, and who Oscar knows. That was the key. I never expected to find an incriminating status message, I just wanted incriminating friendships.

I poked and clicked at underlined hyperlinks until I found Oscar's friends list. Facebook had changed its interface since the last time I was on it. I had closed my account soon after my wife was killed, tired of the deluge of "How are you doing?" messages from all quarters. I hadn't wanted more friends. I had wanted to be left alone.

Oscar had forty-three friends. I took a screenshot of the Friend page, scrolled down, and took another screenshot. I'd peruse the list later. Next, I jumped to the photos. Oscar liked to upload pictures. There were pictures of three guys at a Bruins game, waving plastic cups of beer; pictures of three guys at a Red Sox game, waving plastic cups of beer; and pictures of three guys standing on a beach, waving plastic cups of beer. Clearly Oscar was a man of range and sophistication. Each photo album had a URL at the bottom that was to be shared with "friends and relatives"—and snoops. I ran through the partying photo albums, copying the URLs into a file to examine later. Then I reached a wedding photo album and slowed down.

When it comes to mining social networks, weddings are the mother lode. Most of us have a small circle of friends, and those people show up over and over in casual photos. Weddings, on the other hand, cast a wide net over all your acquaintances.

Casual relationships are like Schrödinger's cat. They have an equal chance of being alive or dead. Since it's uncomfortable and awkward to admit that a relationship has died, we try to leave them in a state of quantum superposition where they could be alive or dead and we don't know unless we look.

Wedding invitations, however, collapse that superposition and make the state of the relationship clear. If you got the wedding invitation, you are in; if you were snubbed, you are out. Wedding lists grow because people would rather spend $25 to feed a guy a rubber chicken dinner than to admit that they don't like him anymore.

The album was called "Stevie's Wedding." I skimmed through the photos looking for pictures of Oscar, and found several pictures of him dancing with a brunette in an electric blue dress that rode high on her thighs and low on her boobs. There was a picture of Oscar doing tequila shots, with limes and salt scattered across the bar; a picture of Oscar raising his glass in toast; and then the picture that I was afraid I would find. I pressed "download." I wanted a copy of this.

I felt a change in the air, as if the gravity around me had shifted slightly in response to a large mass. I looked up and saw the man himself, Oscar Sagese, looming over me. Oscar was leaning down, about to see himself on my computer screen. I slammed the screen shut, not sure whether the download had completed.

Oscar said, "Mr. Graxton wants to talk to you."

THIRTY-TWO

I said, "Who's Mr. Graxton?"

Oscar looked around at the Starbucks. He pulled up a chair, sat down. He had a soft squeaky voice, more pebble than boulder. "Why are you fucking with me? Mr. Graxton says your name is Tucker. He says you're Sal's cousin, and he says he wants to talk to you. He didn't tell me that you were going to play fucking games with me."

I'm a big believer in the scientific method. I was going to get to use it now. I had a theory that Graxton wouldn't hurt me in public. This would be the experimental test. I predicted that I'd remain uninjured. If Oscar beat the crap out of me, my theory would be disproved. I said, "Okay."

I gathered up my laptop and coffee and followed Oscar to Hugh Graxton's table. He looked up at me with a smile that I took to be friendly. He closed his computer and gestured to the chair across from him. "Tucker, have a seat. Want a refill on your coffee?"

I said, "No. I'm good."

Graxton leaned closer and looked at my head. He said, "Jesus, you got the crap kicked out of you. Good stitches, though."

I thought back to the picture I had just downloaded. "Of course, *you* didn't have anything to do with my beating."

A little smile tweaked the corner of Graxton's mouth. He said, "You're Sal's cousin, right?"

"Yeah."

"I see no family resemblance whatsoever."

I said nothing.

"You should take that as a compliment."

"Why? What's wrong with Sal?"

"Nothing. It's just that you seem like a happy guy. Your cousin Sal, on the other hand, is a Grumpy Gus."

"A Grumpy Gus?"

"The grumpiest."

"Hard to argue with that."

Graxton drank his coffee and said, "Still, he's a loyal bastard, old-school."

"Also true. Are you old-school?"

Graxton gestured to his MacBook Air and asked, "What do you think?" A big college ring with a red stone graced Graxton's right hand, flashing as he moved.

I asked, "Where did you go to school?"

"UMass Amherst."

"Zoo Mass?"

Graxton's smile tightened. "C'mon, Tucker, you're better than that. You went to MIT. You going to use that education to repeat tired cliches?"

"How did you know I went to MIT?"

"People talk."

"Which people?"

"I thought you MIT guys were supposed to be *wicked smaht*." Graxton did a poor imitation of a Boston accent.

"We are."

"So use your MIT brain and figure it out. Who do you know that I know?"

"Walt Adams."

"Walt Adams? What does Walt have to do with it? Sure, we've done a little business, but I have to admit that you never came up."

"How much does Walt owe you?" I asked.

"That's between me and Walt. There are privacy laws in this country."

"There are also laws against having someone beaten up."

"I had nothing to do with you getting beaten up."

"So who do you think did?"

"How should I know? Maybe you're an asshole. C'mon, MIT, think. You got any enemies? Anyone threaten you?"

"One guy."

"Who?"

"This little guy named Talevi."

Graxton scratched his ear and said, "Never heard of him."

Oh, Hugh, you big fat liar.

I said, "Sal told me that Talevi was a mean little bastard."

Graxton leaned back forward and said quietly, "So this mean little bastard, what's-his-name—"

"Talevi."

"Talevi comes up to you and threatens you. Probably tells you to stop poking around in this business."

"Yeah."

"So then you *don't* stop poking around and you get the crap beat out of you."

"Right."

"And so your big MIT brain says, 'Let's go visit Hugh out in Chestnut Hill.' Jesus, Tucker, that's right out of *A Beautiful Mind*. Have you been hearing voices or seeing patterns in numbers?"

"No."

"Because it might be schizophrenia."

"I'm not crazy."

"Well, you're not stupid, so I'm at a loss as to why you came out—"

Graxton stopped talking and looked over my shoulder. Jael was standing in the doorway. He smiled and said, "Ms. Navas! You are looking beautiful, as always. I assume you're here with Tucker."

Jael walked into the Starbucks and stopped behind my chair. She said, "Hello, Mr. Graxton."

Graxton said, "Tucker, did you hire Jael to help you with this? That's the first smart thing you did."

I stood next to Jael and said, "We're friends."

"Friends with benefits?"

Simultaneously, I said "No" as Jael said, "Yes."

Graxton grinned, and I whispered into Jael's ear, explaining the phrase "friends with benefits." Then Jael said, "No."

Graxton said, "Jael, your friend Tucker here said that he was threatened by a guy named Talevi."

"Yes."

"So why did he come see me?"

Jael said, "He insisted."

"He's not as smart as he thinks he is," said Graxton.

Jael said, "I know."

I looked from one to the other. "Hello. I'm standing right here."

Graxton's iPhone played "I'm Shipping Up to Boston."

Graxton said, "I've got to take this." He answered the phone and said, "Tony! Guess who I'm talking to? No. It's your old friend Jael Navas … Tony? Tony? Look, don't piss yourself, you don't have to ever go near her again."

Jael tugged at my arm, and we left.

THIRTY-THREE

JAEL PULLED HER MDX onto Route 9 and headed back toward Boston. She asked, "Why were you talking to Graxton? Your plan was to spy on him."

"I was spying on him, actually on Oscar, but Graxton recognized me and wanted to talk."

"Did you learn anything?"

"I learned more from Oscar than Grax—" I was interrupted by my Droid. Usually, the thing just said, "Droid," but I had special songs for some numbers. This one was the Wicked Witch's flying music from *The Wizard of Oz*.

Jael asked, "Is that your phone?"

I said, "Yes. It's a special ringtone."

The theme song ended and started up again, its cyclonic hyperactivity filling the car.

"Who is it?"

"My mother." I steeled myself, took a deep breath, and answered the phone. "Hello, Ma," I said.

"Hello," she said. "I am going to the police station in Boston to talk to Lieutenant Lee. I thought you would like to come."

"Why are you going to talk to him?" I asked.

"He told me to come to the police station. I had no choice."

"Of course you have a choice. You shouldn't even be answering their questions. They think you killed Cathy Byrd."

"That's ridiculous. Of course I didn't kill her. I haven't thought about her in years."

"All the more reason not to talk to them."

"Aloysius Tucker, I am not going to disobey the police. Do you want to come to this meeting with me, or should I go alone?"

"Do you have a lawyer?"

"Of course I don't have a lawyer. I am *not* wasting money on a lawyer when I didn't do anything wrong."

"Oh, for God's sake—"

"Are you coming?"

"Yes. I'll be there in an hour." I hung up and turned to Jael. "Would you drive me to the police station?"

"Would you like me to accompany you inside?"

"Why not? The more the merrier."

I settled into a sullen silence, contemplating my mother and her descent into incompetence. The woman had managed to grow up, get married, buy a home, and raise a son. She had, at one time, been a normal and productive member of society. Now she lived in a trash pile as she contracted in upon herself and rejected a world that she no longer seemed to understand.

Though the red marks on my cheek were gone, I could still hear the cracking sound of her hand across my cheek. Lee had seen it too. Probably made him feel superior, gave him the upper hand. It made me wonder why I was going to this meeting. I knew that she'd ignore my advice and that we'd probably fight. I hoped that Jael, a stranger and a woman, might be a calming influence. Besides, I was curious to hear what my mother had to—

"We are here," Jael said, shocking me out of my reverie.

I said, "Let's get this over with."

THIRTY-FOUR

BOSTON'S POLICE HEADQUARTERS LOOKS less like the home of the first police department in America, and more like the home of a rapidly rising software company. The building dominates a city block on Tremont Street, where it overlooks the transition between the new student dormitory buildings of Northeastern University and the old housing project buildings of Roxbury.

Jael and I entered through a gigantic plaza where flat planes of glass folded in upon themselves to create a lobby. My mother stood in the lobby in her Sunday best, Lee next to her. They were talking and laughing. They looked like they were at a cocktail party. The laughter stopped when they saw me.

I kissed my mother on the cheek. She touched the stitches on my temple and asked, "What happened to you?"

The last thing she needed to know was that someone had kicked the shit out of me in a Quincy Market toilet. I said, "I had an accident on my bike."

My mother shook her head. "Why are you so careless?" Then to Lee, "He was always a clumsy boy."

I said to Lee, "I'm especially clumsy when I ask a lot of questions."

My mother ignored me. "Tucker, you're being rude. Introduce this young woman."

"I was going to, but we were having so much fun with my clumsiness that I didn't get a chance." My mother had, once again, transformed me into a petulant teenager. "This is Jael Navas. Jael, my mother, Angelina Tucker, and Lieutenant Lee of the Boston Police."

Lee asked, "Is she your legal counsel?"

I said, "She's my muscle."

"We're in police headquarters. I don't think there will be violence."

I looked at my mother. "You never know."

Jael said, "It is a pleasure to meet you, Mrs. Tucker."

My mother said, "Jael is such a pretty name. Is it Gallic?"

Jael said, "It is from the Bible."

Lieutenant Lee said, "It's from Judges. Chapter Four."

Jael cocked an eyebrow at Lee. She said, "Very few people know the reference."

Lee said, "Very few people know their Bible."

My mother said, "Even so, it's a very pretty name."

We started walking to a conference room. As we reached the elevators, I asked Lee, "Did I miss anything before we arrived?"

Lee said, "We were talking about the other night."

My mother said, "Yes. I was apologizing for my outburst."

And an apology for the slap? I waited. Nope, apparently not.

Lee said, "I didn't want to be the one to tell her."

"Yes, Tucker," said my mother, "Lieutenant Lee says that you should have told me."

I said, "I would have told you, but I didn't get a chance. I was having trouble finding the right way to say, 'Dad was porking the babysitter.'"

"Aloysius Tucker! I will not listen to that language!"

"Here it comes," I said.

"Don't you give me your smart mouth. Especially not in public."

Lee said, "Tucker, remember the fifth commandment."

I said, "What's the fifth commandment?"

Jael said, "Honor your father and mother."

I said to Jael, "I thought you were on my side."

"It says what it says."

Lee opened the door to a conference room and said, "Let's sit in here."

The conference room held a small round table. We milled about, looking for appropriate seating. When the music stopped, Lee was sitting next to my mother, who was sitting next to Jael. I wound up across from my mother—the fighting chair.

Lee said to my mother, "Let me recap. John Tucker, also known as Little John or JT, was found murdered in front of your son's house. It turns out that JT's parents were Cathy Byrd and your husband. Cathy Byrd was murdered two days ago."

My mother said, "I don't see what this has to do with me."

"You are more than an innocent bystander in all this."

My mother folded her hands in front of her. "That's not true. I didn't know that my husband was having an affair."

"He had more than an affair. He had built a parallel life in Pittsfield."

I watched my mother's knuckles whiten as she clenched her folded hands. She said, "That's ridiculous. I would have known."

Lee said, "How would you have known?"

"A woman knows these things."

Lee looked at me. I gestured. *Please, go on. You're doing so well.*

"Mrs. Tucker, your husband led a double life. Cathy Byrd owned a house in Pittsfield, and she lived there with your husband. Her neighbors thought that Pittsfield was his primary—"

"Really?" my mother interrupted. "With what money?"

"Excuse me?"

"Cathy Byrd was a little girl with no job and my husband was an engineer. I paid all our bills and I did all our taxes. I saw his W-2 form every year. I tracked every penny in our bank account and balanced that checkbook every month. How did he buy a house?"

"Did he have money before you got married?"

"We got married when we were twenty-two. We didn't have any money. All the money in our marriage passed through my hands."

Lieutenant Lee asked, "How old were you when Tucker was born?"

"I was thirty-two."

"You waited ten years?"

My mother reddened. "We had problems conceiving. We didn't use birth control, but—"

I had reddened as well. I asked, "Is there a point to this?"

Lee said, "I'm trying to get a complete picture. The same gun was used to kill Cathy Bird and JT. There has to be some connection."

My mother said, "I don't see how dragging up all these filthy memories is helping. My husband did *not* have the money for a second house!"

"He must have. He bought it with cash."

"Cash? How would he have that much cash? He worked a full-time job, and he didn't gamble. He didn't even buy a lottery ticket."

"He must have kept some records of his activity," said Lee.

I had been sitting in my chair, leaning it back on two legs, arms crossed, frown etched across my face. If I had any brains, if I had the smallest piece of common sense, I would have maintained that position. I would have watched Lee and my mother go back and forth, I would have placed little mental side bets as to how long it could go on. I would have looked toward Jael and rolled my eyes.

Sadly, I did not. My brains were overridden by an urge to tilt my chair down, engage in the conversation, and try to be helpful. If God had been so kind as to give us a chance to press an Undo button once in our lives, I would have used mine to take back what I said next.

"Ma," I said, "didn't Dad have a bunch of engineering notebooks?"

An iron silence gripped the room.

My mother said, "I don't know what you're talking about."

I'm sure there must have been warning signs: pursed lips, pinched eyes, knuckles whitening on her purse. I'm sure there must have been a way that she was trying to communicate to me that she didn't want to talk about the notebooks. Unfortunately, I had slipped into the tactless, fact-based, argumentative world of engineering problem-solving. If there were signs, I missed them.

I said, "You know. The ones with the brown covers and the green graph paper."

Lee said, "Yes. That's exactly the sort of thing. Did he use them as a diary?"

I said, "I think so."

My mother said, "Those are private documents."

"Yeah, but Ma, they're not going to publicize them. They're just going to look through them."

"I'm sure I don't have them. I think they were lost."

I shook my head. "Lost? How could they be lost? You keep every—"

"Aloysius Tucker, I told you that they are *lost*! Are you calling me a liar?"

"No, but—"

"No *buts*! They are lost. You cannot see them."

Lee asked, "Which is it, Mrs. Tucker? Are they lost or are we not allowed to see them?"

My mother aimed her gaze at Lee. "They are lost."

Lee leaned forward. Reached out for my mother's hand. She drew back. Lee said, "We could help you search."

"No. You cannot search my house."

"We would be respectful, Mrs. Tucker. We're trying to solve a murder."

"No! I said *no!*"

"But, why—?"

I said, "Because my moth—"

My mother pointed at me from across the table and looked daggers into my eyes. I felt her finger jabbing me in the back of the brain. "Not a word from you. Not a word! You've done enough."

Jael looked from me to my mother and back with increased interest.

Lee said, "We could get a search warrant, you know."

My mother rose. "I haven't done anything. You cannot search my house!" She moved to leave the conference room.

"We're not done here, Mrs. Tucker."

"I want to leave."

I asked, "Is she under arrest, Lee?"

"No," he said. "She is not under arrest."

"Then I'm leaving." My mother opened the conference room door and was gone.

THIRTY-FIVE

"My God," said Lee. "What just happened?"

I said, "I ask that question every time I see her."

"Why did she get so upset?"

"My mother is a hoarder."

Lee shook his head. "That's a terrible thing to say about your own mother. It might have been true of your father, but not your mother."

"What? No! Not *whore*. Hoarder. Hoar-DER! She hoards things."

"What kinds of things?"

"Paper things. She's saved every scrap of paper that she's come across since my dad died. Her house is almost completely full of paper."

"Well then, she should have the notebooks."

"She might have them, but you'll never find them."

"Why not?"

I shifted in my chair. Jael and Lee were sitting across the table from me. Jael, as always, listened. Lee had a notebook out, his hand poised over the paper with a pen. The pen had a little crucifix on it.

I said, "There are two reasons. First, the information you want is old. Her house is like an archeological dig. The oldest information is at the bottom of the pile. So you'll have to dig through mountains of paper to find something about my dad."

"What's the second reason?"

I paused. I hated talking about my mother's mental illness. People's responses range from judgment (*what kind of son lets this happen?*) to pity (*that must be terrible*). The worst response is the instinctive recoil (*is it catching?*). I wasn't interested in encouraging any of them, so I just didn't talk about my crazy mother and her paper dungeon.

Lee repeated, "And the second reason?"

I asked, "Lee, do your parents live around here?"

"Sure."

"Do you have a key to their house?"

"Of course I do."

"I don't."

"You don't have a key to your mother's house?"

"No."

"Why not?"

"Because she doesn't trust me. She's afraid that I'll come into her house and move a scrap of paper. I'm not exaggerating. I can't move anything. She has a mental map of the place and she thinks that she knows where everything is. If someone moves anything, she feels like she'll never find it. It's as bad as throwing it away, and she never throws anything away."

"So a search would mess up the house."

"Yes."

"But it's worthless scraps."

I pointed at Lee's pen and asked, "How much do you want for that pen?"

Lee looked at the pen, then back at me. "It's not for sale."

"Oh, come on. It doesn't look very expensive. I'll give you two hundred dollars for it and you can buy a nicer pen."

"I said it's not for sale."

"Okay. Five hundred dollars and not a penny more. Wait. I'll negotiate against myself and give you six hundred."

"I will not sell you this pen."

"Why not?"

"My church gave it to me when I accepted Jesus Christ as my personal savior."

"It's just a pen."

"It's not *just a pen*."

"And my mother's papers are not just worthless scraps. She's attached every one of them to my dad and her memory of him. If she loses a piece of paper, she'll feel like she lost a piece of him."

"So if we had her house cleaned out—" Lee started.

"She'd probably kill herself."

Jael was looking at me in a way I'd never seen before. Her eyes had softened, and her perpetually thin lips were a little fuller, a little less pinched. She was falling into the pity camp. I didn't like it.

Lee said, "So what do we do?"

I said, "I don't know what to tell you."

"Look, Tucker, I sympathize with your mother's condition, but I have a murder to solve. Your half brother was killed in front of your house and his mother was killed the next day with the same gun. These events are related and they intersect at your father and the house in Pittsfield. How did your father buy a second house without your mother knowing about it? I suspect he gave a pile of cash to Cathy Byrd so she could buy a house. The source *must* be written in his notebooks."

"You're probably right, but there's not much else you can do."

"There is. Today, I'm going to get a search warrant for that house, and tomorrow I'm going to search it as carefully as possible, hopefully with your mother's help, so we can find something about your father and his second family."

"She won't let you do that," I said.

"That's your job. If you bring me those notebooks by tomorrow, I won't have to search the house."

"And if I don't?"

"Then tomorrow, your mother is going to have a very bad day."

THIRTY-SIX

SAL WAS SITTING IN his usual spot in Cafe Vittoria when Jael and I popped into his window. I waved. He grimaced and gestured us in. As Jael seated herself, he gave her an appraising top-to-bottom inspection. There was nothing covert in his glance, but there was nothing overtly lascivious. While most men look at a beautiful woman the way they look at a sports car, with acquisitive intensity, Sal looked at Jael as if she were a bottle of fine wine. Something to be appreciated but not opened.

He said, "So, Jael. Long time no see. You look good."

Jael said, "Thank you."

I said, "You two know each other?"

Jael said, "I know Sal from my work."

He waved at the barista to bring us coffee and looked at my stitches. "What the fuck happened to your face?"

"Some guy beat me up in the men's room at Faneuil Hall."

"Who?"

After my mother's encounter with Lee, Jael had driven back to my house and had parked her SUV there. Upstairs, Jael had sipped tea in the living room while I sat next to Click and Clack and inspected my laptop.

Oscar's picture was there. It had downloaded before I had snapped the laptop shut. I copied the picture, cropped it, and synced the photos to my Droid. Then Jael and I had taken the train to Haymarket to visit with Sal. If I had needed to talk to Sal about Dad's money, I needed to talk to him about this picture even more.

Sal repeated his question: "Who beat you up?"

In response I took out my Droid and opened the cropped picture and showed it to Sal. It was a picture of Teardrop with his bald head, yellow teeth, and teardrop tattoo bleeding out of one eye. He was laughing.

I said, "This guy."

Sal glanced away from the picture. "Never saw him before."

I hadn't expected it, the bald-faced lie right to my face. I had expected dissembling. I had expected promises to look into it. I had expected an I-told-you-so. A small part of me had even expected a name, the truth. I hadn't expected this, and because I hadn't expected it, I did something stupid.

I said, "You're a fucking liar."

The air froze. Sal turned, his brow furrowing into a mask of concentrated rage, his hand leaving the tabletop and his fingers extending, his shoulders turning, one dipping down away from me, the other twisting toward me as his arm extended and his big fingers seized my shirt front and yanked me from the chair. Suddenly I was ten years old, and my older cousin was bullying me.

Sal raged, "Don't you ever call me a liar!"

The bottle of familial rage that I kept in my chest exploded. Black vapors fumed out and spread through me, darkening my vision, focusing me on violence.

I screamed back, "Liar! You're a big fat fucking liar!"

Sal twisted the T-shirt in his paw and drew back his hand.

I slapped at his grip on my shirt and cried, "Go ahead, you fat fucking liar! Go ahead!"

Sal's weight shifted as he turned his shoulder into the coming punch.

"Enough!" Jael's voice cut through the air. She stood, pointing at Sal, violence in her eyes.

Sal grunted. His shoulder relaxed. His fist unclenched. He looked at Jael and said, "What? You gonna shoot me?"

"Let him go," said Jael. Sal let go of my shirt. I sagged into the chair, covering my face and hiding the shame of my tears. Hiccups broke through as I worked to master myself. I felt Sal's bulk disappear. Then it was back. Sal nudged my hand away from my face. He was holding a shot glass full of clear liquid.

"Wha—" I took a deep breath. "What's this?"

Sal rested his hand on my back. "It's grappa. It's good. Shoot it down."

I knocked back the grappa. Its warmth splashed into my belly and filled my head. My breathing slowed.

Sal raised his glass, drank some grappa. "Why would you call me a liar?"

I looked across the floor and saw my Droid sitting in the corner. Its rubber phone-condom had protected it from the fall. I crawled under the table, my arms unsteady from the combination of adrenaline and grappa, grabbed my Droid, and sat next to Sal. The picture of Teardrop was still there.

I said, "This is a cropped picture. I also have the original."

I flicked the picture to the original and Sal said, "Fuck me."

THIRTY-SEVEN

"Where did you get this?" asked Sal.

"It doesn't matter," I said.

"Did you get this from that son of a bitch Miller? Does the FBI have this picture?"

"How should I know? I got it. I assume they could get it."

The photo glowed on my Droid. It was from happier times, a wedding celebration. Four men, each with a cigar in one hand. Oscar Sagese wore a tuxedo. His arm draped across Hugh Graxton's shoulder. Hugh held a similar cigar, his arm around Sal. Sal wore a big smile, held a cigar, and used his other arm to sideways hug a smaller man into the frame. The smaller man was Teardrop, the guy who had beaten me in the toilet.

I said, "You lied to me, Sal. You said you never met this guy. Looks like you're best buds."

Sal said, "You know what, Tucker? Fuck you." He turned to Jael. "This guy ignores his fucking family all his life, then when the shit goes down, he wants me to trust him."

Sal's words stung. I dug back through my memory. He'd chosen his word well. *Ignore.* Actually, I had done worse than ignore my mother's family, I had rejected them and their worldview—a worldview that ended at Cross Street.

My mother never escaped the North End. Her mind remained trapped in the area bordered by Prince, Hanover, and Commercial Streets. My father, on the other hand, had been a citizen of the world. He read *The New Yorker*, listened to NPR, talked to overseas friends. He had been an engineer, a man of science who built weapons. My mother had been a housewife, a woman of cooking who boiled pasta.

Over the breakfast table, my mother would gossip about what Auntie Rosa had said about Auntie Contessa; my father would speculate about the Iran-Contra affair. My mother gabbed about Nonna's bunions; my father extolled the MX missile. My mother talked about people; my father talked about ideas. At the age of thirteen, presented with a choice between Battery Street and the world, I had chosen the world. I was the guy George Bailey would have been if he had escaped Bedford Falls.

I didn't have anything against my relatives. They simply didn't interest me, just as they didn't interest my father. When he was home he'd let himself get dragged down to Boston for the endless string of birthdays, christenings, weddings, funerals, holidays, and feasts. He never looked comfortable. He sat next to my mother, smiled when required, and spoke when questioned.

For their part, the North Enders never warmed to my dad. The dinner table served people named Gianelli, Testa, Rizzo, and some guy named Tucker. The only name that didn't end in a vowel. They viewed my father as some sort of strange Englishman from a foreign country called Minnesota.

Still, while my father had given me a worldview, he hadn't given me a family. He was an only child and there were no other Tuckers.

I was alone in the world except for my mother and her family, and I had turned my back on them. Sal was right not to trust me.

We were silent.

Sal said, "I need to know where you got that picture."

I slumped in my chair. "I'm so tired of this shit."

"What?"

"You say I ignored my family, and maybe I did, but I was better off alone."

"That's fucking stupid," said Sal. "You don't even know how to be in a family. I never see you at holidays. You never come around. You never say hello. It's a fucking sin that this is the first time you've had a drink with me. You blow off all the good stuff, then show up, dig into everyone's shit, and bitch about how it stinks."

"Hmmph."

"This is a fucking good family, Tucker. You turned your back on us."

I pointed at my stitches. "Yeah. This is what my good family gave me."

"Hey! I had nothing to do with that," said Sal.

I was silent, not wanting to enrage him again.

"I swear on my father's soul," said Sal. "I don't know how that happened."

"Fine," I said. "I believe you."

"You gotta tell me where you got that picture. If the FBI ever gets that picture, they'll make you testify about where you found it. You want to be on a witness list?"

"You're threatening me now? After your little family speech?"

"You are so fucking stupid. There are four guys in that picture who don't want to go to jail. You gonna be the one to put them there? I need to know where you got that, Tucker. I need the negative."

"Oh, Jesus Christ, Sal!"

"Hey. Watch your mouth."

I said. "There is no negative. I got this off the Internet. There could be a million copies. We'd never know."

"The Internet? Some asshole posted this on the Internet? Anyone can see it?"

"Not exactly. It was on Facebook," I ducked my head. "I hacked Oscar Sagese's account."

"What? Hugh's guy?"

"Yeah."

"You hacked his account?"

"Yeah."

"You know, you got a lot of fucking nerve to come in here and judge me."

"I didn't hurt anyone."

"No. You just hack a guy's account and steal a picture that could get him killed. Then you parade it in front of me. You're an asshole."

"I needed information."

"Get the fuck out of my face."

"I can't. I need your help."

"You need my help?" Sal crossed his arms across his chest. "Why should I help you?"

"Because if you don't, I'll tell your mother. I'll go tell Auntie Rosa that you won't help her sister."

"What the fuck are you talking about?"

"Lieutenant Lee from the Boston Police wants to search my mother's house. He wants to know how my father got the money to buy that house in Pittsfield."

"So? Let him search."

"Sal, you know my mother's a hoarder. She can't have police moving her stuff. She'll freak out. She could even kill herself."

Sal said, "I told you, I don't know where your father got the money for that house." He turned to Jael. "This guy never listens."

Jael said, "Perhaps your mother has information."

Sal said, "My mother, huh?"

My Droid said, "Droid." I pulled it out and looked at the number. It came from a 413 area code—Pittsfield. I said to Sal, "I gotta take this."

The voice at the other end said, "Tucker? This is Dave Patterson. We need to talk."

I said, "So. Talk."

"Not like this. I need to meet you. There's a spot on the Pike. If I send you a map link, will you meet me there at ten tonight?"

"Yeah."

"Good."

The line went dead.

Sal asked, "Important call?"

I asked Sal, "You ever hear of a guy named Dave Patterson?"

"No. Go ahead. Ask me if I'm lying. I'll punch you right in the mouth."

"Okay. I won't ask."

Sal stood. "Look. I gotta go. But I remembered something my mother told me. She said that Auntie Angelina had saved all the stuff from your dad's office."

Jael and I stood to leave with Sal. "That figures. She saved everything."

"Yeah, but there was something weird about the way she saved it. My mother didn't tell me anything else, wanted to keep it hush hush, so I didn't dig."

We walked out of the cafe onto Hanover Street and started to go our separate ways when Sal called out, "Hey, cousin!"

I turned. "Yeah?"

"Watch your fucking back."

THIRTY-EIGHT

BOBBY, JAEL, AND I were crammed into Bobby's tiny office, staring at Google Maps on Bobby's computer. Bobby sat behind his desk, working the mouse. I sat next to him, peering at the map. Jael stood behind us, supervising the operation.

Dave Patterson had emailed me a link, and I had emailed it to Bobby. Bobby clicked on the link and Google Maps presented us with a graphical blue flag marking a spot somewhere between nothing and nowhere.

"It's on the Pike," said Bobby.

"Not exactly," I said. "Zoom in."

Bobby zoomed in. The mark was not on the Pike. It was off to the side. Bobby zoomed in further, and Google Maps switched to its street view. We were standing on the Mass Pike, looking west. Bobby rotated the view and the blue flag came into view. It was in the middle of a clearing, bounded by trees on one side and a small river on the other side. Google Maps said the clearing was in Warren, Massachusetts, sixty miles west of Boston, halfway across the state.

I leaned in close, trying to pull details out of the picture. "He wants to meet in a clearing?"

Bobby said, "Yeah. I guess he wants to stop his car, run from the road, say what he wants to say, and run back."

Jael said, "It provides a perfect ambush. A sniper could easily hide in the trees."

I asked, "You think he wants to kill me?"

"The point is that he *could* kill you. We cannot allow him the chance."

Bobby clicked the mouse a few times trying, and failing, to zoom in. "What the hell is that?"

There was a white smudge in the middle of the screen.

Jael said, "Switch to an overhead view."

Bobby zoomed out and switched from map to satellite. The picture was from the summer. The clearing was a bright green, and the trees next to it hid the ground.

"We must set up in these trees. It will be dark, so I will bring my night scope."

Bobby said, "Your night scope? For what?"

"My sniper rifle."

"Your sniper rifle? You can't go walking through those woods with a sniper rifle."

"Of course I can," said Jael. "There is no fence. How else would I keep Tucker safe?"

"He'll be plenty safe," said Bobby. "Patterson is a little dweeb."

I realized that I was a step behind these two. "Safe? Safe from what? What am I doing?"

Bobby said, "Well, obviously, Patterson wants to talk to you, not me. So you go out there and talk to him."

"Talk to him about what? I don't even know what's going on."

"Yeah. And it's gonna stay that way unless you talk to him. Just find out what he has to say."

157

Jael said, "I cannot allow Tucker to endanger himself. I must be in the woods with the sniper rifle."

Bobby said, "What if I say no?"

I said, "Then I'm not going. Either Jael has her rifle or I take Lucy to the movies."

"That's fucking stupid," said Bobby.

I said, "C'mon, Jael. Let's get out of here. Let Bobby go talk to Patterson."

We stood and made for the door. Bobby rattled his mouse at the computer and then pounded the desk with his fist. "Fuck me!"

"Does that mean yes to the sniper rifle?"

"Fucking yes, okay? But I have one condition."

"What's that?"

"I'm coming with you."

THIRTY-NINE

I STILL HAD THE problem of keeping Lieutenant Lee from ripping my mother's house apart. I needed to get those notebooks. They had to be in the house somewhere, but I didn't know where to look. I had one shot left. I called Uncle Walt and he agreed to meet me at a coffee shop in Sudbury.

Jael said, "I will drive you."

"You think Uncle Walt is dangerous?"

"Anyone can be dangerous."

Sudbury Coffee Works sported a large brass teapot hanging from its brick facade. I love places like this—independent coffee shops whose local owners roast their own beans and have committed their livelihood to the creation of a good cup of coffee. The coffee shop had a long, low serving counter, with the roaster sitting out where you could watch it work.

The décor represented the taste of the owner rather than the committee-conceived, focus group–judged, and executive-approved decor of Starbucks. Lively blue and green tables sported artwork secured under clear polyurethane surfaces. Jael sat across from me drinking a cup of tea, while I had opted for a mug of coffee—the

1776 blend, a nod to Sudbury's revolutionary history and its victory in grabbing the 01776 zip code.

Uncle Walt walked into the coffee shop, waved hello, bought a cup of coffee in a disposable cup, and settled down at our table. He pointed at my stitches. "Jesus Christ, Tucker. What happened to you?"

"A bald guy with a teardrop tattoo beat me up in Quincy Market."

Walt's eyes flashed recognition.

Jael asked, "Do you know the man who beat Tucker?"

Walt held out his hand. "Hi. I'm Walt."

Jael shook Walt's hand and said, "I am Jael Navas. I am Tucker's friend."

"Well, good for Tucker! The boy has good taste."

Walt hadn't answered Jael's question, but I didn't want to press. That answer didn't interest me. I assumed that Walt would know Teardrop if he owed Graxton money, and I didn't want to alienate him.

I said, "Uncle Walt, I need your help. It's my mother."

"What about her?"

"The Boston Police are going to search her house. They're going to dig through her crap to find out how my father paid for that house in Pittsfield. They're looking for my dad's notebooks."

Walt drank his coffee. "His notebooks? They've got to be in her house somewhere. I haven't seen that woman in almost ten years, and she had piles of shit even then."

"The piles are bigger now, believe me. Do you have any of his notebooks?"

"Hell no. He never shared those with me. I'm surprised he never put the little locks on them with the little girlie keys to keep everyone out. He was a secretive bastard."

"Tell me about it."

Walt raised his hand. "Don't judge him, son. It's what he did for a living. People forget, we lived through some bad times. We were sure the whole world was going to get blown up, and he was doing his part to keep that from happening. Keeping secrets was part of his job."

"Even from you?"

"Even from me? Tucker, I'm a glorified janitor. Your dad dealt with things on a need-to-know basis, and I didn't need to know shit to sweep the floors. So, yeah, he even kept secrets from me."

"Keeping secrets was one thing; raising me in a lie was another. He stole my brother from me."

Walt grimaced. "Come on, Tucker. He couldn't tell anyone about Pittsfield. Your mother would have divorced him, Sal's family would probably have killed him, and you would have grown up in a broken home. You sure as shit wouldn't have been able to afford MIT."

"MIT wasn't worth being raised by a liar."

"Don't be a baby. You think things are bad between you and your mother? Imagine how it was for him, married to a friggin' devout Catholic who didn't want any kids after she had you. Said that you were too much work and she didn't want another one."

"Yeah, but—"

"You know how a devout Catholic practices birth control?"

"I thought they didn't practice birth control."

"Oh, they practice it—with abstinence. Your mother cut your father off the day you were born. He was going to divorce her sorry ass as soon as you were out of college, but he didn't want your college fund getting caught up in some bullshit Massachusetts divorce court."

"Abstinence?"

"Yeah. So maybe he was screwing the babysitter and maybe he knocked her up. But he did okay by her, bought her a house, was a father to her child. God knows what that cost him."

I crossed my arms and looked out the window. "Whatever."

Walt stood. "Suck it up, son. So you didn't meet your brother. Boo hoo. Go make some friends." He stalked out of the coffee shop.

"Sorry you had to see that," I said to Jael.

Jael said, "Family issues are always difficult."

"You know what I have to do now," I said. I pulled out my Droid and dialed.

"Hi, Ma. I'm in Sudbury. How about if I come over for dinner?"

FORTY

JAEL SLOWED TO A stop in front of my mother's house. If she noticed the mess, she was polite about it. A hoarder's yard is always a mess; once the hoard fills the house, junk spills outside. My mother's yard was no different. Cardboard boxes of paper rested against the side of the house. Paper had escaped the boxes and gotten caught in the long lawn. A row of full recycling bins sat in front of her garage, their contents soggy from repeated rainstorm drenchings. Though recycling bins are uniquely suited to dispose of the papers they hold, these bins hadn't made it to the curb. And they never would.

I climbed out of Jael's car. "Thanks for the lift."

"I'll be back in two hours," said Jael. She drove off to access her armory and load up for tonight's rendezvous with Dave Patterson.

My sneakers crunched on the stone walkway as I approached the door and rang the bell.

My mother called out, "Just a minute." Stacks of paper thumped on the other side of the door.

The door opened halfway and my mother smiled out at me.

This was new.

I stepped through the door and she gave me her cheek. I kissed it.

"I'm glad you called," she said. "You're lucky. I had gravy cooking on the stove when you called. It's good not to eat it alone."

That explained the smile. A good Italian marinara sauce simmers for two hours. After all that time, it tastes better when shared.

Still, I couldn't imagine my mother cooking in this space. I looked around at the stacks of paper and asked, "Is cooking safe?"

The smile disappeared. "Of course it's safe! Do you think I'm an idiot?"

We wound our way through the goat path in the living room. The path forked in what was once the dining area. We took the kitchen branch instead of the bedroom branch.

The kitchen was a small rectangle. The kitchen window peered out from over the sink and gave a view of the back yard. The kitchen's back half-wall stopped three feet from the ceiling. In normal Campanelli ranches, this allowed light to fill the house. My mother had clogged her half-wall to the ceiling with books. Light never reached here.

The sink, range, and oven, however, remained clear of clutter. A covered quart pan of marinara sauce (*gravy* to my mother) bubbled on the stove over low heat. Next to it, water boiled in a larger pan.

My mother dumped a box of ziti into the boiling water and stirred. The ziti frothed for a moment and settled down. "I waited for you to get here before I started the ziti."

I thought about how steam permeates paper to create mold and looked around at the piles of books in the kitchen. My mother had gotten them from yard sales, library fundraisers, and trash cans. In addition to the books on the half-wall, piles of books sat on the floor and on the kitchen table. Some of the books were shredded where mice had gnawed homes for themselves. These were mostly near the floor.

My mother said, "What's the matter? Aren't you hungry?"

I said, "Sure I'm hungry. Can we use my room?"

She smiled and said, "Yes. Yes, of course. Let's eat in your room. You open it up and I'll bring in the food."

I wound my way down the goat path to the door of my room and worked the combination lock. The room was just as I had left it. I turned on the light and found two small folding tables to put in front of our chairs.

My mother liked to eat in front of CNN, so I brought it up on the HDTV. The economy was in the shitter. The Middle East was devolving into a missile fest. A celebrity had adopted an Asian baby and tried to return it. Somebody had been arrested for mistreating a horse. I couldn't believe my mother ate in front of this garbage. No wonder she was crazy.

My mother bustled in carrying two steaming bowls of pasta on a tray. She put a bowl on each table, smiled at me, and went back out again. When she came back she had a bottle of wine, one from Trader Joe's with a rooster on the label, two wine glasses, and a wine opener. She handed the wine and the opener to me and I did the honors.

My mother sat next to me but popped up again and went into the kitchen. She came back carrying a small wedge of cheese and a cheese grater. She held the cheese in one hand and the grater in the other and grated me the perfect amount of cheese. She always got it right. Then she grated some for herself, settled into her chair, and said, "Isn't this nice!"

"It is. Thank you for dinner," I said. I forked ziti into my mouth, tasting the gravy.

My mother's gravy was perfect as always. I had tried to re-create it and failed. When I was married, Carol tried to re-create it. She failed. Determined to succeed, she asked my mother for the recipe but was stymied by directions such as "chop some garlic," "add enough oregano to make it taste good," and "add two bay leaves, unless they're small, then three or four." She watched my mother make it and tried to copy the steps and ingredients, but it never tasted the same. My mother's gravy, like the gravy of all Italian mothers, was her unique gift to me. I was thankful for it.

Our meal together transported me back to the family dinner table. We had occupied three sides of the rectangle. My dad sat at the head. My mother sat kitty-corner on a long side of the rectangle. I sat across from her on the other long side.

A crusty Italian bread on a scarred breadboard waited in front of my dad. He would cut the bread, give the end to me, and the next slice to my mother. A big bowl of pasta sat on the stove. My mother would fill our plates with spaghetti and meatballs, grate cheese onto them, and serve them. We'd eat pasta and talk about nothing and everything: Ronald Reagan, Uncle Walt, my Auntie Rosa's latest drama—all were grist for the mill at our dinner table. At the end of the meal, we'd sop up the last gravy with our Italian bread.

I pointed at the ziti with my fork and said, "This is delicious."

My mother said, "Good. I'm glad you like it."

"It reminds me of dinner with Dad."

At the mention of my father, my mother's face tightened and a line formed between her brows. She asked, "Is it true?"

"About the house in Pittsfield?"

"Yes."

"It's true. I've been there myself. Dad's pictures are all over it with Cathy Byrd and JT."

"Who is JT?"

"John Tucker Jr. Dad's son with Cathy Byrd."

My mother ate a forkful of pasta and said, "I always thought she was too friendly with your father. I never imagined that he would stoop so low as to sleep with the little whore."

"I never would have believed it without the pictures."

We stabbed at our ziti. The TV droned on about some indefinite threat that could only be solved by immediate, but undefined, action. My mother drained her glass of wine and refilled it. I joined her and we finished the bottle.

Emboldened by wine, I said, "We have to do something about that search warrant."

My mother said, "I don't see why. There is no reason for them to search this house."

"I know, but Lee's going to get a warrant anyway. He thinks there are clues in those notebooks."

"That's ridiculous."

"Even so, he says he'll be here tomorrow. If we don't want him to search, we need to give him the notebooks. He needs something to explain how Dad bought a house in Pittsfield for cash."

Our plates were empty. My mother stacked them and carried them into the kitchen. I took the empty wine bottle and the glasses and wound my way through the piles with them. I handed my mother the glasses and said, "They've got to be here somewhere."

She took the glasses and said, "I don't have anything for that detective."

My relationship with my mother had been punctuated by a long string of failures and mistakes. There were events that I should have remembered but forgot, wrongs that I should have forgotten but remembered, things that I should have done but didn't, and things that I did do but shouldn't have. There were fights and absences, disagreements and slights, hurt feelings and mangled emotions. Yet none of those mistakes would match the one that I made at that moment.

I suppose I was driven by the right reasons. I was trying to protect her. I was trying to keep strangers from coming into the house to do exactly what I chose to do when I left that kitchen: climbed off the goat path and waded into my mother's piles.

My mother heard the crunching paper and came out of the kitchen. She asked, "What are you doing?"

"I'm looking, Ma. I'm looking for the notebooks in this pile of crap so I can give them to Lieutenant Lee and keep him from clearing out your house."

I remembered that the piles had started in the corner of the living room nearest the front of the house, away from the front door. I worked my way back there, stepping around stacks of newspapers, junk mail, books, magazines, and the other detritus that most of us ejected from our lives on a daily basis.

My mother said, "Get out of there!"

"They've got to be back here," I said. "In a file. In a box. Somewhere."

"Get out!"

The light from my room spilled into the living room. Still I couldn't see. A lamp was pressed against the front wall, buried by papers. It hadn't been turned on in ages. I turned it on, thinking the light would make it easier to see. The cacophony of printed material got no clearer.

My mother started to pace on the goat path. She yelled at me, "Goddamn you! Get out! Get out of there! You're ruining it! You're ruining everything. I'll never be able to find anything!"

"Find anything? Find what, Ma, what? What piece of crap is back here that you could find? The police are going to tear this place apart. Don't you get it? All this—this—this crap, this shit, is going to get dumped into the front yard and then thrown into dumpsters. All of it, unless I can find something. Those notebooks, or a bank account slip, or a betting receipt, or a cancelled check—something that Lee can use to chase down Dad's money trail."

"There's nothing there!" My mother sobbed. "Nothing there from him. I don't keep it there."

"For God's sake, there must be something."

"Get out! Get out! Get OUT!" my mother shrieked. She ran along the goat path and into the kitchen. I looked down into a pile, saw a manila folder, and pulled on it. It was stuck. I pulled harder and it moved. Something in it looked official. One more pull and the folder came free as its pile gave way and fell across the living room.

My mother screamed behind me as the paper hit the ground. I turned. She had left the goat path and stood right in front of me, holding a kitchen knife in a trembling hand.

"Get the FUCK out of my house! Get out of my house, you goddamn son of a bitch! You bastard! Get out!"

I raised my hands at the sight of the knife, holding the manila folder in my right hand. I said, "Okay. Okay, Ma!"

"Don't call me that! Just get out!"

She backed up onto the goat path, holding the knife in front of her. I climbed out and stood in front of her with the manila folder. I took a step toward her.

"Get out! Get away from me!" She said, tears running down her cheeks, her voice skipping along the edge of hysteria.

I said, "I just want to lock my room."

"NO! No! Get out! The room is mine. It's my house. *My* house! I'm tired of giving you that space and not having enough room for everything I want, having to rent space, use the yard. It's *my* house and *my* room. You get *out!*" She waved the knife at me, and I backed up. She took a step forward.

I said, "Put down the knife."

169

"Get out!"

"C'mon. Please. Put down the knife before you hurt yourself."

My mother's voice was icy cold as she said, "You and your father have ruined me. Now, get out."

I was at the front door. I pulled on the door and got it open to its limit. Then I squeezed out and pulled the door shut behind me. The lock clicked and my mother yelled, "Don't you ever come back!"

FORTY-ONE

I stood in the front yard, trembling, stranded in a suburban wasteland. My mind cranked in a continuous loop, playing and replaying the transition from a pleasant domestic scene of pasta and gravy to a nightmare of knives and screaming.

I didn't want to upset her any further, so I got off her front lawn and stood in the street. Cars and trucks thrummed on the nearby Mass Pike. Trees hid the highway; without the sound, you'd never know it was there.

The neighborhood had no sidewalks here, but it had no traffic, either. The one lane led to a larger cross street after five driveways. I found the cross street and stood on the corner under a street lamp where Jael would see me. I pushed the memory of my knife-wielding mother out of my mind and opened the manila folder. It was the only piece of information that I had been able to wrest from the black hole that was her house.

The folder had twelve slips of paper in it. Pay stubs from the year before my father died. I angled the papers in the street lamp's light to read the numbers. Like other engineers at GDS, my father made a comfortable upper-middle class income, hovering somewhere around six figures.

The income on all the pay stubs was identical. Apparently GDS gave their cost-of-living raises at the beginning of the year. The money was divided among taxes, a 401k, Medicare, Social Security, and my parents' checking account. All the money went into that one checking account, and my mother paid all the bills. There was no way that my father was slipping money out of his pay to cover the expenses of a second family in Pittsfield. This had been a waste of time.

I looked up and down the street. Jael wasn't due for half an hour. I opened my Droid and searched for Lucy's phone number. The picture I took of her at Fenway smiled out at me. That day seemed like it was years ago.

I realized that I hadn't spoken to Lucy today. Funny that she hadn't gotten back to me. I called her cell. She answered immediately.

"How's the face?"

"It's okay," I said. "Thank you for helping me out last night."

"It didn't seem right to say, 'Oh look, my date got beat up. Time to go!'"

"Still, it was good of you get me back to my bed."

"Was your other friend still there when you woke up?"

"What, Jael? Oh yeah. We've been busy today."

"She's beautiful in an exotic sort of way."

Doh! It finally occurred to me why Lucy hadn't called.

I said, "Jael and I aren't dating or anything."

Lucy said, "It's really none of my business."

"No. Seriously. She's a friend of mine who's—well—"

"Yes?"

"Who's really good with a gun."

"You have a friend who's really good with a gun?" Lucy sounded skeptical.

"You don't?"

"No."

"I highly recommend it."

Lucy was silent for a moment, and I let the silence linger. I was happy to be talking with Lucy. The conversation was pushing my mother further and further out of my mind.

Finally Lucy spoke. "How are you feeling tonight?"

I said, "I feel good. The stitches don't hurt much."

"Would you like to come over to my house for a visit?"

My stomach flipped. Imagined images of Lucy's naked body flooded my brain. I took a deep breath and said, "Boy, that sounds great."

"So you'll come over?"

"Sorry, but I can't. I have to be somewhere tonight. I won't get home till late."

"Whatcha doin'?"

I'm meeting a mysterious defense contractor engineer in the woods in Western Mass next to a white dot on the satellite picture. Jael's getting her sniper rifle. It'll be great.

I said, "You don't want to know."

Lucy asked, "Are you going to get beat up again?"

I said, "I doubt it. How about dinner tomorrow? We could go into Cambridge."

"Sure!"

We made plans. As I hung up, Jael's Acura MDX glided down the street. Bobby Miller sat in the passenger seat. I opened the back door and climbed in.

FORTY-TWO

JAEL PULLED AWAY FROM the curb.

"Put on your seat belt," said Jael.

"Yeah, Tucker, put on your seat belt," said Bobby.

"Fuck you," I said.

Bobby turned to Jael. "Somebody is a cranky pants."

Bobby had the seat pushed all the way back, leaving no room for my legs. I slid over behind Jael, grabbed the seat belt, and clicked it into place. "Hey, Bobby, how come you get to ride shotgun?"

"Because I brought a shotgun." Bobby reached down between his legs and pulled up a black weapon. He asked Jael, "Should we give Tucker a gun?"

Jael said, "No."

"Why not?"

"Because the last time he held a gun he nearly shot someone."

"Really?"

"He does not practice proper trigger safety."

Jael was talking about my tendency to let my finger slip over the trigger when I held a handgun. Apparently, that's bad.

"We can probably teach him trigger safety."

"I have tried. He has a mental block."

I said, "I wish you two wouldn't talk about me behind my back."

"I can see that," said Bobby to Jael, ignoring me. "He's kind of a theoretical academic."

Bobby and Jael's yammering kept driving spikes of irritation into my brain. The spikes brought up images of my mother threatening me with a knife, and the whole concoction felt like nitroglycerine.

"Screw you, Bobby. You go out and talk to Patterson if I'm so theoretical."

"He only wanted to talk to you. I'd get nothing."

"Then maybe I'm not so theoretical after all. Maybe I'm useful. Was that why you broke up my date with Lucy?"

"What are you talking about?"

Jael had navigated all the side streets, zoomed down Route 9, and was merging onto the Mass Pike heading west. I was pressed against the side of the SUV as she tore down the entrance ramp.

"If JT's murder is Lieutenant Lee's case, why were you in front of my house? Why call me?"

Bobby said nothing. The car remained silent. I slumped in the back seat and let my mind wander. It meandered over to the question that hung in the air, picked it up, and started poking at it. Why *was* Bobby at the murder scene, and why had he called me out of a Red Sox game to look at a dead guy? I turned the question over, probing it, twisting it, trying to make it fit into the rest of the puzzle.

Now that I thought about the problem, it made no sense that Bobby would have called me. The Boston Police must have been called at the gunshot. Lieutenant Lee was investigating the murder. The FBI doesn't investigate random Boston murders. The FBI investigates bigger things.

What had Bobby said to JT's manager, Paul Waters? He had said that there were "serious concerns regarding the security of the Paladin project." I had assumed that he started investigating those serious concerns because JT had been murdered, but how would he have known about the murder so quickly? He couldn't have. He must have been investigating the serious concerns earlier. He already had serious concerns about JT. He said that he thought JT was a spy. What had Bobby said when we learned that Patterson was sharing a password with JT? He had said, "Figures." The final Tetris piece fell into place and I knew why Bobby had called me.

"You're an asshole!" I shouted toward the front of the car.

Bobby turned. "Who? Me?"

"It sure isn't Jael."

"Why am I an asshole?"

"I figured out why you wanted to get me to the house to look at JT."

Bobby twisted in his bucket seat. "What are you talking about?"

"You thought that JT and I were working together!"

"I did not."

"You absolutely did, you asshole."

"If you call me an asshole one more time, I swear I'm going to give you more stitches."

Jael said, "You two must discuss this later. I am driving."

I said, "Tell me it isn't true. Tell me that you didn't send me that picture of JT to see how I'd react."

"Hey, it worked. That picture got you down there pretty quick."

"I knew it! You *are* an asshole. The only reason that picture got me down there was that JT looked just like my father."

"I know that now."

"So what did you think then, huh? Did you think that JT and I were stealing Paladin secrets?"

Bobby glanced at Jael, back at me. "You shut up about that. That's classified."

"Bullshit!"

"I'm serious. You shut up."

"*You* shut up, you fucking asshole."

Bobby reached for me, but I stayed back in my seat.

Jael said, "I will stop this car."

Bobby said, "Well, he started it."

I muttered, "Asshole."

"What?"

"You heard me."

Jael said, "I am going to turn this car around. Do you want me to do that?"

Bobby and I were silent.

Jael continued, "We cannot go into a dangerous situation with you two fighting."

I said, "Well, it pisses me off that he thought I was a spy."

Jael said, "Agent Miller was doing his job. He cannot let friendship get in the way of that."

Bobby said, "Thank you, Jael."

I said, "Sure, take his side."

Jael said, "There are no sides. We are all on the same side."

Bobby asked, "Tucker, what's wrong with you?"

I crossed my arms. "Nothing." Images of my mother and her knife flashed before me. I pushed them out of the way. "There's nothing wrong."

"Because, I mean, fuck Patterson, you know? We don't have to do this. Let him wander around his fucking field and call you back. We shouldn't have agreed to meet there."

"You mean *I* shouldn't have agreed to meet there. Sorry. I screwed that up too." There was a lump in my throat. *I'm losing my mind.* I couldn't take a deep breath. I folded my crossed arms more deeply, the corners of my mouth turned down.

Bobby said, "You didn't screw anything up. Look, Tucker, I'm sorry. You're right, I was investigating JT. When he got killed in front of your house, I was afraid you were involved."

"Thanks for the trust."

"It's got nothing to do with trust. It's just my job. I get lied to all the time. I check everything. It's what I have to do. I'm sorry that I didn't tell you more that night in front of your house. I'm sorry I didn't tell you to just take off and drive Lucy home."

"Fine."

"I mean it, dude. You're a good guy. You don't deserve any of this."

The lump was back in my throat, my lower lip jutted out of its own accord.

Bobby asked, "You okay?"

I took a deep breath and blew it out. "Yeah, I'm okay." I was not okay.

"You want to head home? We don't have to do this."

"No," I said. "I want to hear what Patterson has to say. I want to know what's going on."

Jael drove on. I sat in the back, closed my eyes, and replayed my dinner with my mother. There was no other conclusion: I had fucked that up. If Lee wanted to empty her house, I should just let that be between them. I owed her an apology. I decided to apologize the next time I saw her.

The apology never happened.

FORTY-THREE

Jael's GPS took us off the Mass Pike at Route 84, as if we were going to New York. We exited almost immediately onto Route 20, the same highway that held GDS and Lotus Blossom. It seemed as if my whole world could be reduced to Route 20 and the Mass Pike. Jael wound her way through dark two-lane country roads with no streetlights.

I looked out the window at the dark woods. "Can we talk about what we're going to do out here?"

"Yeah," said Bobby. "How do we want to handle this?"

Jael said, "The meeting is at ten o'clock. I want to be in place by eight thirty. I would have preferred to arrive in the daylight, but we will have to make do."

I asked, "Why are we getting there so early?"

"To make sure that someone has not set up an ambush before us. It is difficult to approach a hiding place in the woods without making noise. The person who arrives first has an advantage."

Bobby said, "There's three of us. That could be an advantage."

"I do not think so. Three people make three times as much noise. If I were in those woods with my rifle and scope, I could easily kill five men before they found me."

Bobby said, "Well then, let's be glad that you're on our side."

I asked, "What will we do for an hour and a half?"

"We will wait and we will watch. We will not talk."

Jael's GPS led us to smaller and smaller roads. Two-lane roads with yellow lines and guardrails became one-lane roads with only guardrails, and these became one-lane roads where the woods edged right up to the asphalt. Jael parked on one of these small roads. She made no move to get out of the car. We sat as the car clicked and cooled.

"What are we doing?" I whispered.

"Yeah," said Bobby. "What are we doing?"

"We are letting our eyes adjust to the dark. We are going to be walking through the woods. Our flashlights will make us obvious. It is another reason I wish we had gotten here during daylight."

We adjusted for another minute, and then Jael popped the trunk, went around to the back, and hoisted out a rifle and three flashlights. The flashlights had red filters over their lenses. Jael had a smaller GPS in her pocket. She consulted it, and we headed off down the road, Jael carrying her rifle and Bobby his shotgun. I considered picking up a rock.

There were houses at the end of the road. Farmhouses? They sat on the right, with a broad driveway that led to a home and a garage. The nearest home had blue television light playing behind closed curtains. The garage was dark. We sidled past the houses, through the road's dead end, and straight into the woods.

The woods were not as black as I had expected. Partially, it was due to my eyes adjusting to the dark. In addition, somebody had lit the clearing near the highway with a ghostly white light.

Bobby whispered, "What is that light?"

Jael whispered, "I wonder if we are too late."

I said nothing. The light unnerved me. It didn't seem normal to have this white light shining in the middle of the woods. *Don't walk toward the light!* The woods smelled damp, and our feet crunched over thin loam and fallen leaves. It was September. The leaves on the ground would soon be joined by their brethren overhead. The cars on the Mass Pike whooshed past. The sound reminded me of my mother's house. *Don't you ever come back!* Depression drained my energy. I pushed it aside. I didn't have the luxury of feeling sorry for myself.

As we reached the edge of the clearing, Jael touched my arm and put her finger to her lips. We stopped and waited, listening for any sounds other than cars. There was no wind. The woods were silent. After about fifteen minutes, we moved forward into the clearing. I felt like Bambi being led into The Meadow. *Was Man in the woods?* My shoulders hunched in anticipation of a rifle shot as we approached the white statue in the middle of a manicured lawn.

She stood about three feet tall, her pedestal adding another two feet. A small spotlight lit her from below. This was the ghostly light I had seen through the trees. Flowers grew at her feet and bushes framed her. The combination created an eerie shrine.

Bobby said, "It's the Madonna."

Jael said, "Who?"

I said, "Jesus Christ's mother."

Jael said, "I thought Jesus was Israeli. She does not look Israeli."

"What?"

Jael said, "She looks European."

Bobby said, "Have you seen the paintings? So does Jesus. Let's get out of this fucking field."

I said, "Nice language in front of the Madonna."

Bobby asked, "What is she doing here?"

"She seems to be monitoring the traffic."

The Madonna stood between us, her arms extended in prayer, blessing, or supplication. I felt like an intruder, as if this spot was too holy for a meeting with some guy from Pittsfield with a guilty conscience.

Jael said, "This statue could ruin my shot." She looked out at the highway, then at the statue, and finally at the woods. She set off toward the woods halfway between the statue and the highway. We followed. Jael found a level spot on the ground behind a pair of trees about a hundred feet from the Madonna. She lay on her stomach and tested her gun sight. Bobby and I stood behind her.

I asked, "What do you think?"

Jael said, "This is a little closer than I like. The scope limits my field of view. There is almost enough light to use the iron sights, but only near the statue."

"What about just using a handgun?"

"A handgun is only reliable at ten feet."

Bobby said, "Same problem with my shotgun. If I shot from here, I'd be as likely to hit you as Patterson."

I said, "That statue creeps me out."

"Is the Madonna a bad omen? I thought she was considered to be good."

"No, she is good. I just—I don't know. Something about her bothers me."

"You are as safe as possible in this place. We are the first ones here. We'll see anyone who approaches. I suspect Patterson will park on the highway and climb over the traffic barrier. I will be watching him in the rifle scope. If he shows a gun, I will shoot him."

Bobby said, "Sounds like a plan."

"Yeah. I'm just being silly. Let's do this."

Jael said, "Then please sit down and wait."

I sat with my back against a tree, alone with my thoughts. They weren't good thoughts. My energy drained as depression settled into my gut. My mother had threatened me with a knife to defend a pile of garbage. What did that say about our relationship? Probably more than I wanted to admit.

My parents had been married ten years before I was born. Dad had told me that the delay, and my only-child status, both spoke to infertility rather than choice. They had started trying for a child immediately. It was ten years and two miscarriages before their efforts paid off. After that, my mother wasn't interested in getting pregnant anymore.

I looked out at the Madonna and thought about Mary's immaculate conception. She'd had a baby with no sex. My Italian cousins liked to think that their mothers had pulled off the same trick. The Catholic Church, with its ban on birth control, had enforced the idea of having sex only for procreation. Uncle Walt was probably telling the truth about my mother cutting Dad off in the bedroom.

"Someone is coming," said Jael.

A car had slowed to a stop along the Mass Pike and parked in the breakdown lane. The strategy spoke of a quick meeting, because eventually a state trooper would investigate the car. We waited and heard someone tromping through the brush between the road and the shrine.

The thin figure of Dave Patterson padded into the clearing. He walked into the Madonna's light.

"Tucker!" he called. "Are you here?"

Jael settled down and put her eye to her gun sight. Bobby nodded. I stood and strode out onto the short grass. A faint whiff of car exhaust wafted across the clearing as Patterson saw me and approached. He engaged in the ancient practice of demonstrating that he didn't have a weapon, raising his hands, palm outward. I did the same, though I had backup he didn't know about.

"Why couldn't we do this over the phone?" I asked.

"I'm worried about a wiretap," Patterson said.

"On a cell phone?"

He laughed. "Are you crazy? If the FBI wants to hear your conversation, they hear your conversation. It doesn't matter what kind of phone you use."

"Why would the FBI care about our conversation?"

"Hey. You're the one who rousted me with that fat bastard Bobby Miller. Remember? You tell me why he would care."

I decided to let him bring up Paladin. "JT and his mom had just been killed. We were talking to Paul Waters and he told us about you."

"So JT never asked you for help?"

"Is that why he was in front of my house? To ask for help?"

"He didn't ask you?"

"I never met him."

Patterson's thin features crunched into a rodent glare. "So you and Agent Miller didn't know about Talevi's deal with JT?"

"Why does everyone keep talking about Talevi?"

As if in answer, the brush erupted in urgent crunching and two men ran from the highway and into the field. Patterson and I had been blinded by the light around the statue and hadn't see them park behind his car. I heard a voice.

"Hey, Tucker! How's the face?"

I knew the voice. It was Teardrop.

I called, "Why don't you come over here and check it out yourself?"

Teardrop entered the Madonna's circle of light. Talevi stood next to him. Teardrop was between Talevi and the woods.

Talevi said, "Mr. Patterson, are you getting the Paladin documents I need?"

Patterson said, "Look, Mr. Talevi, I can't get those documents. I don't work at GDS anymore. I don't have access to the downlink design."

"JT said that Tucker would be able to help him. Perhaps he can help you."

What?

Patterson said, "I can't get back into GDS."

Talevi said, "And you, Mr. Tucker, can you get the downlink design?"

I said, "I don't know what you're talking about. What's a downlink?"

Talevi said to Teardrop, "They're useless. Shoot them." He turned to leave. "Shoot them both."

Teardrop produced a handgun and shot Dave Patterson in the chest. He aimed the gun at me, but I was already moving to put the Madonna between us. He squeezed off a shot. It missed.

Jael's rifle cracked and Teardrop's bald head snapped sideways. He didn't look surprised. He didn't look scared. He just looked empty as he sank to his knees.

Talevi bolted, covering the ground across the clearing in seconds. Another rifle shot rang out, and Bobby ran out of the woods. He chased Talevi into the brush. The shotgun boomed, but Talevi's tires squealed away a few seconds later.

I looked around. Patterson lay on his back, his long thin legs crumpled beneath him. Teardrop lay on his side, his tattoo obliterated by a bullet hole. The Madonna stood between them, her pure white stone miraculously untouched by the blood around her.

FORTY-FOUR

Bobby stormed out of the brush and advanced on the bodies. He checked their necks for pulses. Finding none, he rose and looked down at them. Jael had emerged from the trees and stood by my side. Bobby nudged Teardrop with his toe.

"I know this guy," said Bobby. "He's Stevie Donato. Worked for your cousin."

"Sal sent him?"

Bobby shrugged. "There isn't much Stevie does that Sal doesn't know about."

"It looked like he was working for Talevi," I said.

Bobby said, "Yeah. I know. Makes no sense. The Mafia doesn't do espionage. Or at least they didn't. What did Talevi say to you?"

"He wanted Paladin's downlink information."

"Did he."

"Patterson said he couldn't get it. Talevi asked me if I could get it, but I didn't know what they were talking about, so Talevi decided to shoot us."

"That's it? He didn't say anything else?"

"He said that Talevi had been working with JT."

Bobby said, "I was afraid of that." He looked at the Madonna and back out to the highway.

I asked Bobby, "Did Talevi kill JT? It would have been nice to tell me that."

"I have no idea who killed JT." Bobby looked at Jael. "What do you think?"

Jael said, "I think that Talevi has decided that his operation is a failure. He is now cleaning up loose pieces. Tucker is no longer safe."

Bobby blew out a big sigh, walked in a small circle on the grass, and stood looking out at the highway for a moment. He turned back to us. "Let's get out of here. I don't want you guys answering questions from the staties."

We collected our flashlights, made sure that Jael's shell casings were picked up, and headed back into the woods.

Bobby stopped walking once we were in the middle of the woods. He turned to us. "I'm about to share secret information from the US government."

I said, "Do I need to sign a nondisclosure agreement?"

"No. You need to keep your mouth shut and not tell anybody, and I mean *anybody,* about this for any reason. You got that?"

I said, "Yeah."

Jael said, "Understood."

Bobby looked at her and asked, "Are you even a US citizen?"

Jael remained silent.

"Goddamn. Motherfucker. Shit!"

I said, "What's the big secret?"

Bobby said, "Do you know what I mean when I talk about intelligence chatter?"

"Yeah. Little bits of data pointing to something."

"Right. So, we've been getting chatter lately that the Iranians are looking to buy secret information about the Paladin missile system."

"The one that shot down missiles in Iraq?"

"Yeah. The one that Israel will use if their situation with Iran turns into a shooting war."

"Oh, crap," I said.

Jael muttered something in Hebrew. From the tone, I took it to mean, "Oh, crap."

Bobby continued, "Of course, chatter that the Iranians are looking to buy secrets is nothing new. They're always looking to buy secrets. So we put this information on the back burner and waited—until we got the second piece of intel. We learned that someone in Massachusetts says he can sell the kind of information the Iranians are looking to buy."

"What kind of information?"

"The Paladin missile uses radar to track its targets and a big computer to hit the target."

"Okay."

"The problem is that the computer is too big to fly. So the missile gathers its radar data and uses a radio downlink to feed the information into the computer. Then the computer sends back guidance instructions."

"Talevi asked for information on the downlink."

"Right. If you have the right information about the downlink, you can disrupt the guidance and the missile will be useless."

"So JT and Patterson were selling information to Talevi?"

Jael said, "That is a reasonable theory."

I said, "Thanks."

She continued, "On the other hand, there are two questions that the theory does not answer."

Bobby asked, "What are those?"

"If JT and Patterson had the information, then why doesn't Talevi already have it? Why has he decided to abort the mission and kill his contacts—and Tucker?"

Bobby said, "Good point. What's the second question?"

"How do young men like JT and Patterson get connected to an Iranian spy such as Talevi? Contacts such as those take years to develop. One cannot simply ask for the information in a first meeting. One must understand the contact and the pressures on him to manipulate him."

I said, "Jael's got a point. I heard that JT had just started on the Paladin project. How would Talevi have known to talk to him?"

Bobby said, "That's why I want to keep this investigation a secret. There's more here to unravel. Talevi has some other contacts out there."

We emerged from the woods without using our flashlights and snuck past dark houses into Jael's car. Bobby let me ride shotgun on the way home. We drove away as Klieg lights snapped on in the woods. The crime scene technicians had started work.

We found our way back to the Pike and headed east. I looked into the night and thought about JT being a spy. It explained surprisingly little. Specifically, it didn't explain why he had been in front of my house holding my childhood drawing of the Paladin. Did he think I had coded the downlink into a crayon scrawl? I would have used yellow for the downlink if I had known it was there. Yellow is the perfect color for drawing something that should be invisible.

Jael drove down the Mass Pike, back toward Boston. We were silent. As we passed through Framingham, I took a habitual glance toward my mother's house. My mother's house is about three hundred yards from the road where a wall of dirt, shrubs, and trees shields it from the Pike. Normally I can't see any evidence of her house, or any other.

Tonight was different. Tonight I could see a column of smoke billowing into the sky, inky black smoke, lit from below by a flickering orange light and shot through with cinders of burning paper.

Lots of burning paper.

FORTY-FIVE

WE ARRIVED WITH THE fire trucks, but the house was already lost. Orange flames boiled out of the windows and through the front doors. Flames broke though a window on the side and shot out into the night. They'd immediately latched onto the maple tree outside my mother's window.

I ran toward my mother's bedroom. The heat buffeted me, but I fought through it, trying to reach the window, shielding my eyes and yelling for her. The buffeting turned to stinging. I stepped forward into the pain.

"Ma!"

Gloved arms grabbed me and pulled me backward.

I struggled for the window. "My mother's in there!"

One of the guys yelled, "You'll die here!"

They pushed me out onto the lawn away from the flames. Cool air washed over me. They handed me off to the fire chief, turned, and ran back toward the house. I struggled after them, but the chief held me.

"They've got protection. You'll get burned just standing near that thing."

"My mother doesn't have protection!"

"They're doing all they can. You watch from over there." He handed me off to Bobby and Jael, who led me toward a lawn across the street, then turned. "Do you know why this place is burning so fast?"

I looked at the paper shooting into the sky through a new hole in the roof. It hadn't occurred to me that my mother would have filled the attic with paper. I said, "She's a hoarder."

"Sweet Jesus." He turned and called out, "We've got a hoarder! Maximum fire load! Defensive strategy! Defensive strategy!"

I stood on the neighbor's lawn as the hoses swung away from my mother's house and started soaking the neighboring houses and the trees. I could see two firefighters trying to check my mother's bedroom; they couldn't even get close. Flames melted the window frame, popped the glass, and shot into the night. The firefighters retreated. The skin on my hands ached where I'd been burned.

The chief made eye contact with me and shook his head. Then he went back to directing the effort to save the rest of the neighborhood. More trucks showed up. None of them wasted water on my mother's little house. The heat drove me and the other spectators down the street. The house became an x-ray of itself. Orange flames filled every window and door, silhouetting the walls and roof. Fire broke through the roof. Flames shot into space.

I stood across the street. A memory dragged and pulled at my mind: gin rummy. My mother and I would sit at the kitchen table, alone because my father was away on business or whatever, and play game after game of gin rummy. I was thirteen and had gotten skillful enough that I had a fifty-fifty chance of winning. My mother would ask me about school and try to listen when I described the program I was writing on my new computer.

Gin rummy morphed into thoughts of tonight's dinner and the few pleasant moments we'd had in front of the television, where nobody could have distinguished us from a normal mother and son enjoying their time together.

Bobby and Jael stood beside me. Jael placed her hand on my shoulder. She murmured, "*Hamakom yinachem eschem b'soch sha'ar availay Tzion v'Yerushalayim.*" I didn't know what it meant, but her touch, and her gentle voice, broke through the fragile wall I had built against my emotions. A tsunami of sorrow pummeled me. I grabbed Jael. She pulled me close as sobs punched their way out of my gut.

I don't know how long we stood like that, but when the sobbing stopped, I released Jael and stood between my friends, watching my mother's house burn to the ground.

FORTY-SIX

THE CASKET RESTED AT the head of the small funeral parlor, flowers covering its oak lid, which remained closed tight against the horror of my mother's remains. They told me that someone had broken the front window while she slept and poured lighter fluid down the drapes. A single match and the mountain of paper did the rest. She hadn't made it five feet from her bedroom before she had been overcome by smoke. They assured me that she was dead before she felt the heat of the fire. A small blessing.

I sat next to the casket, wearing a black suit and accepting the condolences of a line of fellow mourners. Auntie Rosa, my mother's sister, sat next to me. The mourners had formed a line that snaked from the room's front door past the casket and on to me. The women talked quietly together and looked at the name cards on the flowers. The men stared straight ahead, lacing their fingers together to form an empty basket that they let hang in front of their suit pants.

They each knelt in front of the casket, the married couples often kneeling together, and, perhaps, said a short prayer. Some reached out and brushed their fingers across the polished oak, murmuring last wishes to my mother, maybe encouraging her on her new journey.

Finally they stood, gazed upon me with sorrowful eyes, and offered their condolences.

"I'm sorry."

"Thank you."

"She was a great lady."

"She was."

"How are you holding up?"

"Okay."

"It's a terrible thing."

"I know."

"I'm so sorry."

"Thank you."

"Sorry for your loss."

"Thank you."

"She was a great lady."

"She was."

"What can you do?"

"Remember her, I guess."

There were handshakes and kisses on the cheek for me and hugs for Auntie Rosa, the surviving sister and the last surviving child of Luciano and Belinda Testa.

The initial rush of mourners passed. I sat staring into space, trying to remember how many times my mother had dragged me through a mourning line. I had knelt next to her, my father refusing to get close to the dead. While my mother whispered a Hail Mary next to me, I folded my hands and peered closely at a real dead body, its lips pressed together, prayer beads clasped in its hands. I couldn't fathom the stillness of the dead, and I'd have sworn that the chest rose and fell in tiny increments. Then my mother would grab my hand, and we'd share our condolences.

"You look sad. Would you like some candy?"

A little girl stood before me in a blue, frilly dress. She held out her hand, displaying an orange funeral home candy.

"Maybe candy would make you feel better," she said.

Maybe she was right. I took the candy.

"Thank you," I said. "What is your name?"

My Auntie Rosa intervened. "This is your cousin Maria."

"I was going to tell him that, Nonna."

I said, "*Nonna*? You're Auntie Rosa's granddaughter?"

Maria said, "My daddy is over there." She pointed at Sal, who held forth in a small knot of men that included, improbably, Hugh Graxton.

Auntie Rosa said, "You don't remember Maria? She's our little surprise."

I covered, "Well, she was so small the last time I saw her."

Maria said, "Yes. I'm older now. I'm nine."

I smiled, couldn't help myself. "Wow! You're an old lady. Sal is my cousin."

"I know that. Daddy said that Auntie Angelina who died was your mom, and that you were his cousin. You look really sad."

"I am really sad," I said, deciding to change the subject. "If Sal is my cousin and you're Sal's daughter, then I guess you're my second cousin?"

"No, silly. You are my first cousin, once removed."

"I am?"

"Yes. If you have a baby, then the baby would be my second cousin."

I turned to Auntie Rosa, pointed a thumb at Maria. "She's only nine?"

Auntie Rosa said, "She's a smart one."

Maria said, "If you have a baby boy, then I could marry him because we'd be second cousins."

I said, "Really. Would you like to marry a baby boy with the name Tucker?"

"Well, sure. But I think I should babysit for him first to see if I like him."

"That's an excellent plan," I said.

Maria said, "Bye-bye," and ran to join a small knot of kids around the candy dish.

The orange candy melted and filled me with artificial orange goodness. The goodness spread through me and lifted the weight from my mind. I looked around the room, at all the mourners, most of whom I did not know, who had made time to come here and provide a featherbed of support for Auntie Rosa and me.

This was my family. These people had made the time to pay their respects to my mother and offer their support to me. I had done nothing to deserve this other than to be born to Angelina Testa, who had married John Tucker to give birth to me. The orange candy melted away, leaving nothing but sweetness.

I cast my eyes around the room and saw movement at the entryway. A new mourner, someone who was clearly not at home in the traditions of an Italian wake. Lucy wore a blue dress and held her purse to her chest. I rose, waved, and met her at the doorway.

Lucy gave me a peck on the cheek. "Tucker, I'm so sorry about your mother."

"Thank you," I said by rote.

"I'm sorry I'm late. I had a little trouble finding the funeral home."

"I'm glad you're here. It's good to see you." I took Lucy by the arm and brought her into the parlor. It was time to share this family, such as it was. I walked up behind Sal, who was gesticulating at Uncle Walt. Sal turned. I said, "Let me introduce Lucy. Lucy, this is my cousin Sal."

Lucy shook Sal's hand and said, "Hi. I'm Tucker's girlfriend."

My heart jumped in pleasant surprise. *Girlfriend? Well, what do you know about that.*

FORTY-SEVEN

THE LAST TRACES OF Lagavulin Scotch dripped onto my partially melted ice cubes. I gave the bottle a little shake, looked down its neck, shook it again, and rested it next to Click and Clack's tank. The boys were awake, keeping me company under a small pool of light in my kitchenette. A pad of paper lay on the counter before me, its top page blank except for a moisture ring from my glass. The ring was the only progress I had made toward writing my mother's eulogy.

I said to Clack, "You know, in some places Catholics don't write eulogies."

Clack did his statue impersonation.

"I know, right? Lucky bastards."

I had started the job in my home office, sitting in front of my Linux box, facing a blinking cursor. I had realized that I couldn't write a eulogy on my desktop computer, so I had switched to my laptop in the kitchen. The blinking cursor was in a different place, but that didn't help me write.

Obviously, the pain of the wake was blocking my eulogy writing. I opted for self-medication. I grabbed a half bottle of Lagavulin from the cabinet, a rocks glass, and some ice. Poured myself a drink and stared at my screen, downed the smoky liquid, poured myself another glass, and watched the cursor blink on the white screen. I couldn't write a eulogy while distracted by my background picture of Fenway Park, so I set the editor to full screen mode. The empty eulogy filled the screen. The cursor blinked at me.

"I don't know what to say," I'd told Clack. Clack waived a claw.

"You're right, buddy. I can't do this on a computer. It's too personal."

I'd closed the laptop, brought it back into my office, and returned with a pad of paper and a pen. The pen had MIT emblazoned on it. I had bought the pen just after my parents had dropped me at school. It was my first independent purchase.

My mother had cried that day—not in a big flamboyant way, but sniffling, her eyes puffy as she kissed me goodbye.

"I'm just ten miles from home, Ma," I'd said.

"You're all grown up," she had said. "It doesn't matter how far away."

I had turned from her with a jaunty "here I come, world" step, and entered the dorm. I never slept in my childhood bedroom again.

My glass had gone empty. I had refilled it. Now it was empty again and I was staring at the blank paper, trying to dredge up memories of my mother so I could share them, while at the same time pushing them away because they hurt. I remembered the time that she called me a "baby" on the playground. I think I was seven. Then there was the time she slapped me in the face for saying, "goddammit, Ma." There was the time we ran into Mr. Musto, my middle school math teacher, in the supermarket, and she commended him on being able to teach "my little retard." I couldn't count the number of times she had called me a son of a bitch, apparently missing the irony of the insult every time. Why couldn't I remember the good times?

There's a story about a funeral in a Jewish *shtetl*. The rabbi was presiding over the funeral, standing over the body of a horrible man who had hated everybody in the village. Everybody in the village had returned the favor. Still, the villagers had come to his funeral.

The rabbi asked, "Will anybody say something nice about this man?"

Silence.

The rabbi said, "Surely, somebody must have something nice to say about this man."

Crickets.

The rabbi said, "We are not leaving this funeral until somebody says something nice about this man."

An old guy in the back of the crowd shouts out, "His brother was worse!"

Could I say that about my mother? Perhaps say, "She was kind of crazy, and her last parenting act was to threaten me with a knife, but there must be others who were worse."

I said to Click, "They probably don't want to hear that. They probably just want to hear about the times she was a normal mother."

I tried to remember normal times. Christmas mornings. Breakfasts. Gin rummy. Watching TV. They all slipped away into darkness, replaced by a knife waving on a goat path in a filthy house.

The empty glass tugged at me. I tottered over to my booze cabinet and pulled out a bottle of Johnny Walker Red. Said to Click, "I'm drunk enough that this will taste okay. You want some?" Click demurred. I refilled my glass.

Lucy had offered to keep me company tonight. I had thanked her but said no. I needed to write this eulogy, and I had guessed that it might take all night. I drank some Johnny Walker Red. I was right; I was drunk enough that it tasted okay.

I pictured the people who would sit in the audience at the church. Auntie Rosa would be sitting out there. Sal would be there. So would Sal's sisters, Cousin Adriana who lived in the North End and Cousin Bianca who lived on Long Island.

Cousin Bianca was now Bianca Goldman, having married Ben Goldman and converted to Judaism. It had nearly killed Auntie Rosa, and my mother wasn't too happy about it either. Yet the Goldmans would surely be there, with their unbaptized son, Jake.

My mind skipped and jumped around the family tree, around my dad and his philandering, around the dead second family, Talevi and his threats, Graxton and his loans, Sal and his brutishness.

There must have been something to write, but I never found it. I woke up the next morning, my head pounding, my alarm clock blaring, and the pad of paper on the counter having nothing more on it than another moisture ring and a new whiskey stain.

I got dressed, put the empty sheet in my pocket in case something came to me, and headed toward the North End.

It was time to bury my mother.

FORTY-EIGHT

I CLIMBED THE SMALL pulpit on the altar at St. Stephen's Church in the North End and gazed out at the audience of mourners. The audience gazed back, faces empty, silent, waiting for me to say something about my mother's life. I reached into my jacket pocket, pulled out the sheet of paper from last night, still blank. I traced my finger around the whiskey stain. My head pounded. I didn't know what to say.

St. Stephen's Church sits on Hanover Street in the North End. It's down the street from Sal's haunt at Cafe Vittoria, and across the street from the famous Paul Revere statue. If Paul Revere's horse were to jump off his pedestal and gallop across the street, he'd run right through the St. Stephen's doors.

Bulfinch designed the church in 1803 for a Congregationalist parish. It looks more like a town meeting auditorium than a Catholic Church. Jesus did not hang from an outsized cross over the altar. Instead, a little platform allowed the speaker to see to the back row. I stood on the platform facing two columns of long pews. An empty balcony ran around the church's long rectangular space. The organ filled the balcony across from me. The woman sitting at the organ rested her hands in her lap and glanced down at her watch.

My mother's casket lay before me, its contents positively identified by dental records. Auntie Rosa had picked the casket. She sat in the second row, Cousin Sal on one side of her and Cousin Adriana on the other. The women wore black dresses and long, somber expressions. The rest of the Rizzo/Testa/Goldman clan sprinkled itself through the church. Uncle Walt sat in the middle of a pew, his face upturned toward me. Jael and Bobby sat together in the back. Hugh Graxton sat behind Sal.

Sal crossed his arms and frowned at me, his index finger tapping his elbow. He was right. I needed to say something.

"My mother made gravy for me—" My throat dried. I coughed. Started over. "She made gravy for me the night she died. I have always thought of her gravy as her special gift. It was the best gravy in the world, and she was the only one who could make it. Auntie Rosa's gravy is excellent, but it's different. My gravy is okay, but it's not as good."

Where was I going with this? I looked out across the audience.

"The thing is … she had her problems. You know. Her housekeeping wasn't the best." A nervous chuckle skittered through the family. "She sometimes lost her temper. She sometimes took things personally. Even so, I always knew that she was doing her best. I always knew that she loved me the best way she could."

Grief filled my throat and pulled my cheeks tight. "She was my only mother. There's nobody else who will love … I'll never taste her gravy again."

I looked into audience. Bianca was sobbing into her husband's shoulder. Auntie Rosa dabbed at her eyes. Sal's mask had cracked and he reflected my grief. Their emotions flooded into me, overwhelming my defenses. Tears slid down my cheeks. Bobby handed Jael a handkerchief. *Jael was crying.* Seeing her break destroyed my last defense against the emotions that pulsed within me. I knew what to say.

I let the rage overwhelm me. "But we all know that she didn't just die!"

My family settled in for the last lines of a good Catholic eulogy. They expected me to say how my mother didn't just die, that she lives on in Jesus. That this woman who never went to church, didn't make confession, and didn't believe in Communion, was going to bypass all the church's dogma and go straight to Heaven. That she was in a better place. That her suffering had ended. They expected me to spout the comforting cliches of a funeral service, but I didn't.

"My mother didn't just die," I repeated. "She was murdered!" I pounded my fist on the lectern. "Someone burned down my mother's house and murdered her!" I pointed at the casket. "She had many faults, but she didn't deserve the life she got. She didn't deserve her hoarding sickness. She didn't deserve a cheating husband, and she didn't deserve a son who visited her only twice a year. She deserved so much more than any of that. And she is going to get it."

The crying in the audience had stopped. They stared at me, eyes wide.

"And I *swear*, with God as my witness, that I will *find* whoever murdered my mother and kill them."

I folded the stained, blank paper, put it in my jacket pocket, and looked from person to person. Every one of them dropped their eyes as mine met theirs. Every one, that is, except Jael. When we made eye contact, she met my gaze and nodded her confirmation.

I leaned into the microphone. "May this be the will of God."

FORTY-NINE

"Tucker, you put the *fun* into *funeral*," said Hugh Graxton.

"Shut up, Hugh," said Sal.

"Yeah," Uncle Walt said. "We just buried the guy's mother."

Graxton gave Walt a hard glance, but he shut up.

The fire was dying in Antico Forno's brick fireplace, my family's traditional post-funeral restaurant. Attending funerals as a child, I would sit in front of that fireplace, watching the shifting logs reduce themselves to ash while my mother and her family transitioned from mourning to eating to drinking to laughing; returning to life after spending the day wallowing in death. At my father's funeral, the owners of the restaurant had ignored my ID and let me drink wine along with my family, while a younger cousin watched the fire. My mother's funeral was no different, though instead of me, my first cousin-once-removed Maria Rizzo sat in front of the ashes. The funeral was over. Only six of us remained, sitting around the table.

Death, the great leveler, makes for strange table companions. The FBI man Bobby and the alleged Mafiosos Sal and Hugh Graxton ringed the table alongside Walt, Jael, and me. Uncle Walt drank a Pabst Blue Ribbon. Sal and I drank limoncello, an unholy matrimony of lemonade and grain alcohol that Sal had made in his apartment. Jael, Bobby, and Graxton drank Scotch.

The limoncello slurred my speech. "Yeah. Shut up, Hugh."

Sal said, "Though I have to admit, that was the most fucked-up eulogy I've ever heard. I thought Father Dominic was going to fall off his chair."

I said, "It's true. I'm going to get whoever killed my mother."

Sal said, "Hey, don't get me wrong. I understand the urge. Burning? That's a fucking horrible way to go. Still, having fifty witnesses who can say that you promised to kill the fucker looks bad in court. It's even worse if one of them's a priest and the other is an FBI agent."

Graxton said, "They don't teach you this stuff at MIT?"

"How to get away with murder? No. Must have been a Zoo Mass elective."

Bobby said, "I didn't hear anything incriminating."

Sal said, "There you go, Tucker. The FBI's got your back."

"We live to serve," said Bobby.

Jael leaned forward. "The problem is not getting away with the revenge. The problem is taking revenge on the right person."

Graxton said, "Yeah, Tucker, listen to Jael. You had better be absolutely positive that you've got the right person."

Sal said, "I say fuck revenge. It's a sucker's game."

Bobby said, "Really, Sal? Never thought I'd hear that from you."

Sal said, "The first step in revenge is to dig two fucking graves."

Jael finished her Scotch. "If you find the right person, it is not revenge. It is justice."

Sal said, "*If* you find the right person."

I had a plan for that. It was time to put it into motion.

I drained my limoncello. "The right person is going to come to me."

Sal finished his limoncello and poured us another. "Why?"

There are all sorts of lies. There are lies that keep trouble from starting: *No, that doesn't make you look fat.* There are lies that smooth over missed appointments: *Stupid BlackBerry!* There are lies that hide your second family: *Honey, I have a meeting in Pittsfield.* Then there are the lies that can get you killed. I was about to tell one of those.

"I have my dad's notebooks," I said.

Bobby said, "What?"

I continued the lie. "They were in a shed in the back yard."

Sal said, "Shred them."

"I'm not going to shred them. I'm going to use them to find my mother's killer."

Sal said again, "Shred the fucking stuff. Get out of the revenge business. It's dirty."

Bobby said, "Sal's right about that. But don't shred them, give them to me. You gotta let it go."

I looked at Jael and asked, "Should I let it go?"

Jael said, "Were you serious about what you said in the church?"

"I swore to God, didn't I?"

"Many people swear to God. Few of them know what it means."

Bobby said, "So you think the person who killed your mother will want the notebooks? Do you have any idea who it is? If you do, give me the notebooks and let me do my job."

I drained my drink and reached for the icy blue bottle that contained Sal's hooch. I poured myself a glass and drank. It was really good. The lemons were the perfect dessert flavor. The sweet end to the spaghetti dinner, though Antico Forno was also unable to replicate my mother's gravy.

I looked straight at Graxton, said, "I have no idea who killed my mother."

"Don't look at me when you say that," said Graxton. "I had nothing to do with it."

Outside the window a young couple examined the menu, trying to decide whether to eat here or at one of the hundred other restaurants in the North End.

I pointed. "You see those two?"

Everyone looked. Graxton said, "Yeah?"

"They had nothing to do with it." I finished my drink and stood. "As for the rest of us, we played our parts."

FIFTY

JAEL AND I WALKED down Salem Street, the bricks doing their best to catch my limoncello-addled feet. When we reached the end of the street, we crossed into the park that bisected the city. I let Jael lead the way. We turned at the park, turned again at Hanover Street, and continued on toward Government Center. I thought we were heading for the train station at Haymarket, but Jael had planned a detour.

Just before we reached Congress Street, Jael turned and led me into the ghostly, smoking chimneys of the New England Holocaust Memorial. The chimneys, square towers of glass etched with six million numbers, towered above us. I followed Jael, craning my neck to see the top of the each chimney. She stopped and stood in a chimney marked as Auschwitz-Birkenau.

I yearned to lean against the glass, but the feeling that I'd be stepping on the dead kept me standing. "Why are we here?"

Jael stood on a grate by the first tower. An unpleasant steam wafted up, enveloping us. "I come here when I am upset."

"Why are you upset?" I asked. "I mean, beyond the obvious."

"I wish you would not improvise."

"Improvise?"

A tourist pushed past on the way to examine other death towers. Streetlights pushed through the etched glass, making Jael's eyes glitter. "Do you have the notebooks? You've never mentioned a shed."

I looked beneath the grate. Warm steam and an LED star field confronted me. I looked away. Toward the end of the Memorial a woman crouched in the path, touching the small stones that edged it. Limoncello and fatigue bore down.

"No. I don't have the notebooks."

"Then you were improvising at dinner."

"Yes."

"I wish you would not do that. It is impossible to predict what will happen."

"No, it's not. It will get a rise out of whoever who killed my mother."

"It will get you killed. Someone may try to take the notebooks. They will not accept 'I made it up' as an answer when they torture you for them."

"I was hoping you would help me avoid that."

"I will help you, but I may not succeed. I could also be killed."

The thought jolted me. I had always though of Jael as a force of nature, permanent and invincible. But that was foolishness. She could die because of me. I was okay with exposing myself to danger in this plan, but I had compromised her. My cheeks reddened as shame trumped fatigue.

I said, "I'm sorry. You're right. It was a stupid thing to do."

"Yes," said Jael. "It was."

"What do I do now? Go back and tell them I was lying?"

"No. The pillow has been torn and the feathers are scattered. There is no way to get them back. We must move forward."

"How?"

"You must cast the net farther. There is another who must hear your claim."

"Who?"

"Your friend, Lucy."

"Lucy?"

"She has been involved with this situation since the start."

"How could Lucy be a spy? She has had nothing to do with this."

"Lucy was with you when JT was shot. She may have been providing a diversion."

"That was a coincidence."

"Also, she was with you when you were beaten."

"That's just silly."

"If I were spying on you, that is exactly what you would say about me." Jael's eyes took on a perky twinkle. She batted her lashes and said, in a perfect Southern accent, "Why Mr. Tucker, you flatter me with your attention."

I stared at the transformation. "My God. Who are you?"

Jael's eyes returned to normal. "I am your friend."

My Droid played the Boston Bruins theme song. Bobby.

"Give me those fucking notebooks, you moron," said Bobby.

I watched Jael touching the numbers on the glass column and said, "I don't have them. I made it up."

"Christ, Tucker. I wish you wouldn't improvise."

FIFTY-ONE

LUCY EDGED HER WAY to the rim of the small dock and looked back at me, her smile as wide and bright as the cloudless Indian summer morning. The dock stood in the middle of the Boston Public Garden. I wrapped an arm around Lucy. She rested her head on my chest and we waited for our turn to ride the Swan Boats. Tomorrow the boats would be put away for the winter, but today they were playing host to the diehards who wanted to get in one more ride.

I'm not sure what was in the water in late-nineteenth-century Boston; those people were construction maniacs. They built the nation's first subway station, won the first American League pennant, and planted the nation's first public botanical garden, starting work on the Boston Public Garden in 1856 and finishing it by 1859.

The Boston Public Garden features a small manmade pond. The pond is long, thin, and pinched in the middle where those same nineteenth-century Bostonians built a little suspension bridge across it. The Swan Boats began operating in 1877 and have been gliding under that bridge ever since.

The hot weather had abbreviated Lucy's outfit. Her short cotton skirt stretched across her hips and moved with her thighs, while her white tank top scooped to expose a tiny bit of cleavage. My stomach did a pleasant flip as my body responded to hers, my first pleasant feeling since I had buried my mother a week ago.

Lucy wore sunglasses but still shaded her eyes with her hand. "Here comes our boat."

The Swan Boat crew unloaded the previous passengers at the other end of the dock and slid the boat down to our end. Lucy and I were first on the dock and would be sitting in the front row, confident that there would be no waves breaking over the prow of our fine craft on this perfect September day. The boat glided to a stop. I guided Lucy in ahead me, admittedly driven less by chivalry than by an opportunity to look at her hips in that skirt.

I sat next to Lucy. She tickled my ear with her lips as she whispered, "No life preservers?"

I said, "We're only thirty feet from the shore. If we sink, I promise I'll carry you to safety."

"I'd be all wet and muddy. Would you still want to carry me?"

"I'd especially want to carry you."

Lucy giggled and nuzzled my neck with her nose. She said, "I'd like that."

A shiver rolled through me and I said hoarsely, "Me too."

The boat set off. Its captain, a blond college girl with a steady hand on the tiller, pedaled evenly to drive the boat forward. Swan Boats have always been pedaled. We were riding in one of the newer Swan Boats, designed and built in 1918, back when the Red Sox were a dynasty led by Babe Ruth.

I put my arm around Lucy's shoulder. She nestled into me as we watched the Public Garden glide past. People sat on the shore, some having picnic lunches, others sleeping.

Swan Boats make one circuit of the barbell-shaped lagoon. The first turn is around a small green cupola sitting the middle of the water. Ducks rested on the cupola, staring at us as if to say, "We are off the clock." Other ducks followed the Swan Boat, picking up pieces of popcorn tossed by children sitting behind us. The captain guided the boat in a circle around the cupola. Lucy sighed in my arms. Somewhere in the park, Jael watched over us. I told her that it wasn't necessary for her to watch me, but she reminded me what happened the last time I went on a date with Lucy.

I squeezed Lucy's shoulder, said. "Arrgh. She's a fine ship."

Lucy snuggled in. "What a beautiful day. You seem relaxed."

"I love the Swan Boats," I said. "I rode them all the time."

"This is my first time. There's so much I haven't seen in Boston."

I didn't answer. My comment about riding the Swan Boats had bumped my thoughts against the empty place in my mind recently occupied by my mother.

Lucy looked up at me. "What's the matter?"

"Just thinking about my mother. She took me on the Swan Boats a couple of times a year."

"Oh. Tucker, I'm sorry."

I said, "Thanks. I suppose there's not much to do about it. I can't avoid everything that reminds me of her."

"It's only been a week since the funeral. It'll get better. I promise."

We snuggled as the boat approached the lagoon's constricted center near the suspension bridge. A little girl in a pink summer dress sat in her father's arms and waved at us. We waved back. Her father smiled. They slid from view as we passed under the bridge.

Screens kept pigeons from nesting in the bridge's nooks and crannies. I looked down at Lucy and kissed her as if we were in the tunnel of love. She returned the kiss, her lips softening, and her tongue touching the edge of my lip. She hummed a happy little sigh, then we were back into the sunlight, heading toward the island that filled the other end of the lagoon's barbell shape.

The island had originally been a peninsula, but it had attracted so many nineteenth-century lovers that the city forester decided to sever the connection to the land. Now a narrow channel cut between the island and the edge of the lagoon. Like the Straits of Magellan, this channel tested the Swan Boat captain's mettle. Our captain navigated the strait easily.

I closed my eyes, summoned my strength, then lied to Lucy. "The person who torched my mother's house was an idiot. He didn't burn the notebooks."

Lucy said, "What notebooks?"

The lie stuck in my throat. I worked to get it out.

"My dad had notebooks that he used as diaries. I think someone burned my mother's house to hide them, but they were in a shed."

Lucy said, "What will you do with them?"

"I don't know."

She settled back into the crook of my arm. "I'm sure you'll do the right thing."

We were silent as the boat headed down the final stretch. My mood had been broken. Guilt sloshed around in my gut. Lucy didn't seem to notice. Instead she put her hand on my bare, suntanned knee, and ran her finger a few inches up from the kneecap. Then she circled the knee with her finger and rested her hand on my thigh.

She said, "I think we should get some lunch and bring it back to your house."

"That's the best idea I've heard all day."

As we left the Public Garden, my Droid played "Extreme Ways." Jael's ringtone.

"Where are you going?" she asked.

Lucy didn't know Jael was watching us. I said, "Hi, Jael. Lucy and I were just hanging out at the Public Garden. We're going to grab a cab and get some lunch."

"I will not be able to watch you if you take a taxi," said Jael.

"That's okay," I said. "I'm good. We're going to grab some lunch over at Whole Foods. You know. The one near my house?"

"Understood."

She hung up. Knowing her, she'd be at the Whole Foods before us. Naturally, we wouldn't see her. Once Jael goes into her stealthy protective mode, she's almost impossible to find.

Lucy asked, "Have you known Jael long?"

I said, "Yup. She's an old friend."

"How come you two never got together?"

"It's never been an option. We just don't relate that way. You've met her. Could you see her on the Swan Boats?"

Lucy tugged on my arm, lowering my head. She kissed me on the lips for a long time. "Let's get lunch."

Normally I walk everywhere in Boston, especially on a beautiful fall day. Today, however, paranoia drove me to hail a cab. We took the cab over to Whole Foods Market behind Symphony Hall.

The Whole Foods market on Westland Ave occupies the first floor of a circular parking garage. The building looks like a tire that had been left on its side, with the Whole Foods occupying the bottom tread. I got a basket and carried it as Lucy chose strawberries, apples, exotic cheeses, and crusty bread for lunch. As we walked, Lucy rested her fingers inside my elbow. When our hands touched, our eyes would lock. Sometimes we'd kiss.

I led us back to my house, Lucy's arm through mine, her breast pressed against my bicep. It's a ten-minute walk from the Whole Foods to my place on Follen Street. It seemed to take an hour.

We walked over the spot where JT had lain and climbed my front steps. I disengaged my arm and unlocked the door. Said, "Ladies first," and ushered Lucy into the doorway. Before closing the door I looked out into the street. I couldn't see Jael, but I figured she was out there. I gave her a thumbs-up sign and a bye-bye wave, letting her know that I'd be staying in. Then I closed the door.

We climbed the narrow steps to the apartment. Lucy led the way, her black skirt sashayed before my eyes. When we reached the top of the stairs, Lucy stood to one side as I worked the lock. I opened the door and we stepped inside.

I placed the groceries on the kitchen counter as Lucy closed the front door and grabbed me from behind. She wrapped her arms around my chest, pressed herself into my back, and slid her hands down my stomach. I turned and her mouth found mine. We kissed and stumbled our way to the bedroom. Once there, Lucy pulled me onto the bed, then she hiked up her black skirt and straddled me.

I ran my hands up her thighs, sliding the skirt around her waist. She pulled off my T-shirt and I pulled off hers. Her bra went next. Lucy's bare breasts brushed my chest as she leaned in to kiss me.

Jael popped into my head. *Isn't this exactly what Lucy would do if she were a spy?* The thought disappeared as Lucy unzipped my fly.

Afterward, we spooned naked on the bed, Lucy's butt curving against my stomach as she dozed. My arm lay over her hip, my hand resting between her breasts. My other arm had gotten caught under the pillow that cradled her head. It tingled with nervy pain. Lucy's hair tickled my nose. I shifted my weight, tilted my head away from Lucy's hair, couldn't get comfortable. I disengaged myself, pulled on my underwear, and padded out to the bathroom, closing the bedroom door behind me.

In *Three Days of the Condor* Robert Redford tells Faye Dunaway, "I just want to stop it for a few hours." Then they have sex and he's all happy and relaxed. Why wouldn't that work for me? The guy in the mirror didn't look relaxed. He looked harried, annoyed, and guilty about lying to his girlfriend.

"You're a retard," I told him.

FIFTY-TWO

THE FRUIT AND CHEESE in the Whole Foods bag called to me. I washed my hands, emptied the bag, and began assembling a fruit plate. Perhaps lunch would drive Jael's warnings from my mind and let me enjoy my afternoon with Lucy.

My Droid said, "Droid." Uncle Walt.

"Hey, Tucker. I'm just calling to check up on you. How are you doing?"

"Great, Uncle Walt. You know. Considering."

"Yeah, I know. Listen. I'd like to take you out to dinner tonight. I got something to show you."

I thought about Lucy in my bed: her long legs, firm butt, and the soft smile that crossed her face when she was pleasured. "Sorry. I've got plans with Lucy tonight."

"Lucy? The girl from the wake?"

"Yeah, that Lucy."

"Bring her along. I'll treat you both."

I floated at the edge of a whirlpool, feeling myself sucked toward an inevitable decision.

"What's this about?"

"I can't really do it justice over the phone."

"Lucy and I are about to eat now. We won't be going out for dinner."

"Well, drinks, then. After-dinner drinks."

The whirlpool increased its sucking power.

Walt said, "Just name the time and place. This is important, Tucker. I need your help."

"It's got to be tonight?" I asked.

"Yeah."

"Okay. Meet us at Stoddard's near the Boston Common at eight tonight."

"What's the address?"

I heard the bedroom door open behind me and turned. Lucy stood in the doorway, unapologetically naked. My eyes widened. My breath shortened. I gaped at Lucy's flat stomach, curving hips, and long legs. Her breasts rose from her chest, beckoning me to touch them.

I said, "Google it, Uncle Walt. See you at eight." Terminated the call.

Lucy asked, "What's up?"

"My Uncle Walt called to invite us to dinner."

"Us?"

"Yeah. But screw that. I talked him down to having a drink at Stoddard's."

Lucy stepped close to me and placed her palm on my chest and gave me a light kiss on the lips.

"Does he always invite you out?"

"No. This is the first time ever."

"That's not good." Lucy turned and headed for the bathroom.

"What do you mean?"

She paused at the door. "Random dinner invitations from relatives are never good news." She disappeared into the bathroom and closed the door.

I continued to assemble the fruit plate. There were blueberries, strawberries, an apple, assorted cheeses. I arranged the blueberries in the center in a pile, ringed them with strawberries, sliced the apple and cheese into wedges and interspersed the wedges between the strawberries.

The result looked like the Wheel of Fortune. I didn't like it, and was considering another arrangement when Lucy came out of the bathroom, still naked. She said, "Yum!" and picked up a strawberry.

I watched the muscles of her back move under her satin skin as she chose some blueberries. I moved behind her and put my hands on her hips, kissing her on the neck. She stepped back, grinding her ass against me.

I said, "Much as I hate to suggest it, would you like a T-shirt?"

She turned, put her arms around me, kissed me on the lips. Blueberry.

"No thanks," Lucy said as she slipped her thumbs into my underwear, kissed my chest as she slid them to the floor. Rose and gave me another blueberry kiss. "There's nothing more organic than nude lunch."

No arguing with that. We took the fruit plate to the couch in my living room. Lucy curled up, her red toenails contrasting nicely with the black couch. She leaned in to kiss me. Her hand brushed the scar on my upper arm, and she sat back.

"Where did you get this?" she asked, running her finger over the scar.

"A guy shot at me once with a machine gun."

"Shot *at* you? It looks like he shot you."

I raised my arm and looked at the scar. "He mostly missed. He's gone now."

"What happened to him?"

"Jael."

Lucy had been about to bite into a large strawberry. Paused. "Do you think she can protect you?"

"Uh-huh. Why do you ask?"

"Haven't you noticed that the bullets keep getting closer to you? Your half brother was shot when we were at the ball game, his mother was shot just before you arrived at her house, and that Dave Patterson guy was shot right in front of you."

I had nothing to say to that. I slid closer to Lucy, pressing my naked hip against hers. Took the big strawberry from her hand and held it out to her. She took a bite. I kissed her strawberry-stained lips and ran my hand lightly over her breast. She moaned and lay back on the couch.

The rest of the fruit plate remained untouched until that evening, when we finished it and headed out to Stoddard's to hear Uncle Walt's big secret.

FIFTY-THREE

Stoddard's sits near Downtown Crossing in a building that survived the Great Boston Fire of 1872. A wooden bar, carved in Europe and echoing the building's architecture, graces one wall. Wooden Corinthian columns frame mirrors and bottles of top-shelf liquor, while Doric columns sit above the bar's trolley-track footrest. Framed corsets decorate the rest the of bar, a reminder of the building's original tenant: Chandler's Corset Store, the nineteenth-century's idea of Victoria's Secret.

I love Stoddard's for two reasons. First, it has old-fashioned lampposts installed in the middle of the floor, so you can lean against a lamppost, one knee bent, and rest your foot on the base while you drink your beer. Second, it has twenty silver beer taps that run the length of the bar and five ale casks tapped at the end of the bar. The twenty-five taps deliver a rotating assortment of outstanding microbrews.

Lucy and I stood under a lamppost. She nursed a white wine, while I had already downed half a pint of Mayflower Pale Ale, brewed right near the Plymouth Rock boulder.

Lucy looked around at the small crowd. "Should we get a table?"

"No. I want to keep Uncle Walt standing. That's the key to short meetings. If we sit, there's no telling when we'll get back home."

"Don't you like Uncle Walt?"

"I like Uncle Walt just fine. I just don't like mysterious dinner invitations."

"You should have just said no."

A jolt of irritation rippled across my belly. Lucy was right, I should have just said no. I pursed my lips and drank my beer.

"Maybe I should go," said Lucy.

"I'd hate to end our day like this," I said. "I had fun."

"Me too. It's just that—"

Walt burst upon us. "Hey, kids! How are you doing? Let's grab a seat!" Walt strode to the empty bar and sat at a seat with an empty chair on either side. He patted the chairs and tilted his head. *Come on over.*

Lucy glanced at me. I shrugged. We climbed into the seats on either side of Uncle Walt. The unoccupied bartender greeted us.

I said, "Uncle Walt, you remember Lucy."

Walt took Lucy's hand and said, "How could I forget this gorgeous creature. Tucker, you are a lucky guy."

Lucy extricated her hand. "We're both lucky."

I caught the bartender's attention and changed the subject, "Pabst Blue Ribbon, Walt?"

Walt said, "Screw that. We're celebrating. I'll have a Jack Daniels. Make it a double, neat. You guys want one?"

I looked across Walt to Lucy, who placed her hand over her wine glass. I drained my beer and looked to the bartender. "Geary's Pale Ale."

The bartender brought the drinks. I had just tilted my Geary's when Walt shot back his double Jack Daniels. Lucy's eyes widened.

Walt said to the bartender, "Another."

I said, "Jesus, Uncle Walt. What's your hurry?"

"I'm celebrating. That's why I called you."

"Okay. What are we celebrating?"

Walt reached into his back pocket and pulled out a glossy brochure. The brochure featured a large DNA molecule, superimposed over a mountain. The name *MinCare* dominated the top of the brochure. "We're gonna make us some money. You too, Lucy."

"What's that?" I asked and regretted it immediately.

"That, Tucker, is a ground-floor opportunity for us. This Min-Care stuff is the reason I'm so healthy. I never realized it until one of the guys at the gym let me try some. It's all in the min—" Walt's voiced faded into a dull drone of minerals, DNA, free radicals, cellular membranes, quick twitch muscle, the evolutionary history of man, and finally the health of barnyard animals.

I broke into Walt's spiel. "You mean these are vitamins."

"Not just vitamins. Supplements. These supplement the things that you're not getting into your body because you're not a caveman anymore."

The corner of my eye caught Lucy, the biology teacher, rolling her eyes and knocking back her wine.

Curiosity destroyed my good sense. "What does this have to do with making money?"

This gave Walt the opportunity to flip to the back of the brochure. It displayed a diagram that looked to me like a binary tree, the type I would use to store data in alphabetical order and retrieve it quickly. Apparently, binary trees could also be used to make money.

Walt said, "This is the payment plan. Each person has two people direct to them, then …" And he was off again. There was a power leg and profit leg, and Walt was certain that Lucy would be his power leg and—no offense, Tucker—I would probably be the profit leg. Then the money from the power leg would meet the profit leg…

A bartender noticed Lucy's empty glass and refilled it. I had hardly touched my Geary's as I sat in slack-jawed amazement at Walt's ability to rattle off long strings of meaningless business gibberish.

Finally I broke in. "But I don't need any money."

Walt blinked. "What do you mean, you don't need any money? Everyone needs money."

"I've got money."

Lucy watched the conversation.

Walt said, "No. You earn money with your time. I'm talking about residual income, Tucker. The money just rolls in like you were living off your investments."

"I do live off my investments."

Lucy reached across Walt and touched my hand. "And he's handsome and good in bed."

Walt looked back and forth between us. "Jesus, you guys are in love."

Lucy pulled her hand back and I looked into my beer.

Walt continued, "Don't deny it, Tucker. Did you tell her you love her?"

This had to end. "Walt, does this have to do with the money that you owe to Hugh Graxton?"

Walt glared at me and shot down his Jack Daniels. He tipped his glass to the bartender. "Another."

"How much do you owe the guy?"

"It's none of your goddamn business." The drink arrived. Walt shot it down. "Another."

I caught the bartender's eye and shook my head. Made a writing motion it the air. *Check, please.*

Walt caught my movement and said, "No. One more, one for the road."

"Walt, I think you're done. If you drink any more, I'll have to take your car keys."

Walt stood, stumbled back a step, gave Lucy a sidelong glance. *Now you're scoping out my girlfriend?*

Lucy caught the glance and said, "I think it's too late. You should take his keys."

Walt leaned on the bar and rummaged in his pants. Pulled out a big black key fob and slammed it on the bar. "You want my fucking keys? Go ahead. Take 'em. Take the whole fucking truck, and the payments."

"Jesus," I said. "I don't want your truck."

Lucy said, "I think you should take his keys anyway."

"Walt, c'mon. It can't be that bad. How much do you owe? Maybe I can help."

"I don't wancha goddamn help."

Damn it. The slurring had started. I took the keys. Walt would have to spend the night on my couch.

The check came. I signed for it.

"Whacha doin'?" demanded Walt. "This was supposed to be my treat. It's my fucking party."

"C'mon, big fella." I said. "Let's get you to my house."

"I gotta take a leak."

Walt broke away and stumbled around, looking for something.

I pointed at the staircase. "Bathrooms are downstairs."

Walt teetered off.

Lucy said, "Shouldn't you help him?"

"Help him walk down the stairs and take a leak? It'll just aggravate him. I suspect he's got practice doing this."

Lucy pulled me close. Her blue eyes bore into mine. "I had a fun day."

"Me too," I said. "Sorry it ended this way."

"There will be more fun days." Lucy gave me a white wine kiss that lasted until Walt slammed his hand on my back. My front tooth clicked against Lucy's. We both said, "Ow!" and put our hands to our mouths.

"Let's roll," said Walt.

FIFTY-FOUR

WE GOT UNCLE WALT up the steps and out onto Temple Place. It was going to be a long walk back to his car. We led him up Temple toward the Boston Common.

"Where did you park?" I asked.

"Underground. In the garage."

The Boston Common Garage has three exits. I needed a hint. "Where did you come up?"

"Near the baseball field."

We reached the corner of Temple and Tremont. Walt fumbled at the walk button until he got it.

Lucy watched Walt's attempts to operate the walk button. "Why do guys drink like that?"

I shrugged. "It makes us sexy."

Walt leaned against the pole, burped, spit into the gutter, and let out a heavy sigh.

Lucy said, "I see what you mean."

We crossed Tremont Street. I tugged Walt down the street. "The ballfield is this way."

A circular plaza held the visitor's information center, some benches, and a few statues. Walt stopped at the Statue of Learning. It featured a boy reading a book and sitting astride the globe as if it were a Hippity Hop. Walt pointed at the statue. "What the hell is that?"

I said, "It's a kid reading a book. C'mon, we have to get you to your car."

We led him into the Boston Common. The Common is the oldest city park in the country (take that, New York). It was originally used to graze cattle and hang Quakers. Now it provides a communal lawn for apartment dwellers.

Walt pulled back. "I'm not going in there."

"In where?"

"The Boston Common at night. You're gonna get us killed!"

Lucy and I made eye contact behind Walt and rolled our eyes. I said, "For God's sake. It's a lawn. It's fine. Besides, there's three of us."

"No!" Walt pulled his arm out of my grasp and stumbled toward the Hippity Hop boy. "I'm not going. It's not safe!"

He tripped and fell against the statue. For a man so worried about crime, he was close to getting himself arrested. I grabbed Uncle Walt's arm again to steady him. "We need to get your car, Walt."

"I'm not going!"

I led Walt over to a low stone bench near Tremont Street and said, "Sit. I'll go get the car. What level is it on?"

Walt said, "The bottom." Then he listed to the right, fell over, lay on his back, and started snoring. Lucy and I stood over him.

I said, "Just so you know, he's not a blood relative. I don't have his DNA."

Lucy said, "I wonder if he's got any DNA left."

Walt snored. I pulled his wallet out of his jeans and found the ticket for the parking garage. I considered handing the wallet to

Lucy but decided that it was important to keep the package in one piece, and shoved the wallet back into Walt's pocket. He brushed at my hand in feeble protest. More snoring.

"I'll go into the garage and find his car. It should be easy with the key fob." I pressed the button a few times. "Could you stay with him so he doesn't get arrested?"

"Sure," said Lucy.

"Thanks! You're a trouper."

"I know."

I set off across the Common. Uncle Walt's ravings had put me on edge. I peered around the park, looking behind trees and inspecting bushes. Nobody in the shrubbery. Nobody behind a tree. Lampposts dotted the wide path. I walked past a couple strolling down the path, the woman holding the man's arm, her head tucked in against his shoulder. Lucy had walked with me the same way as we went to Stoddard's. The posture was unmistakable: a woman in love.

I walked on, reminiscing about my afternoon with Lucy and fending off Jael's warnings about her. I could not imagine that Lucy was a threat, at least not in the way that Jael suggested. The threat from Lucy didn't come from anything that she would do to me. It came from the way she looked into my eyes as we rocked together. She had been so happy, so content to be in my arms and intertwined with me. She had not been having sex with me. She had been making love to me. My stomach warmed at the thought.

An entrance to the garage loomed out of the lawn. The Common Garage featured three such entrances, each a small building that protected a payment kiosk, an elevator, and a staircase. I looked through the glass doorway—empty. I entered and pushed the elevator button. The elevator whirred as I slid the parking pass into the kiosk. It asked for money. I paid for Walt's parking.

The elevator door yawned open. My hands twitched as adrenaline trickled through them. Jael was out there somewhere, hopefully watching Lucy. I entered and pressed the button for the bottom level. Gravity faded then returned as the elevator descended. It slid down the shaft, stopped at the bottom. The doors slid open. I peeked out. There was nobody near the elevator.

I stepped out into the garage, pausing at the little handrail that kept people from running out into the roadway. I pressed the key fob and Uncle Walt's pickup truck responded with a beep from second row over. I looked down the rows of cars, couldn't see anyone. It was late.

I moved down the wheelchair ramp and beeped the truck again. It responded. My ears triangulated the sound. The truck wasn't in the second row of cars. It was in the third. I looked around again. My sneakers squeaked over the concrete. Somewhere a car clicked and cooled.

As I passed the second row of cars, one of them started. It pulled out and headed down the garage toward me. It didn't accelerate, and the driver didn't seem to notice me. Still, I wasn't taking any chances. I stepped between two parked cars and walked into the third row, keeping an eye on the windows of the moving car. If one of them started to open, I would dive. The car glided down the row, turned, and followed the exit signs.

I slid between the parked cars and emerged onto the third row, beeping Uncle Walt's truck. It was halfway down the row. As I headed for the truck, another person turned into the row heading toward me, a woman pushing a stroller.

I don't know what made me suspicious. It was probably the baby stroller. She was a short woman. As I got closer, more of her features revealed themselves in the dim light: short, brown hair, an oval moon face, dark eyes. She moved easily, pushing the stroller with a confident gait, looking at the cars as if finding the one she had left behind. A big, pink, poofy diaper bag hung over her shoulder.

That was another clue that something was wrong. How did she not know where her car was? If she didn't, wouldn't she just beep the car with her fob? Then again, the stroller held a sleeping toddler, a girl—judging by the pink outfit. Maybe she didn't want to wake the baby.

Intuition is cursed to be the Cassandra of mental faculties, especially in men, and particularly in me. My intuition was screaming that something was wrong with this woman, pushing her baby through a parking garage late at night, looking for a car that she must be able to recognize, and timing her walk to meet me at Uncle Walt's truck.

But the logical part of my brain, and especially my ego, wouldn't listen. What was I supposed to do? Run away? *Why did you run, Tucker? There was a woman. A woman with a baby stroller. It was horrible!* The presence of the child protected me. Who would shoot me in front of a kid? I was clearly paranoid.

When we were ten feet from each other, the woman made eye contact. I stood by the truck and called out to her. "Hi! Can I help you?"

The woman said, "No. I'm fine." She reached into her diaper bag and pulled out a gun, aiming it at me in one fluid motion.

The intuition I had ignored had served at least one purpose. It kept me from being surprised at the sight of the gun and had caused me to make a plan in case I saw one.

I thought, *My God. She* did *have a gun*, and hurled the key fob right at her solar plexus. Adrenaline caused my throw to sail a little high. Instead of hitting her in the stomach, Uncle Walt's key fob, shaped like a heavy little brick, hit her right between the eyes.

"Bastard!" she screeched as she fired the gun. The gun's explosive boom reverberated off the concrete ceilings and floors. It was the loudest thing I had ever heard. It woke the toddler, who started to wail. I turned and ran for the garage door.

"Goddamn you!" the woman called and took another shot. The bullet whizzed by me and hit the back wall of the garage. I had put an extra twenty feet between me and the woman and risked a look over my shoulder, figuring that she would stay with the stroller. Instead, I saw her shove the stroller next to the truck and run after me.

I ran down the row toward the back of the garage while the woman began slipping between the parked cars. She was going to cut me off at the door. I needed to cut the corner. I ran between two cars, but got hung up on the mirrors between the cars and lost ground.

We were in the second row of cars. The baby's crying echoed in the empty garage.

The woman called out, "Momma's right here, honey!"

The gun boomed as she took another shot at me. The bullet burned across my back like a match being struck.

I ran away from her, dodging as I went. Another booming roar from the gun, and then the whizzing sound of the bullet. The baby cried, and the woman swore, "Fuck!" I bolted across the last row of cars. Her next shot slammed into the wall by me as I hit the door to the staircase that led to the surface. I crashed through the door.

As I started climbing the steps, I slowed. I thought there was no way she'd leave her baby in the parking garage. I was wrong. I heard the door open behind me.

She called out, "Goddamn you! I'm going to shoot your balls off!"

"You'll have to catch me, you psycho bitch!"

"You are a fucking dead man!"

I think I hit a nerve with *psycho bitch*.

I didn't think she'd shoot at me with her baby in the stroller, and I didn't think she'd chase me, and I didn't think she'd come up the stairs. Now I didn't think she'd follow me out into the Common, but I had lost confidence in my ability to predict her actions. I kept charging up the stairs. I had an advantage on her. I could take the stairs two at a time. Still, it wasn't much.

Her gun roared in the stairwell. The bullet ricocheted off a railing and clipped me on the head. Lights flashed across my vision. Blood poured into my eyes and the staircase tilted beneath me. I began taking the stairs one at a time. I could hear her behind me, but I was almost to the top.

I turned a corner on the stairs and saw another woman in front of me. She also had a gun, and she had it aimed right between my eyes.

"Get down," said Jael.

I dropped and she fired.

Jael called, "If you come any closer, I will kill you."

There was silence. The woman below called, "Jael, is that you?"

"Monica needs you, Lyla," Jael answered. "Go to her."

Lyla said, "Oh, shit!" Her footsteps clattered down the stairs and the door opened to the sound of the baby crying in the garage. The sound disappeared as darkness closed in.

FIFTY-FIVE

I'VE HAD ALL SORTS of hangovers: little hangovers from sampling fifteen different types of beer at the Sunset Cafe; big hangovers from a night that started in beerworld, traveled through whiskeyland, and ended in tequilaville; and vomity hangovers from drinking a bottle of triple sec on a dare. All these hangovers came with a headache, and none of those headaches were as bad as the one that I had right now in a hospital bed at Mass General.

My eyes fluttered open.

Somewhere Lieutenant Lee said, "He's awake."

I said, "Water," and Jael handed me a cup with a bendy straw. The water tasted like plastic, but it washed away the cotton in my mouth.

Bobby's face loomed before me. "Holy crap, Tucker. I hope you feel better than you look."

"I don't."

"That's too bad, because you look like shit."

"Thanks." I reached up and touched a bandage across the back of my head. The hair around the bandage was gone.

"Stitches?" I asked.

Bobby said, "Yeah. Seven or eight. You were bleeding all over the place when they brought you in."

"Where's Lucy and Uncle Walt?"

Lee said, "You were alone."

"No, I left them on a bench. I was getting Uncle Walt's car because he was so drunk."

Jael said, "I went to the bench after the ambulance arrived. They were gone."

Lee said, "Jael tells us that Lyla Black tried to kill you."

"Lyla Black?"

"A suspected professional killer," said Lee. "She's thought to work for the Rizzos."

A spike of pain shot through my head. I winced and said, "What?"

Lee said, "This Lyla woman has been known to work for the Rizzos. Sal Rizzo tried to have you killed."

Bobby said, "C'mon, Lee, that's a stretch."

Lee asked, "You haven't seen the pattern here?"

"Which pattern?"

"Someone has been killing his family—"

Bobby said, "Shut up, Lee."

Lee said, "One by one. I don't think it's an outsider."

A blast of pain in my head squeezed my eyes shut and forced a groan out of me. Someone said, "You all have to leave. Mr. Tucker is spending the night."

FIFTY-SIX

I woke in the middle of the night, needing to use the bathroom and wondering where I was. *Right.* I was in the hospital. Light from the hallway streamed into the dark room. I found my way to the bathroom. When I came out, I saw a head outlined against my window.

"Are you feeling better?" asked Jael.

I didn't have the energy to be startled. "Yeah. My head has stopped hurting."

"They gave you something for the pain. You should go back to sleep."

I sat on the edge of the bed and drank some warm plastic water from a cup. "Have you heard from Lucy?"

"I haven't been looking for her. She was with Walt when I followed you into the park. I'm sure she went home."

I lay back on the bed, eyes wide open. Sleep was unreachable.

"I need to get out of here."

Jael said, "You are safe here. There is no need to hurry back into danger."

"I can't just lie here."

Jael rose and walked toward the door. "Then come with me. Bring your camera."

I grabbed my Droid and followed her out of the room, past the nurses' station. Jael nodded to the nurses, who nodded back.

I asked, "How long have you been here?"

"I did not leave. There was a low chance that you would be found here, but I wanted to be sure. This is a secure floor." Jael pointed to the entry doors and said, "Visitors must be buzzed in. If somebody had asked for you, I would be notified."

There was a waiting room at the end of the hallway. We entered and I stopped, gaping at the view of the city. The secure door made sense now. I turned around and looked at the hospital floor with new eyes. Rich mahogany doorways with tasteful woodwork frames graced each hospital room. The medical dread that permeates hospitals had been attenuated by opulence.

I asked Jael, "What floor is this?"

"Phillips 22."

That explains the woodwork.

There comes a time toward the end of a tycoon's life when the only thing money can buy is a comfortable hospital room with a beautiful view. The Phillips floors of the Mass General Hospital fulfilled that dream. The Phillips floors mixed the luxury of the Ritz with the prestige of Mass General. Ted Kennedy had stayed on the Phillips floors. They are the *crème de la crème* of the hospital experience.

The waiting room lived up to the Phillips experience. Demure beige furniture fronted floor-to-ceiling glass windows, commanding a panoramic view of Beacon Hill. The brightening night sky suggested that sunrise was close at hand, but street lamps still twinkled on the narrow streets of the Hill.

I looked down on the little brick houses, then out to the State House, with its golden dome, and beyond it to the Financial District. It was as if the wealthy and powerful in Boston were being afforded a last chance to look at their lives. *There's my house. There's my power base. There's my money.*

Our height revealed the old contours of the land. Beacon Hill sloped toward the river. I imagined the trees that preceded the brick houses. Beyond Beacon Hill lay the Boston Common, with its deadly garage.

I said, "I know you don't trust Lucy, but I think I love her."

"Yes," said Jael. "I can see that."

The sky brightened. Headlights glided along Storrow Drive and across the Longfellow Bridge. It would make a beautiful picture. I raised my Droid and was lining up the shot when the Droid said, "Droid." I had a phone call from an unknown number.

"Hello?"

A man's voice said, "Good morning, Mr. Tucker."

"Who is this?"

"I have left a gift at your apartment. Your friend, who is here with me, would be grateful if you would look at it."

"Talevi. Is that you?"

The call died and my phone became a camera again.

I forgot about taking the picture.

FIFTY-SEVEN

M Y MOTHER'S MAIL SPLASHED across my kitchen counter and spilled onto the floor. The new pile merged with a previous pile, creating a suffocating mound of crap. She'd been buried a week; her hoard was looking for a new home. I'd been piling it up but hadn't noticed how bad it looked until Jael stood in my kitchen.

I said, "What a mess."

Jael asked, "This is your mother's mail?"

"Yeah. I had it forwarded to me."

Jael picked up a menu from a Framingham pizza shop. "Why have you kept it all?"

The hoard squatted on the counter, inviting me to help it grow. A Macy's catalog sat on top. It said, *How could you throw me out? She loved Macy's.* A bill rested on the edge of the table, threatening to fall to the floor. It said, *You can't throw me out. I might be her last bill.* The circulars, envelopes, credit card offers, magazines, and newspapers formed a chorus of whispers: *You'll forget her without us. She'll be gone. Save us and save her.*

I said to Jael, "You're right. This stuff has got to go."

I went into the kitchen, fished around under the sink, and pulled out a plastic garbage bag. I started throwing mail into the garbage bag, looking for something that wasn't addressed to my mother. I tossed catalogs and magazines and solicitations. Bills went onto the counter. There were heating bills, electrical bills, her phone bill, and a bill for a storage facility. Apparently my mother had outgrown the house and had rented extra space. There was a cable bill, a lawn service bill, and a security company bill. Was I really going to pay the security company, given that she was murdered?

Jael said, "Can I help?"

I handed her a garbage bag. "Yeah, thanks. Just throw everything that's not a bill in this bag. I hope there's some mail in here for me."

"You look unhappy."

"Of course I'm unhappy. My mother's crap is filling my life. Where is this goddamn 'gift'?"

"You should not talk like that. It is profane."

I stopped shoving crap in the bag and considered Jael, a killer who objects to profanity.

I said, "I'm sorry."

Jael stepped into the hallway and returned with something I had overlooked as I ran up the staircase. She asked, "What is this?" and handed me a yellow padded envelope that had no stamp and the name TUCKER written on it in black magic marker. I squeezed the envelope and heard paper crinkle. It contained something hard, and something soft. My Droid spoke up, "Droid." Uncle Walt. I put him on speaker, put the Droid on the counter.

"Tucker, where's my truck?" asked Walt.

I turned the envelope over in my hands. "Where are you?"

"I'm at the Starbucks in Boston."

"There's a Starbucks every ten feet in Boston. Which one?"

243

"How the hell should I know?"

"Look out the window. Is there a street sign?"

"There aren't any street signs in Boston."

"Just look."

I heard some grumbling and "excuse me's" as Walt moved through a crowd.

"The sign says Cambridge Street."

I said, "You're right down the street from Mass General. How did you get there?"

"The cops picked me up last night after you and Lucy left me on the bench. They thought I was a drunk."

"You were a drunk. What do you mean, Lucy left you on the bench?"

"I mean that I was sleeping and two cops grabbed me and put me in their car. Lucy wasn't there."

"Where is she?"

"How should I know where she is?" Walt snapped.

I tore open the envelope and shook it. Uncle Walt's key fob fell out. The last time I had seen this, I was throwing it at Lyla.

I said, "I guess your truck is still in the garage."

Walt shouted into the phone, "Why the hell is it in the garage? You were supposed to get it!"

I shook the envelope some more. Nothing came out. I reached inside and pulled out a slip of paper. The paper was a handwritten note.

Call Me. I have your friend. Here is proof.

It was signed *T* and had a phone number. *Friend? What friend? Proof?* I showed the note to Jael.

She read it and asked, "Lucy?"

Walt shouted from the speakerphone. "Tucker! Tucker! Are you still there? Are going to come get me or what?"

244

The proof was stuck in the padded envelope. I tore the envelope open and the proof fell onto the table. I thought about my night the other night with Lucy, and how she had curled up on my couch, tucking her red toenails against the black leather.

A pinky toe had fallen onto the countertop. It had red polish, the only scrid of color on a waxy bit of flesh and bone. The toe had been cut off, just after the first knuckle. My gut convulsed. Bile rose in my throat. I forced it back down.

"Tucker! Are you still there?" Walt called over the speaker.

I grabbed the Droid off the counter. "I gotta make a call. Take a cab to my house and I'll give you your keys."

I hung up on him and dialed the number on the note.

FIFTY-EIGHT

"Did you like my present?" asked Talevi. He was speaking through the speakerphone on my Droid, which lay on the kitchen counter once again. Jael listened with her typical impassive stillness.

"You are a sick bastard," I said. "You didn't need to cut off her toe. I would have believed you had her with a phone call."

"That was not proof that I have her, Mr. Tucker. As you say, a phone call would have sufficed. It is my proof that I will hurt her. That toe is almost a vestigial organ. She will survive. She will even be able to run. Assuming that she keeps both of her feet."

"You sick fuck!"

Jael touched the phone, muting it. She said, "That will not help. Find out what he wants." She unmuted the phone.

I said, "What do you want? My father's notebooks?"

"I have no interest in your father's notebooks. I want what I have always wanted. The plans to the Paladin downlink."

"Jesus, Talevi, let her go. How am I supposed to get the plans to the downlink?"

"That is not my problem. That is your problem."

"Why would you even think I could get them?"

"Because your brother thought you could get them."

"My brother was an idiot. I don't even work at GDS."

"Goodbye, Mr. Tucker. Call me tomorrow with the plans, or you will receive another envelope."

The phone call winked off the Droid's screen. Talevi had hung up. I pounded the counter. My mother's mail scattered to the floor. I crouched to the floor, picking up mail and shoving it all into a garbage bag. *Fuck the bills. They'll send more.* I knotted the bag and threw it by the front door. "What am I supposed to do? I can't get those plans. I need to call Bobby."

"That would be a mistake," said Jael.

"How can calling the FBI to rescue Lucy be a mistake? This is Bobby's investigation."

"Bobby Miller is a good man, but he must prioritize the plans over Lucy's life. He will not save her."

Stress pinched the muscles in my neck, driving a pain spike into my eye. I winced and rubbed my temples, my thoughts getting crammed into a desperate corner. "What did JT want from me?"

"If Dave Patterson were not dead, he could have told you."

I sat at my now-clean counter and watched Click and Clack, willing the stress in my neck to subside. Patterson. What did I know about him?

"All I know about Patterson is that he knew Talevi," I said.

Jael searched through my cabinets, found the Advil, filled a glass of water, and put four of the orange pills on the counter in front of me alongside the water. "Pain will not help."

I took the Advil. "And Talevi knew Patterson."

Jael said, "Patterson was unable to get the plans for Talevi because he was no longer at GDS. Why did he leave GDS?"

"His boss told us that he was fired for sharing his password."

"Who did he share with?"

"JT. And JT had the deal with Talevi."

Jael said, "Your brother was a spy. He was buying the plans from Patterson."

"By getting the password."

"Yes. GDS mistook the password sharing for simple policy violations. They fired Patterson and changed the password."

"Those paranoid bastards," I said. "Their system worked and they didn't even know it."

"JT could not get the plans without the password," said Jael.

"That's why JT came to me. He thought he had a crooked half brother who could hack the account."

"Could you hack the account?"

"Probably. If I could get into the GDS building."

The intercom buzz broke through our conversation. I slipped off the kitchen stool and pushed the talk button.

"Hello?"

"It's me, Tucker. It's Walt."

FIFTY-NINE

Uncle Walt stared at my Mr. Coffee as it dripped out sweet hangover medicine. He looked bad and smelled worse. Gray bags hung beneath his eyes, his skin was the color of wax paper, his hands trembled.

I said, "You don't drink very often, do you?"

"No," he said. "Last night got out of hand. All I remember is you going to get my car. What happened to you?"

"Someone tried to kill me."

"In the parking garage?"

"Yeah."

"I knew it! I knew that parking garage was a death trap. This whole city is a pit."

"It had nothing to do with the parking garage."

I got a Museum of Science mug out of the cabinet and put it in front of Walt, poured him a cup of locally-roasted Bitches Brew coffee from Wired Puppy. I offered Jael a Red Sox mug. She passed, so I used it myself. The coffee was perfect. Walt took a sip of the sweet blend of African beans and said, "Jesus, what is this shit? You should get some of that Dunkin' Donuts coffee."

Dunkin' Donuts coffee tastes as if someone had ground up an ashtray, put it in the coffee filter, and run dishwater through it.

I said, "Sorry. I ran out."

"Damn shame."

"We've got a much bigger problem. Do you remember Lucy?"

"Your girlfriend? The one from last night?"

"Yeah. She's in trouble."

"What do you mean?"

I spent the next five minutes filling Walt in on the envelope and the phone call with Talevi. I showed him Lucy's toe.

"Jesus!" Walt clamped his hand over his mouth. I felt sorry for him.

I told him about the downlink information and how it was in Dave Patterson's account. I told him my plan.

Walt said, "I'm not sneaking you into GDS to steal secrets."

"You have to. Talevi will cut Lucy into pieces."

"I'm sorry, but I can't help with that."

"You have to help. She's an innocent bystander."

Walt looked at Jael said, "He's just not getting it."

Jael said, "The data is secret for a reason, Tucker."

"What, now you're on his side?"

"This is not a matter of sides. This data Talevi wants will allow Iran to disable Paladin missiles, correct?"

Walt said, "How should I know? I sweep the floors."

I said, "That's why you'd be the perfect person to sneak me in." I turned to Jael. "Yes. The data would do that."

Jael said, "Israel uses the Paladin missiles for defense."

Walt said, "I'm not sneaking you in."

I said to both of them, "I'm not talking about giving Talevi his data. I'm talking about getting a clean copy of the document so I can trick Talevi into the open. I'll change the numbers. I just need a clean copy on GDS letterhead."

Jael said, "So you would not provide the real data to Talevi?"

"No. Of course not. The guy is a psychopath."

Walt said, "I'm not doing it. If you get caught we'll all get arrested, and I'll lose my pension. I'm two years from retiring. I've been working toward this my whole life, and you want me to throw it away?"

"You're going to let him kill her?"

Walt picked up his key fob off the kitchen counter. He stood. "I'm sorry your girlfriend's in trouble, Tucker, but there's nothing I can do."

He walked out of my apartment, letting the door close behind him.

I said, "Goddammit!"

Jael said, "This was easily predictable."

"Why?"

"Talevi has leverage over you. The problem is that you have no leverage over your uncle." She reached into her handbag and pulled out a cell phone. Started dialing.

"What are you doing?"

"Arranging some leverage."

SIXTY

Hugh Graxton sat in his customary spot in the Chestnut Hill Starbucks, his MacBook Air open on the table in front of him. Oscar Sagese hulked next to Graxton, the spot on the table in front of him occupied by a vente cup of coffee. Jael and I stood in front of Graxton.

"Well, well, Oscar," said Graxton. "Look. It's your hacker buddy."

Oscar stood. Jael shifted her weight.

He pointed at my chest. "You fucked me, Tucker."

Oscar was at least six foot four. I said, "Uh—sorry."

"Sal made me close my Facebook account."

"That's a shame."

"A shame? A fucking shame? All my friends are on Facebook."

I raised my hands. "I know you probably don't want to hear this, but it was probably for the best."

Oscar stepped toward me. He shouted, "What the fuck do you know about the best?"

Graxton said, "Oscar, you need to use your inside voice."

I said, "If you're on Facebook, the FBI can get all those pictures, all your statuses, they can even get a list of your friends. It's like handing them evidence on a silver platter."

Graxton said, "The man is right, Oscar. You were lucky he was the only guy to get them before you deleted them."

I decided not to mention the fact that Facebook might have not deleted the pictures. Internet pictures are like a tattoo; they're out there forever.

Graxton said, "Check Tucker for a wire, Oscar."

Oscar grabbed at me, his meaty hands batting me around as he pounded my check and back. He ran a hand up each thigh, and whacked me on the left nut with his fist. It wasn't much of a punch. A love tap in the balls, so to speak. Still my eyes fluttered shut as the pain washed over me.

Oscar said, "He's okay. You want me to check her?" He took a step toward Jael, who arched an eyebrow.

Graxton said, "It's your funeral, buddy. As much as I'd like to see what would happen, I might need you functional later. Why don't we take Jael at her word? Are you wearing a wire, Jael?"

"No," said Jael.

"That's good enough for me," said Graxton. His eyes lingered on Jael's face, and her eyes found his.

I said, "Do you guys need some time alone?"

"No," said Jael. "We do not."

"You're in enough trouble, Tucker," said Graxton. "You should shut up now."

"Can we get down to business?" I said.

"By all means. Oscar, I think Tucker is about to owe us a big favor."

Oscar sat, "Favor, my ass. I'm not doing him any favors. Fucking hacker."

Graxton sighed and pulled out his wallet. Stripped out a fifty and handed it to Oscar. "Go buy me a *Wall Street Journal*."

Oscar said, "Can't you just read it online?"

"I like the smell of newsprint, okay? Now, go get me a *Wall Street Journal.*"

Oscar stood, grunted, and lumbered out of the Starbucks, folding the money into his pocket.

With Oscar gone, Graxton said, "Tucker, you seriously destabilized that boy. I think Facebook was his drug of choice."

"I think there's an online twelve-step program. You should Google it."

"He has serious anger-management issues. He needs to beat somebody up."

I considered Oscar's size and the latent violence that came off him like body odor. "Well, that can't be good."

"It's not. This is a major pain in the ass. So you should know that the only reason I'm talking to you is that you're Sal's cousin."

Jael coughed into her hand.

"And because Jael asked me to. Two. There are two reasons."

"And a fanatical devotion to the Pope," I said.

"What?"

"I can give you a third reason to talk to me."

"Really? How?"

"How much money does my Uncle Walt owe you?"

"I told you. He doesn't owe me any money."

"Look, I'm not wearing a wire and I won't tell anyone. How much?"

"It's none of your business."

"C'mon, Hugh. Work with me."

"Get lost."

Jael said, "Mr. Graxton, this is not helpful."

"I'm not here to be helpful."

"I'll make it worth your while," I said.

"Really? How?"

"I'll pay it."

"You're going to pay me Walt's fifty grand?"

I blanched. "That much? He owes you that much?"

"Why would you pay it?"

I told Graxton about Lucy and Talevi, how I needed Walt to get into GDS, how I didn't have any leverage. Then I shared my plan.

Hugh said, "I like it. If Walt gets you into GDS, you pay me sixty thousand dollars."

"I thought it was fifty."

"There's a ten-thousand-dollar change fee. It's like the airlines."

"Screw that, Hugh. Why should I pay ten grand more?"

"You're desperate to save Lucy, right?"

"Yeah. I told you that."

"So for ten thousand you get a little negotiating lesson: don't bring your desperation to the table."

I crossed my arms, "Hmmph. Fine."

Hugh picked up his iPhone. "Now, let's call Walt."

SIXTY-ONE

My Honda Accord Zipcar rested in blissful anonymity in the Russell's Garden Center parking lot. I had chosen the Accord because it was the least likely car to be remembered by eyewitnesses. Ornamental shrubs dotted a flat landscape that led up a low rise to hothouses and long buildings that sold houseplants and garden supplies. Global Defense Systems lay beyond those buildings across Route 20.

Hugh Graxton parked his BMW next to my Accord. He and Oscar climbed out. I felt exposed in front of Oscar without Jael, but I had left her in Boston. If I got caught doing this, I'd be arrested. If Jael got caught, there'd be an international incident. Of course, that wasn't to say there wouldn't be one anyway. The closer I got to the idea of espionage, the more my stomach tightened. It thrummed like a bass drum as I saw Walt emerge from the one of the hothouses.

Walt approached and called, "Tucker? What are you doing with him?"

Graxton put his finger to his lips and turned to walk away from the buildings and into the scrubby brush behind the Garden Center. Nobody noticed us disappear from view.

When we were hidden, Walt approached Graxton. "What's this about?"

Graxton nodded to Oscar, who punched Uncle Walt in the stomach.

"Hey!" I said.

Oscar glared at me and Graxton said, "You shut up now and let the man work. You're getting what you want."

Walt was doubled over. He straightened partway and said, "What was that for?"

Oscar slapped Walt across the face with an open palm, knocking him to the ground. Oscar closed in, aiming a kick.

Graxton said, "That's enough."

Oscar lowered his foot. I saw a light tremor in his arms. He was itching for Walt to give him an excuse.

Walt stayed down, cradling his red cheek.

"Walt," Graxton said, "you owe me money."

"Yeah, but—" started Uncle Walt.

"But what, Walt? What? You're going to pay me now?"

"You know I can't pay you now."

"Then how did Oscar surprise you with a punch in the stomach? You didn't pay me. Why shouldn't you get a punch in the stomach?"

Walt rubbed his lip and spit onto the ground. There was no blood. "What's Tucker doing here?"

Graxton wrapped an arm around my shoulder. "Tucker here is paying off your debt."

"What?"

Graxton strode over to Walt, grabbed him by his blue button-down shirt, and pulled him to his feet. He held Walt close. Walt scrabbled at Graxton's fist where it held his shirt. "What do you want from me?"

Graxton released the shirt. "It's simple, Walt. I want you to sneak Tucker here into GDS so he can steal some secrets and save his girlfriend. That's all. I just want you to enable a heartwarming tale of love and espionage."

"I can't—" started Walt.

Graxton raised his hand. "Don't even."

"I'll get fired. I'll get arrested. I'll lose my pension."

"Your pension? Walt, are you worried about outliving your money?"

"Well—"

"Oscar, you hear this? Walt doesn't want to outlive his money." Graxton bore into Walt. "Trust me, shithead, you're not going to outlive anything."

"I'll pay you. I swear!"

Graxton straightened his jacket and said, "You're not going to pay us. Tucker's going to pay us, right after you get him into GDS. C'mon, Oscar."

Oscar lumbered over to Graxton, passing Walt. Oscar raised his hand, and Walt flinched as Oscar patted his head. Oscar and Graxton walked out of the woods, side by side.

I turned to Walt. "I need to do this."

"Don't you talk to me," Walt said.

"I'm sorry."

"Shut up."

I shut up.

Walt squatted and drew a rectangle in the dirt. "This is the building. Meet me at this back corner in fifteen minutes. I'll get you in a side door."

"We're not using the lobby?"

"I don't want us going into the lobby together, you idiot. Once you're inside, I'll get you to Patterson's old computer. Then you're on your own."

He stood, turned, and walked away.

I called out. "I'm sorry, Uncle Walt!"

Walt turned. "Fuck that uncle stuff. We're done after today, you hear me?"

I heard him. Didn't blame him a bit. I'd be done with me too.

SIXTY-TWO

I APPROACHED THE SECURITY guard at the entrance of the parking lot.

I said, "I'm here to see Mindy Frank."

The guard held out his hand. "ID?"

I handed him my driver's license. He compared it to my face. I waited for some hidden mechanism in security theater to kick in and bite me in the ass. For example, they might realize that I didn't know a Mindy Frank. They didn't.

The guard handed back my license. "Thank you, sir."

I walked into the lot and followed the visitor parking down the building as if I were looking to meet up with someone. When I reached the end of the building I turned around the corner, out of sight out of mind. Ten minutes had elapsed. I reached the end of the windowless building and found a side door. The door opened. Uncle Walt beckoned me inside.

Walt handed me a visitor's badge with an indecipherable picture on it. "Here."

"What's this?" I asked.

"It's a visitor's badge that somebody threw into the trash."

I read the badge. "My name is Carmen Hazleton?"

"Sure," said Walt.

"That's a woman's name."

"No it's not."

"Yes it is."

"Deal with it."

We climbed a flight of stairs and walked past the military shrine, which honored young people from every branch. Some were grim in their army uniforms. Others smiled. Most had a generic, blue portrait photo background, while some stood in front of flags, and one had his own full-length portrait superimposed behind his head. It looked like a military baseball card. I wondered if a jammed Paladin missile would fail to save one of the kids in the pictures. A picture of a blond girl in a blue uniform caught my eye. She smiled through her nervousness, the smile ending at her eyes. I was going to save Lucy, but Talevi would never get this data.

The facility was huge. I followed Walt past the cafeteria, down the hallways, up a staircase, through a tunnel connecting us to another building, down a staircase, past a convenience store, and through another connecting tunnel. Without Walt, I'd never find my way out. As we walked, people smiled at Walt, greeting him with a "Hiya, Walt!" Walt plastered a smiling grimace on his face and waved at them. The sweat on his bald head ran down his temples in rivulets.

Walt stopped walking and pointed into an empty cube. The name plaque was blank, but a PC sat on the desk. Walt said, "This was Dave's cube when he worked in Wayland. Can you get his password off it?"

"It depends if they deleted his account."

"I've got whole rooms full of old computers that GDS won't throw away. They keep everything. I'll bet the account is still on there. They probably just changed the password."

I inspected Dave's PC with mixed feelings. On the one hand, I needed to get his password and find the data that would save Lucy. On the other, I didn't want to believe that GDS would make it as easy as I feared. I crawled under the desk, looked at the back of the PC, and found a security hole big enough to kill all the kids in those pictures.

SIXTY-THREE

LATE IN 2009, A worker at the Iranian nuclear enrichment plant in Natanz plugged a USB stick into his PC and unwittingly brought down the Iranian nuclear weapons program. When the stick entered the computer, the Stuxnet virus woke up and copied itself into the system.

The virus had been traveling across the Iranian countryside, hopping from computer to computer through infected USB sticks. It was a clever virus, created by a large and probably international team of engineers. It carried within it a valid security certificate from a semiconductor company in Taiwan. The certificate had been stolen.

Ensconced in its new home, the virus began to look around, searching the PC for Siemens Step7 software. Normally the virus couldn't find the software, and in that case it would shut down and wait to infect another USB stick. But that day was a good day for the virus because the Siemens Step7 software was in place. Now the virus knew that this PC controlled an industrial system. It performed its final check.

Stuxnet looked through the software to see if this PC was connected to a piece of industrial hardware called a frequency converter. Specifically, it looked for a frequency converter that had been designed and built in Iran, and when it found it, it knew that it was sitting on a PC that controlled a key piece of the Iranian nuclear weapons program: a uranium enrichment centrifuge.

Then all hell broke loose.

The virus inserted itself between the centrifuge and the monitoring systems on the PC. It began to manipulate the speeds of the centrifuges, driving them too fast then too slow, breaking them down. At the same time, it controlled the monitoring display systems on the PC so that the Iranian operators couldn't see what was happening. All they knew was that their displays showed normal operation while their centrifuges were being destroyed at a record rate.

Iran's security forces descended upon the engineers, digging through people, looking for the spy who was sabotaging their weapons program. The head of the program resigned. This whole time, Stuxnet continued to destroy equipment. This went on for months, until a Belarusian antivirus company found Stuxnet.

Nobody is saying who wrote the Stuxnet virus, but the lesson was clear: USB ports are festering petri dishes of computer infection. Because of that, I had expected and partially hoped to find the USB ports on Dave's machine to be filled with epoxy. They weren't.

I was sitting in a US defense contractor's office with a USB stick in my hand and an open USB port in front of me. All the walls, locks, security cards, and secret-keeping efforts of the US government were about to fail.

Still, GDS had one final defense against me. They could have upgraded their computers to Windows 7, but they hadn't. The Windows XP login screen presented itself.

Oh my God! Our tax money at work.

This was security theater at its most theatrical. GDS, a company that went through the trouble of looking at my driver's license and making visitors leave their cell phones at the desk, couldn't bring itself to upgrade its PCs to Windows 7 even though Microsoft had stopped supporting XP. Too bad for GDS.

My USB drive contained a copy of Ophcrack, a piece of software that could decrypt Windows XP passwords in record time. I turned Dave's computer on and Ophcrack took it over, sidestepping Windows and booting to the Slax Linux operating system. A friendly green clover appeared on the screen.

"What are you doing?" asked Walt. "The screen's all messed up. That isn't Windows."

"I'm cracking Dave's password."

"Jesus, you know how to do that?"

"Yup. What are you doing here? I thought I was on my own."

"I don't want you to get caught and start talking." Sweat dripped off Walt's chin.

"Well, keep an eye out for security."

Ophcrack started running. It showed me a list of accounts, including dpatterson. I removed all the accounts from the list but Dave's. I didn't want to waste time or know more secrets than were absolutely necessary to save Lucy's life.

I clicked the "Crack" button and Ophcrack went to work, traversing lists of known passwords and hints. The old PC was slow and there was no way that GDS would use a simple password. This would take a while. I settled in and watched the screen.

I considered the fact that I'd probably spent at least a year of my life waiting for computers, watching progress bars inch across screens as the computers compiled my code, copied my files, downloaded my movies, or simply booted. A full year of staring straight ahead, emptying my mind, stretching, breathing, conversing on Twitter. These little waits were never long enough to allow me to do something useful, but they weren't so short that I didn't notice them. They held me in suspended animation as I waited for some machine to do something that seemed important at the time.

A hand grabbed my shoulder and I jerked my head around.

"Aren't you done yet?" asked Walt.

"No! Will you please leave me alone and let me do this. I'll call you when I'm ready."

"This is killing me," Walt said.

"Just go watch for security," I said.

"And then what? You don't have a real badge."

"This isn't helping."

Walt went back to his post, I turned back to the machine. *Holy crap!* Ophcrack had found the password already:

```
Administration123
```

Seriously? What a crappy password. I didn't even bother copying it. I had memorized it in a glance.

I turned off the machine, let it reboot to Windows. Entered dpatterson and the password. Dave's PC came to life and we were ready to start digging through his files. I spun in my chair and called out, "All set!"

A jacketed security guard stood behind me, his arms crossed, his jarhead crew cut eclipsing the fluorescents behind him.

He pointed at my visitor badge and asked, "Where's your escort, Carmen?"

SIXTY-FOUR

My eyes widened as my face flushed full red.

Poker Face Tucker. The unreadable man.

I jumped to my feet and pointed at the spot in the hallway where Walt stood watch. "He's right over there."

No Walt.

The guy looked at the spot and back at me.

"You can't stay here without an escort."

"Well, I know that. I just don't know where he went."

"What's his name?"

I figured I had done enough damage to Uncle Walt and told a stupid lie. "Bob Baker."

"What were you doing on that computer?"

"Fixing it."

The "fixing it" lie wouldn't have worked with a piece of technology that functioned reliably. *What are you doing with that screwdriver? Fixing it. Right...* But it would always work with a PC.

The jarhead stepped into the cube and peered at Dave's screen.

"What's wrong with it?" he asked.

"The usual."

"Piece of crap, huh?"

"Yup."

"Why would Bob have you fixing his computer instead of the IT department?"

I was caught. I hadn't thought ahead. I had been playing checkers when I should have been playing chess.

"Um … not the computer as much as a piece of software."

"What software?"

"The compiler."

"What's that do?"

"It compiles."

The guard looked into my wide and twitching eyes.

He said. "Look, you can't stay here without an escort. Come sit in the security office with me until we find … what did you say his name was?"

"Bob Baker."

"Like the gameshow guy?"

"That was Bob Barker."

"Let's go back to my office and find Mr. Baker. He needs to learn that he can't leave visitors alone."

Jarhead walked down the aisle between the cubes and gestured for me to follow. If we got back to his office, which probably locked from the outside, he'd find out that there was no Bob Baker. Then I'd be locked in and arrested.

I cast about for a plan as I followed him. I didn't know how far we had to walk to get to his office, but I didn't want to step inside. We walked past gray fabric cubes, knots of engineers, and a poster with a finger poised over pursed lips exhorting people to be careful with secrets.

Jarhead asked, "How do you know Bob, Mr."—he read my visitor badge—"Mr. Hazleton?"

"Yeah."

The guard peered closely at the indecipherable blob of a picture. "Isn't Carmen a woman's name?"

"That's what I kept telling my parents, but they said I was named after my uncle Carmen."

Jarhead gave his head a small shake. "And how do you know Bob?"

"He's a customer."

"What company do you work for?"

"Zariplex." There was no such company. The easily-checked lies continued to flow from my adrenaline-charged mouth.

We approached an office with solid walls and a locked door, built across the hallway from a window. Wetlands glimmered outside the window. We were in the back of the building. The security guard waved his badge in front of the door. The lock popped with a loud click as it came free. He rattled the door open and put his arm around my shoulder to usher me inside.

The time for cleverness was over. When his fingers touched my shoulder, I spun away from them and ran.

"Goddammit!" the guy yelled. "Somebody grab him!"

Startled engineers flashed past me as I ran. Given the choice between tackling a fleeing fugitive or freezing, most people will freeze. I took advantage of the freezing and then threw some more confusion into the mix.

"Run!" I yelled. "He's got a gun. He's says he's going to shoot people!"

The employees of GDS could either believe that I was a fugitive, or that someone had launched a killing spree. They chose to believe what the TV news had taught them was most likely: the killing spree. They turned and ran alongside me.

There were five of us running down the hallway. A woman in the group stopped to pull the fire alarm. *Now, why hadn't I thought of that?* Confused people stepped from their cubes.

"He's got a gun! Run!" someone shouted. Crowds of engineers jostled out of the aisles. My small group of runners was snowballing into a mob. I heard the news of the gun spreading to the edges of the mob as it grew. Then the crowd piled up as people pushed their way through a small set of double doors. In the distance I heard the guard yelling, "There is no gun! Somebody grab that guy!"

I blended into the crowd, allowing myself to be jostled and pushed through the glass doors and out into a courtyard behind GDS. People streamed out of all the doors as the alarm cleared the building. They moved toward the edges of the parking lot. It was as if I had kicked over an anthill.

Once out of the building, my group slowed and blended into the mass of people streaming away from the doorways. I followed the crowd around the building and into the gigantic parking lot.

My plan, if you could call it that, was breaking down. People were gathering at the far end of the parking lot and the parking lot was surrounded by a tall chain-link fence. Guards stood at the entrances to the compound, blocking the car and sidewalk exits. To get out of GDS, I'd have to walk alone across the lot with all the guards watching.

I separated myself from the crowd and walked with purpose toward the visitor's parking lot through the hot sun. The mob noises died away and I was alone, walking in a zig-zag pattern through parked cars toward a black Buick Regal, the car closest to the gate in the visitor's lot. I needed to move fast before a description of me got from the guard inside to the uniformed guards at the gate.

As I neared the car, a guard approached me. He was fit and wore a blue rent-a-cop shirt. The shirt had short sleeves that showed off his biceps. He wore black pants and black running shoes. Soccer? Baseball? Wrestling? The kid was an athlete. I wasn't. If he tackled me, I'd stay down.

"Sir, you need to get to a rally point."

I kept walking. "A what?"

"A rally point, sir. When there's an evacuation, we need everyone to get to a rally point."

I kept walking and pointed at my badge. "I'm a visitor."

The guard fell into step next to me. "Yes, sir, especially as a visitor. Your escort needs to account for you."

I walked past the Buick toward the exit. Twenty feet to go.

"He and I got separated in the crowd."

"You need to go find him, sir."

Walking.

"How am I supposed to do that? Look at this mess!"

I waved my arm toward the crowd and the guard ignored me, keeping close to me as we walked. I stopped at the gate. Cars whooshed past on Route 20 in a continuous stream in both directions, trapping me against this side of the road.

"Sir, you need to go back to a rally point. When people start to go back into the building, go sit in the lobby. Let your escort account for—"

The guy's handheld radio crackled to life. He held it to his ear. I heard the word "Hazleton" come from the speaker. He looked at me, glanced down at my badge, and grabbed me with his free hand. Bad move. He should have dropped the radio and used two hands.

I shook my arm free and ran straight into the traffic on Route 20. I timed my run so that I was headed straight for the side of a car.

As the car passed, the one behind it hit his brakes and blared his horn. That got me past the first lane.

I wasn't as lucky on the second lane. Time slowed as I glanced at the driver. I expected to see someone with wide eyes, braking wildly. Instead I saw a teenage girl texting on her cell phone. I was gonna die. I dove across her path.

Her bumper slammed into the sole of my sneaker, tearing at my ankle and flinging the shoe down the street. Its impact knocked me down to the edge of the road outside Russell's Garden Center. I climbed to my feet and saw the guy in the uniform putting up his hand to stop traffic across the highway. I turned and ran into Russell's. My ankle protested at the first step. Grinding pain shot through my leg. Hot parking lot gravel dug into my now-shoeless foot, then I bolted through a wooden building full of hoses, fertilizer bags, and plants. The loamy smell of organic fertilizer filled my nostrils. I saw a clawed tool on a shelf and grabbed it.

I dodged past dawdling shoppers, ignoring the screaming pain in my ankle, thankful that it functioned at all. The ankle pain overrode the pain from gravel cutting into my foot. I stopped to pull off my other shoe, gasping as I stood on the bad ankle. Then I ran for my life. Green carts littered the walkways and forced me to sidestep left and right. Behind me, I heard the guard yell, "Grab him!" The crowd was full of suburbanite husbands buying bougainvillea with their wives. Some moms found their kids and picked them up. Nobody was going to grab me.

I got to my Zipcar and unlocked it just as the guard caught up to me. He reached for me and I clawed at his hand with the tool, my eyes wild as pain gelled into anger.

"Get the fuck away from me!" I yelled at him.

He took another step, but I was between two parked cars, and he could only get at me head on. I lunged and swiped with the claws of my tool. "Get away!" He shrank back and I jumped into the car. He sprang forward again and grabbed my collar. I reached out and pulled the car door closed. It jammed against his forearm.

"Shit!" he yelled and pulled his arm out. I pulled the door shut and locked it. He was walking in a small circle behind the car, cradling his arm in his hand as I backed toward him. He jumped aside and looked at me with hurt surprise as I put the car in gear, spun the wheels on the gravel, and escaped the parking lot.

SIXTY-FIVE

By the time had I parked my Zipcar and hobbled home, my ankle pain had become a dull throb. There was more mail in my mailbox. I grabbed it, hobbled up the stairs, and limped through my front door. Once inside, I tossed the mail on the counter and climbed onto a kitchen stool to inspect the damage. I pulled off the sock and put the ankle on the counter in front of Click and Clack's terrarium. It was purple.

"What do you guys think? Do I need x-rays?"

The hermit crabs clung to the sides of their log and ignored me.

"You're right, guys. I should just put some ice on it and see how it goes."

I was wrapping a gel pack in a towel when my Droid played the Bruins Theme song. Bobby Miller.

"What the fuck did you do?" Bobby was upset.

"What are you talking about?"

"Don't you bullshit me, you asshole!" He was really mad. "You got into GDS, broke into their computers, created a panic, attacked one of their guards, and pulled a fire alarm."

"I did *not* pull a fire alarm. And besides, who says it was me?"

"The guard who remembered your name from your driver's license, Aloysius."

Burned by security theater.

Bobby continued, "Now you're sitting in your house like nothing happened."

"How do you know I'm in my house?"

"Because I'm in the fucking FBI and you have a cell phone, that's how."

Hmmm. Maybe it was time to part ways with the Droid.

I lay the gel pack across my ankle. Its throbbing made me testy. "So why aren't you arresting me? You want me to drive to your office and save you the gas?"

"I'm not in my office. I'm calling from home. I want to hear what happened."

There was no point in keeping Lucy's kidnapping a secret if I was going to prison. "What happened? I'll tell you what happened. That guy Talevi kidnapped Lucy and sent me her toe in an envelope. He wants to trade Lucy for the plans to the Paladin."

"So you were going to turn over US government secrets? We got thousands of kids out there who will get killed if Talevi gets this stuff."

"I wasn't going to give him anything. I was going to get the Word document, randomize the numbers, and give *that* to Talevi. I'd get Lucy and he'd get nothing."

"That is a fucking stupid plan."

"You got something better?"

My ankle was starting to feel better. I put the phone on speaker and found the big bottle of Advil I kept over the sink. I ran some water and took four pills. At this rate I'd need to buy another bottle soon. Maybe I should buy stock in Advil.

Bobby said from the speakerphone, "Tucker, you still there?"

I called out, "Yeah, I'm here. I just don't know what to do."

"Wait a second. I got another call." Bobby beeped off the phone.

Silence. I poked through my mail. Something caught my eye: an envelope in the pile addressed to my mother in blue cursive script. I'd seen this bill before. It was the only one with real handwriting. The person had written up another one, trying to get paid. I opened it and my heart did a little skip. It was from my mother's storage place.

Bobby's voice hissed through the speaker. "Tucker, are you there? Boston PD is coming to arrest you. They can't have you; I need you. Get out of there!"

SIXTY-SIX

NOTHING'S BETTER THAN A rooftop patio. You can sit under a humid July night sky, drink a Dogfish IPA, and soak in the skyline. Today the patio was going to be part of my home-field advantage.

I pulled on socks and sneakers, shoved my mother's storage bill into my pocket, and climbed the stairs, ignoring protests from my ankle. Reaching the top, I burst out onto the roof. It was a cool September night. I heard someone knocking on my apartment door. "Mr. Tucker! This is Lieutenant Lee of the Boston Police." I'd left the door open as a distraction. It would buy me some time.

I padded across the wooden patio and climbed over the wall. I jumped down to the rooftop with a gravelly crunch. I winced with pain and fear of noise. It would only take a minute for them to search my condo. I didn't have much time. I'd need to use the fire escape.

I ran to the top of the fire escape and peeked over the roof, dipping back when I saw a cop in the parking area watching the ladders. That wouldn't work.

Sneaking away from the police was going to be a lot like breaking into a computer. The obvious approaches are always blocked by intricate passwords, firewalls, and virus-detection software. The key is to understand your opponent's assumptions and use those assumptions to your advantage. The assumption here was clear. The police had covered the front door. They had covered the fire escape. They were in the apartment. They assumed the building was now secure, because they thought that I couldn't get to another building.

The houses on my block run together, creating a single structure with a common roof. A firewall separates the buildings. Switching buildings was simply a matter of climbing over the two-foot firewall between them. I ran to the first firewall and clambered over it. Then the next, and the next. When I got to the last building, I climbed onto their rooftop patio and entered their hallway. Piece of cake. The cops had my building secure, but not this one.

I limped down the staircase. I would run out the front door, bang a right, and lose myself in the park behind the houses. It was perfect. I opened the door, stepped into the sun. Lieutenant Lee barred the steps.

"Aloysius Tucker, you are under arrest."

SIXTY-SEVEN

"Aw, shit," I said.

Lee waited at the bottom of the stairs, arms folded across his chest. "Please don't swear. Come down here."

I limped down the stairs. My ankle pulsed pain up my leg. "What are you arresting me for?"

"Your sins are many," said Lee. "Trespassing. Espionage. Murder."

"Murder?"

"Assault."

"Assault?"

"Jaywalking."

"Jaywalking? That's bullshit. You can't get charged with jaywalking in Boston."

"You can in Wayland. Please turn around, lean against the banister, and spread your legs."

Lee ran his hands over my body, searching for a weapon.

Other officers had formed a loose circle watching the arrest. Lee turned to them and said, "Thank you, officers." The crowd broke up.

Lee said, "Please put your hands behind your back."

I said, "Seriously?"

"It's procedure."

I put my hands behind my back. As I felt the handcuff ratchet over my wrist, I heard Bobby Miller's booming voice. "Lee! What the fuck are you doing?"

Lee stopped working. One handcuff dangled off my wrist behind my back.

"There is no need for profanity, Agent Miller. I'm arresting Tucker."

"What for?"

"Trespassing—"

"Trespassing? Are you shitting me?" Bobby stood next to me, facing Lee.

Lee said, "Espionage."

"Espionage? What the fuck do you know about espionage? I doubt you can even spell it."

"Agent Miller, I'm confused. What is the problem?"

"The problem is that *I* am investigating the espionage around here, and *I* never asked you to arrest Tucker for anything. You had one fucking job, Lee. You were supposed to figure out who killed Tucker's brother."

"I am doing that."

"You're doing a shitty job. Since you've been on this case JT's mother was murdered in Pittsfield, Dave Patterson was killed in Warren, Tucker's mother was burned in Framingham. On top of it, last night someone kidnapped Tucker's girlfriend, Lucy."

"The girl from the first night?" asked Lee.

"Yes, her. You have a fucking statewide crime spree with a US government defense contractor involved. I'm taking over this case, and I don't want you fucking it up by arresting the one guy who's made any progress on solving it."

I said, "Thanks, Bobby."

Bobby said, "Shut up!"

I shut up.

Bobby continued, "Lee, I need Tucker free. We've got an Iranian trying to buy US secrets."

I said, "Talevi. He's the one who took Lucy."

Lee said, "Talevi? The drug importer?"

Bobby said, "Tucker, didn't I tell you to shut up? Now shut the fuck up."

"But I—"

"Shut up!"

I had brought my hands from behind my back. The handcuff still dangled from my wrist. Bobby pointed at it. "Take that off him," he ordered Lee.

Lee said, "I don't appreciate this treatment, Agent Miller. This is my jurisdiction." But he did as he was told.

Bobby said, "Don't you fucking get it, Lee? I need Tucker. I need him to save the lives of some poor kids in the Army who are going to get the shit blown out of them if Iran figures out how to jam the Paladin missile. Get your head out of your ass and look at the big picture."

Lee looked toward the sky and sighed. He said, "Give me strength."

The uniformed Boston cops and their cruisers had disappeared, but now a new cop car drove down Follen. When the car reached us, I heard the car's GPS lady say, "You have reached your destination." The cruiser said WAYLAND POLICE on the side.

A cop climbed out of the car carrying an envelope. As he approached us, Bobby dropped his key ring on the ground.

The new cop said, "I'm looking for Aloysius Tucker."

I said, "I'm—"

Bobby stood quickly, elbowing me square in the balls on the way up. *Twice in one day.*

I covered my crotch. This was a bad one. "What the fuck, Bobby?"

Bobby said, "Oh Jesus, dude. Did I get you? I'm sorry."

The new guy said, "I have a warrant to arrest Aloysius Tucker."

Bobby said, "Who are you?"

"I'm Lance Jacobson, Wayland Police. I need to arrest Aloysius Tucker."

It takes about ten seconds to feel the wave of pain from a good strike to the balls. Mine hadn't come yet. Still, I wasn't talking. I was standing, hands on knees, waiting.

Lee reached for the envelope and said, "Let me see that." He read off, "Trespassing, assault, assault with a deadly weapon? What was the deadly weapon?"

Jacobson said, "A cultivator."

Bobby said, "A cultivator? What the fuck is a cultivator?"

The pain hit. I said, "Urrggg."

Jacobson said, "It's a gardening tool. It has claws."

Bobby took the envelope from Lee and said, "Give me that."

Lee said, "A cultivator is a deadly weapon?"

"Cultivator my ass," said Bobby.

Jacobson said, "Plus, this Tucker guy closed a car door on the GDS security guard's arm. That's another deadly weapon."

I sank to my knees, "Uhhhhhhhnnnng."

Bobby asked, "Did he break the guard's fucking arm?"

"It caused a contusion. A severe contusion. Is Mr. Tucker around here? This is his street."

"Ohhhhh," I moaned.

Jacobson asked, "Is that guy okay?"

Bobby took Jacobson by the arm and led him away. "He'll be fine. Listen, let me keep this warrant."

"Who are you?"

"Bobby Miller. FBI." I imagine that Bobby showed Jacobson some ID, but I didn't see it. I was crawling across the brick sidewalk.

Lee followed them and said, "We are looking for Mr. Tucker. When we find him, we'll serve him."

"Hey, I need that warrant," said Jacobson.

Bobby said, "Don't worry about it. If I can't serve it, I'll get it back to you. We should catch him today, and it would be good to have a warrant ready to go."

I heard Jacobson's car door open, then close.

Bobby said, "Here's my card. Give me a call."

The cop's GPS lady said, "If possible, make a U turn." Then he was gone.

Lee said to Bobby, "Do not betray my faith in you, Agent Miller." He left us in front of my house.

I rolled onto my back on the sidewalk and reached into my pocket. My mother's unpaid bill was still there. If I was right, I was going to be able to get some answers about my father. I hoped it would be enough to save Lucy.

SIXTY-EIGHT

My injured ankle crackled as I limped toward St. Botolph Street to grab another Zipcar. A Honda Civic named Buford waited for me on West Newton Street. Bobby caught up with me. "Hold up a minute."

I limped on. "Can't stop. I need to save Lucy."

Bobby grabbed my arm. "Will you wait a second?"

"No." I kept moving.

"Don't make me arrest you."

That stopped me. "You're gonna arrest me now? After crushing my balls and lying to that guy from Wayland?"

"You committed a fucking crime, Tucker. What are we going to do about that?"

"I'm not going to do anything about it. You are going to do something about it."

"What am I going to do about it?"

"You're going to make it go away."

"Bullshit on that!" said Bobby.

"Fuck you then, Bobby. Arrest me."

We stood, facing off, my bad ankle complaining about the uneven bricks that made up the sidewalk. Bobby turned away from me and walked in a little circle uttering a mantra of profanity. "God-dammit, motherfucker, shit!"

I crossed my arms, spat my words. "Do you know how happy I was when you called me?"

Bobby stopped swearing. "What?"

"Do you know how happy I was, at that ball game, with Lucy? I was fucking happy."

Bobby said nothing.

"It was our third date, the Sox were winning, I was with a hot girl who I really liked and who seemed to like me. I was probably even going to go home with her."

"What's this—"

"I'll bet that she would have been my girlfriend. We'd be spending the fall watching the Sox, having dinners. She would probably have had some of her stuff in my house by now."

"What's your point?"

"My point is that you fucked that all up. You, my friend, de-stroyed it. If you hadn't called me, I was going to spend the night at Lucy's house. You guys would have cleaned up my street and the next day I would have never known about JT."

"I don't—"

I pulled out my Droid and flipped to Bobby's picture of JT. "But you had to send me this. You know what I thought this was? A pic-ture of my dad."

"I know."

"I thought this was a picture of my dad. My old dad. The guy who was faithful to his wife, who didn't have another family, and who didn't have another son who got his name and who was his favorite."

"Look—"

"That was back when I had a mother—"

285

"It's not—"

"So you fucking owe me, Bobby. You fucking owe it to me to go out there and do whatever it is you people fucking do to make these things go away."

Bobby opened his palms. "It's not so easy."

I stepped close to him. Crushing pain radiated from my ankle. "That's your problem. Not my problem. Go figure it out, because I'm going to try to save my girlfriend before Talevi hacks some other part off of her and sends it to me in a box."

I turned and limped down the street.

Bobby called out, "Let me help you. We can get him."

"I'll call you."

I rustled the handwritten bill in my pocket, making sure that I had kept this last ticket to saving Lucy. It was a long shot, but it was all I had.

SIXTY-NINE

YouStoreIt Self-Storage in Framingham had been hiding in plain sight just off the Mass Pike. I had driven past it dozens of times on the way to visit my mother. I never knew she had a unit here. The building matched the drawing on the handwritten bill. A tall lobby faced customers, while a phalanx of garage doors, entry-ways to storage, ran down the side of the low building.

I pushed through the glass doors into the office. An older woman sat behind the desk, wearing a red YouStoreIt collared shirt and jeans. She had crinkly eyes and weathered skin. She watched a large HDTV that was mounted on the wall as talking heads blabbed on the screen and words scrolled across the bottom: *Iranian Saber Rattling.*

I asked, "How's the news?"

She answered with a husky smoker's voice. "The world's ending tomorrow. It has been for years."

I placed the bill on her desk. "I'm here to pay Angelina Tucker's bill. I'm closing the account."

The woman picked up the bill. "I'd been expecting this. Poor Angelina. Are you her son? Are you Aloysius?"

I nodded.

"I'm so sorry for your loss."

I nodded again. "Thanks. I'm surprised she mentioned me."

She held out her hand. "She talked about you all the time. I'm C.C."

We shook. "Did you know my mother well?"

"She used to come here every week. Usually on Sundays, but sometimes she'd come if the world's news got especially bad."

"Really? What's here?"

C.C. peered at me. "You don't know?"

"No. I never knew my mother had this place."

"That's so sad. I would have expected her to share this with you. You're John's son, after all."

"Shared what?"

"I'll show you."

We left the office and walked through the cool September air. Summer was definitely over. YouStoreIt consisted of three long buildings with wide white doors spaced along the sides. C.C. led me to the closest building and we walked down its length.

"Your mother had a ten by ten unit," C.C. said. "About the size of a small office. That's obvious considering how she used it."

"Used it?"

"You'll see."

We reached a unit. C.C. consulted a strip of paper and entered an access code. "The code is 0723," she said.

"My parents' anniversary," I said.

"That's sweet. I never knew that." She pushed a button. The door rattled open, and I dropped through a hole in time.

SEVENTY

I WAS TWELVE. A thin gold strip demarcated the blue hallway rug from the rust-orange rug in my father's office. My father's shag was holy ground, not to be touched by twelve-year-old feet. I stood on the edge of that gold strip and looked in at my father's desk, easy chair, and filing cabinet. My foot itched to touch the rusty carpet. I inched it forward.

"Aloysius, what are you doing?" my mother called out, poking her head out of the kitchen.

"Nothin'," I said, drawing my foot back.

"Don't you go in there. That's your father's office."

"I know."

"He's got secrets in there. You can't see them."

I wondered at my father's secrets.

"Ma," I called to my mother. She was back in the kitchen. "Why does Dad have the secrets in his office?"

My mother called back, "It's his work. He does work for the government."

"Why do they tell him secrets?"

My mother's head appeared from the kitchen, looking at me down the hall. "Because they trust him. They know he's a good man. Come away from there and take out the trash."

Now the adult me was standing next to C.C. expecting to find the golden border to my father's office. There was none, just as there was no rust carpet. The floor was concrete, but the office was set up just as he had it: desk facing the door, his chair behind it opposite a Barcalounger. A two-drawer filing cabinet completed the triangle.

C.C. said, "You can go in."

"Yeah," I said. "I guess I can."

The taboo washed over me as I stepped into the office. C.C. switched on a lamp next to the easy chair. "Your mother didn't like the overhead fluorescent."

I edged around the desk and pulled my father's chair out. The desktop was empty but for a green blotter with leather down the sides, a GDS mug filled with mechanical pencils, and an ashtray made out of a hunk of twisted metal, a souvenir of a missile test. I considered sitting in my dad's chair but remained standing.

"What did she do in here?" I asked.

"When I saw her, she was sitting in the easy chair. I think she talked to your father when I wasn't around."

I remembered now. I'd find my parents in the office when I got home from school. My father sitting in the desk chair, and my mother in the Barcalounger. The desk chair stood as solid as ever, made of sturdy wood with leather on the seat and back. Dust grayed the brown leather. The chair beckoned, but I'd never sat on it before and I couldn't now. It was my father's.

I ran my hands over the desk, feeling the depth of the dust, and opened the top drawer. It held an engineering notebook dated from the November before my father's death with a dash for the ending date. It was his last notebook.

My mother had never had the notebooks in her house. I could have saved her if I'd known about this room. I could have saved her if I'd been the kind of son she trusted. Too bad I wasn't.

I opened the large desk file drawer and saw other notebooks lying flat in it. The top notebook had an ending date that matched the beginning date on the current notebook. Judging by the size of the pile, decades of notebooks were stacked in there.

"Well, I'll leave you to it," said C.C.

"Thanks. I'll be clearing this place out soon." I imagined taking the heavy desk home and replacing the Ikea thing I had today. That would have to wait. I moved to the filing cabinet. A small metal frame looked out from the top drawer. It held a slip of paper that said *A-L*. The bottom drawer said *M-Z*. The *P*'s would be in there.

I slid the drawer open. Ran my finger down to the *P*'s and pulled out a folder. My father's precise lettering labeled the folder with Sharpie permanence. It said *Paladin*. I lifted the Paladin folder out, put it on the desk, and opened it. My old crayon drawing looked back at me: the secret plans to the original Paladin.

The old leather of the Barcalounger crunched as I sat in the big chair and laid the plans across my lap. The cover was the same one that JT must have pulled out of the archives. He had gotten to see my father's secrets. Another win for him. I opened the front page and read the introduction. It was written in the stilted engineering-speak that was popular today on Wikipedia. It described the architecture of the Paladin missile.

Paladin had two pieces: a ground unit and a missile. The missile used a data downlink to send radar information to the ground computer; the ground computer sent instructions back to the missile. I flipped to the table of contents and found the downlink frequencies. These were the numbers that could save Lucy's life. They'd be obsolete now, but Talevi wouldn't know that until Lucy was safe.

I flipped open my cell phone and called Talevi.

"I have what you want," I said.

"I doubt that," said Talevi. "I heard that you failed completely."

"Who told you that?"

"It does not matter."

"Well, they were wrong. I've got your Paladin specs right here. I'm looking at the downlink information. I want to talk to Lucy."

There was silence over the line. I wondered if the call had been dropped.

"You still there?" I asked.

"Yes," said Talevi. "I will set up an email drop where you can send the file. Then I will tell you where to pick up your friend."

"Bullshit. I've got a paper copy and I'm going to trade it for Lucy, assuming she's still alive. I want to talk to her."

Talevi sighed into the phone, then said, "Here."

Lucy said, "Tucker?"

I said, "Yeah. It's me. I'm going to get you out of there."

"Oh God! Please listen to me, don't trust—"

I heard a slapping sound, and the phone clattered in my ear. Lucy cried out. Then Talevi's voice.

"You see. Your friend is still alive."

"If you hurt her again, I will fucking kill you, Talevi."

"Let us not be dramatic. How shall we trade?"

"Some place public. You give me her, I give you the plans."

"Yes, I assumed you would want to meet in a place public. Go to Dalton Street in front of the red bar. We will make the exchange. You will give me the information, and I will give you Lucy."

"Okay." My mind was cranking on how to get Jael involved.

"You should know one thing before we meet," said Talevi.

"What's that?"

"If I see any sign of that Jew sniper or your fat FBI friend, I will kill you and your lover before I become a martyr. Meet me in one hour."

SEVENTY-ONE

JAEL NAVAS, THAT JEW sniper, leaned over her rifle and considered the sight lines.

"This is an impossible angle," she said. "I cannot defend you."

We were standing on the sixth floor of the Hilton's parking garage trying to see the sidewalk in front of Bukowski Tavern. A wide concrete barrier, five feet tall, blocked our view.

Jael continued, "I would have to climb this wall and lean over it. He would see me."

We walked through the empty garage to another wall that faced the Mass Pike. The concrete here formed a set of Venetian blind louvers. Jael crouched against the wall and poked her rifle through.

"I still cannot see the tavern," she said. "I can only cover you if you stand away from the tavern entrance." She pointed to the bridge where the Mass Pike ran under Dalton Street. It was twenty yards from the rendezvous point.

"Okay." My fingers tapped against my leg, burning off nervousness.

"If they move to the spot in front of the tavern, then you must run away from them down Boylston."

I looked out at the spot. It was across the street from the Capital Grille. Tall windows overlooked the meeting. I wondered if Talevi would be willing to conduct business there.

Jael said, "This is a very bad idea."

"Yeah?"

"I see no way that Talevi lets either of you live."

"If he kills me, you'd tell Bobby about him. That should be enough insurance."

"We could tell Agent Miller about Talevi right now. It is not too late."

I fitted a Bluetooth headset into my ear. "He'll kill Lucy."

Jael took a small sip of air and almost whispered, "He will not let her live, regardless."

"I have to try."

"He will kill you both."

"Not if you can get a shot. I'll stay on the bridge."

Jael fitted her own Bluetooth headset. "Yes. Please."

"Please?"

"Please do not make me watch a friend die."

I entered the narrow elevator and pressed the button for the first floor. "Nobody's going to die today."

The doors closed. I don't think Jael believed me.

My cell phone played "Extreme Ways." I activated my headset. Jael's voice filled my ear. "I am here."

"Okay."

I positioned myself in the middle of the Dalton Street bridge and leaned against the railing. The sun dropped toward the horizon over Framingham, Pittsfield, and all things west. Clouds scuttled red and low across the sky. Cars slid past in the waning rush hour, their tart fumes irritating my nose. I felt Jael's presence over my shoulder, imagined the sniper rifle at the ready. Wondered what was in her crosshairs.

A black Lincoln Town Car glided past me and stopped in front of Bukowski, out of Jael's line of sight. *Dammit!*

"They've parked in front of the bar," I said into my headset.

"Do not approach them," said Jael.

Talevi stuck his head out of the front passenger window.

"Do you have what I want?" he called.

I pulled the Paladin plans from under my jacket and waved them. "Right here."

"Bring them!"

"I want to see Lucy."

"You will see her when you bring the plans here, or you will never see her again."

I said into the headset, "They're going to bolt."

"Let them go," said Jael.

Talevi pulled his head back into the car. The red brake light dimmed as the car started to roll forward.

"Wait!" I yelled. I ran for the car.

"No!" said Jael.

I stopped at the car and the back door opened. A brown-skinned man pointed a machine gun at me. Lucy was behind him on the floor, duct tape covering her mouth, her arms pinned behind her back. She looked at me, her eyes wet and pleading.

"Get in the car," said Talevi, "or we will kill you in the street."

Jael heard the command over the headset. She barked, "Do not get in the car! Run!"

I heard a skittering sound overhead. Jael must have shifted positions and climbed the concrete railing. Talevi looked up and saw something.

"The Jew! Kill him and go," he said.

The man with the machine gun pointed the barrel at my chest. I was going to die in the street. I jumped off the curb and, pushing the gun up, slid into the car.

I heard Jael yell, "No!" It wasn't coming from my headset. A rifle shot cracked and a hole appeared in the Lincoln's hood.

Talevi shouted, "Drive!" and the driver punched the accelerator. The car leapt away from the curb and shot down the street.

Talevi turned and pointed a pistol at my forehead. He motioned to the guy with the machine gun who was sitting between Lucy and me. He said something in a Middle Eastern language. Mr. Machine Gun ripped the headset from my ear and threw it out the window.

Talevi waved the gun at me. "Give him your phone."

I handed the Droid to Mr. Machine Gun. He threw it out the window as well. I heard it clatter, skid, and fall out of earshot.

Talevi placed the muzzle of the gun against my forehead. "Put your hands behind your back."

I did as I was told and Mr. Machine Gun ensnared my wrists in a zip tie. Then he slapped a piece of duct tape over my mouth.

Talevi sat back in his seat, facing forward. He said to the driver, "Take us somewhere we can dispose of them."

As the car's driver pulled away from the curb he said, "I know a good spot."

I knew the driver's voice. It was my cousin Sal.

SEVENTY-TWO

THE HARD PLASTIC OF the zip tie cut into the flesh of my wrist as I slouched on the floor of the Town Car. It was rush hour, and we were stuck in traffic heading out of Boston. Talevi, not wanting us to attract attention with our taped mouths, had told Mr. Machine Gun to force us to the floor.

Lucy looked at me and then looked away. Her eyes were distant and slack. She had given up hope. She struggled to get comfortable, inching away from me. I tested my ties and wondered how long she had been trapped like this.

Sal had lurched the car through traffic and, judging by the signs I could see from the floor, was now bumping along Storrow Drive. Talevi was not happy. "Why are you going this way?"

"It's the fucking rush hour, Talevi. What did you expect?"

"Why are you leaving the city?"

"Because I don't shit where I eat."

Don't shit where you eat. I shifted my shoulder against the car door and remembered when Sal had given me that advice. We were at Auntie Rosa's for Christmas Eve dinner. Steam rose off of lobsters in a pot in the middle of the table. We had laid into the arthropods with nutcrackers and melted butter.

I told Sal, "Hey, I met this hot girl. I think she likes me."

Sal pushed a finger through his lobster's tail, expelling the meat from the other end. "Yeah? What's her name?"

"Carol."

"How did you meet her?"

"We work together."

Sal dunked his lobster meat into the butter and pointed it at me. "Don't shit where you eat." He took a bite of the green tomalley-laden flesh, and the conversation had moved to the Bruins.

I moved my shoulders to relieve the pressure and looked up through the back window of the car. The yellow tiles of the Callahan Tunnel sped past. We were heading to the North Shore.

Lucy was scrunched into the side of the Town Car. Her eyes were closed, and her head rocked back and forth. She was gone. Lost in whatever comfort she could find in oblivion.

God reached into my mind and took his customary place in a doomed man's thoughts. I had completely rejected the Catholicism that Sal celebrated on Easter and Christmas, weddings and funerals. I imagine Sal would never confess to a priest that he had killed his cousin, or helped spies from Iran steal his country's secrets. *For the sin of treason and murder, I give you 50,000 Our Fathers and 28,000 Hail Marys.* I had bailed on Catholicism. What good was it when it would let your cousin shoot you in the head? I hoped I was right about there being no Jesus, because if I was wrong I was going to spend a long time in Hell.

I stretched my legs and waited, watching the darkening sky through the windows. Sal made a series of turns and then the car started bumping along an unpaved road. There were no trees in the windows and I saw a seagull fly overhead. It was probably going to get a tasty brain treat in a few minutes.

Sal stopped the car and said, "Let's do it here."

SEVENTY-THREE

MR. MACHINE GUN HADN'T tied our ankles. I considered the option of kicking him in the face. But then what? It wouldn't knock him out, and he'd either kick me in the face or shoot me with the machine gun. Didn't seem like a win. Rage coursed through me. *Then again, it might be a good way to go.*

Sal and Talevi climbed out of the car and opened our doors. My head and shoulders lurched into space as the door's support disappeared.

Sal looked into the car and said to Machine Gun, "You didn't tie their fucking feet? What's wrong with you? If one of them starts running we'll be out here all fucking night."

Machine Gun took two more sets of plastic zip ties and slipped one set over Lucy's ankles. He cinched them up, running his hand up her thigh as he did so. Lucy ignored him, but I didn't. I slipped past reason.

Machine Gun slipped a loop over one of my ankles. As he reached for the other ankle I kicked him square in the nose with the heel of my shoe, catching him at the bridge. Blood spurted across the car. Machine Gun's eyes rolled back in his head. He let out a shuddering sigh and fell to his side.

Sal, standing outside the car, said, "Goddammit, Tucker, now look what you did." He reached over me, putting a knee into my chest and wrestled my second ankle into the restraint. He zipped the tie, then put his ear next to Machine Gun's mouth. He backed out of the car, crunching my chest.

Lucy was out of the car. Talevi had dragged her away. I was left lying on my back, looking up at Sal through the door.

Sal called out, "Hey, Talevi! Your fucking idiot back here just got himself killed."

Talevi appeared. He climbed over me and felt Machine Gun's neck. Machine Gun wasn't moving. He slapped at him. "Sami? Sami! How did this happen?"

"Tucker kicked him right in the fucking nose."

"Sami is dead!"

"I told you he was dead. Tucker killed him." Sal tapped me lightly on the cheek with open fingers. "You popped your cherry, little cousin."

Talevi let off a string of what must have been Persian expletives and dragged me from the car next to where Lucy was kneeling. He dropped me and I fell to my side. "Kneel next to her."

I lay on my side and said, "Fuck you," through the tape. It came out as two grunts.

Talevi kicked me in the stomach. "Kneel!"

Sal said, "What the fuck, Talevi, we're not making some fucking snuff film. Let's just do it and get out of here."

Talevi pulled my jacket open and saw the Paladin plans. He smiled, reached in, and grabbed the plans by the binding. I tried to pin them with my arm, but he gave a hard yank and they slid out. My breath wheezed through my nose. Lucy shuffled on her knees and whimpered, the gravel digging into her skin.

I rolled to a sitting position and then to a kneeling position next to Lucy. I had gotten her killed. The least I could do was kneel next to her. The gravel dug into my knees.

Sal crunched behind us and waited. I heard metal on leather as he slid his gun out of his holster, then a double metallic click as he jacked a bullet into the chamber. *Blood's supposed to be thicker than water. What bullshit.*

They say you see your dead relatives when you go to Heaven. If I went to Heaven, I didn't want to see anyone except my mother. I wanted to meet the beautiful young woman who had borne me before she was twisted by rage and betrayal.

Talevi stood in the headlight, flipping through the stolen plans. He started reading slowly, then flipped pages faster and faster. He stormed over to me. Kicked me in the leg, and shook the book in my face. "I have this version, you idiot! I've had it ever since your father gave it to me twenty years ago!"

My father? My father? In the preternatural slowness of my last moments, the shattered jigsaw picture of the mystery coalesced in my mind like a movie played backward. Talevi had provided the final, unimaginable clue. All the pieces fell into place. JT's murder became the inevitable result of desperation and betrayal played out over twenty years ago. I saw it all, and I was grateful to have the gift of this epiphany just before I died.

I reached out with my bound hand and touched Lucy. She would not die alone.

Talevi yelled, "Fool!" and threw the book into the gravel. He waved his hand at Sal. "Shoot them. Shoot them both."

Sal said, "Right."

He pulled the trigger twice, putting two bullets into Talevi's chest. Talevi looked at his chest, looked at Sal, and reached for a gun. Sal put four more bullets into him, ranging from Talevi's navel to his forehead. Talevi stumbled in front of me and fell into the gravel. His head hit the stones with a sickening crunch as he emitted a rattling final breath.

SEVENTY-FOUR

SAL RIPPED THE DUCT tape from my mouth in a single searing swipe. "Didn't I tell you to mind your own fucking business? Where am I going to get another heroin connection?"

He knelt in front of Lucy and worked the tape loose. Lucy whimpered as he pulled at the adhesive. Once the gag was gone, Sal pulled out a Leatherman and snipped the ties at Lucy's wrists and ankles. She wrapped her arms around herself and sank lower into the gravel. Sal snipped my ties and I grabbed Lucy and pulled her close. She dug her fists into my back, as her sobs broke through. Tears splashed across my cheek.

She said, "They grabbed me when I was sitting next to Walt."

I just held her close. "I'm sorry. I'm so sorry."

Sal crouched next to us. He touched Lucy on the shoulder and said, "I needed to get Talevi out here to finish him. I'm really sorry you had to be scared for so long."

"I heard Talevi talking to you on the speakerphone about killing us," said Lucy.

"I know," said Sal. "I know you were scared. You did great. I know guys who have sh—Well, never mind. You did great. I was hoping Tucker would figure out a way to let you know."

I said, "Let her know what? I was scared too."

Sal turned to me, his gorilla brows knit close. "You? Why were *you* scared?"

"Why was I scared? I thought you were going to shoot me in the back of the head."

Sal stood. "Why?"

I stood. "Why? What do you mean why? You were working for Talevi, you drove us out here, you said you would kill us."

"You asshole!" Sal slapped me across the face. Pain exploded through my cheek.

I stumbled and fell to one knee. Lucy screamed.

I said, "Jesus, Sal. What the fuck?"

Sal loomed forward over me. "What the fuck? What the fuck? What kind of an animal do you think I am? You thought that I would really fucking kill you? My cousin? My mother's nephew?"

I said, "What was I supposed to think?"

Sal raised his fist. I flinched. He lowered it. "You were supposed to think that we were fucking tricking Talevi. You were supposed to know, *fucking know*, that I wouldn't kill you. That I would rather die than kill anyone in my family."

Lucy stood, slid a little behind me, supporting me as I faced Sal's rage.

Sal continued, "You were supposed to know that you're my fucking cousin and that this motherfucker"—he kicked at Talevi's corpse—"would never come between us. You were supposed to fucking know what it means when I come to your mother's funeral, or that we spent Christmases together. You were supposed to fucking know what family means."

"I'm sorry, Sal," I said.

"Did I ever do anything to hurt you? I mean, when you weren't calling me a fucking liar and stealing pictures that could get me sent up for twenty years? When you weren't being a complete fucking know-it-all South End shit who's ashamed of his family, ashamed of his roots?"

"No, Sal. You never did anything to hurt me."

"Did I ever give you one fucking piece of bad advice? I told you fucking weeks ago, *weeks* ago, not to dig into this fucking thing. I told you to leave it alone. I told you to stay away from Talevi. I told you to ignore the whole fucking mess. You think I did that for my health, because I had something to hide? I did it because I didn't want you to get hurt. Now look at you. Your mother is dead. Lucy got taken. You made me shoot Talevi, and none of this fucking stuff would have happened if you had listened to me."

"I'm sorry."

"What's wrong with you?"

I stared into the dark stones before me, unable to meet Sal's eyes. Lucy hugged me and I put my arm around her. Shame crowded my face. I wished with everything I had that she hadn't seen this, that I had understood my cousin.

I said, "I'm so sorry, Sal. Can we go home?"

SEVENTY-FIVE

WE DROVE BACK TO Boston in silence. Sal had taken us to a long marshy road in Revere, where the rushes did their intended job and concealed the corpses we left behind. Talevi and Sami were seagull food. Lucy curled against me in the back seat, her bare foot tucked up under her with a bandage over the spot where Talevi had cut off her toe. As we drove over the Tobin bridge, I borrowed Sal's phone and texted Jael.

```
I'm safe.
How?
Sal saved me. Long story. Meet us at my house.
```

I called out, "Hey, could you take us to Follen Street?"

Sal said, "Whatever."

We lapsed back into silence as the sun set and we slipped into night.

Sal pulled into a spot in front of my house. Jael's MDX was parked down the street. She got out, walked toward us.

Sal saw Jael and said, "None of this ever gets mentioned again, *capisce?*"

"Yeah," I said.

Sal turned to face Lucy. "You too, honey. Please. Don't tell anyone. If you say anything, Tucker and I will go down for it."

"Why would I go to prison?" I asked.

"Because you fucking deserve to, you shit. I'd see to it."

Lucy said, "I promise. I won't say anything."

Jael stood next to the car. She ran her finger around the bullet hole she had created in the hood. She rapped on the tinted window and peered in. We opened the car doors and climbed out, standing in a small circle over the memory of JT's chalk outline.

Jael said to Sal, "Thank you for saving Tucker."

Sal said, "Yeah. No problem."

Jael asked, "How did you know?"

"Lyla works for me. I heard that she shot up the Commons garage and I asked her about it. She told me that she was working for Talevi."

I said, "She tried to kill me."

"No, shithead, she did not try to kill you. If she'd tried to kill you, you would be dead."

Jael said, "This is true."

Sal said, "She told me that she was supposed to be a distraction."

"A distraction? She nearly shot me."

"You pissed her off when you hit her in the face with those keys. She kinda loses her shit sometimes."

Another piece fell into place.

"By the way," said Sal, "she's really sorry. She didn't know you were my cousin. She's sorry she shot at you."

"Well, that's comforting," I said. "Tell her no hard feelings."

"Good," said Sal. "You don't want her mad at you. She's fucking nuts."

"Really."

Jael said, "She is not well."

Sal said, "Talevi had tried to hire Lyla to drive the car and kill you two. She called me and I told Talevi that she was busy. I volunteered to be Talevi's gun."

I tried again. "You can't believe how sorry I am for doubting you."

"Whatever," said Sal.

I said to Jael, "Please do me a favor and take Lucy to Mass General to get her toe fixed up."

Lucy said, "You're not coming?"

I looked at the ground. "No. There is something I have to do. I'm sorry."

"You seem to be apologizing a lot today," said Lucy. She turned and limped toward Jael's MDX. They climbed in and drove down the street. I waved at Lucy. She ignored me.

I said to Sal, "I need one more favor."

"You want me to tuck you in?"

"No, I need a gun."

"Why?"

I knew who had burned my mother's house down and why. I told Sal.

Sal said, "You don't want a gun."

"Why?"

"Because you aren't a fucking killer, that's why."

I relived the moment when my heel connected with Sami's nose. I felt the crack in my foot as the thin bones of his nose were driven into his brain. I watched again as his eyes rolled back in his head and blood spurted down my shoe. I remembered the feeling when I saw his shuddering last breath and realized what it meant. I had killed the man who was about to kill Lucy and me.

It felt good.

It shouldn't have felt good. It should have filled me with remorse. I should have spent time imagining the wife who wouldn't see him again, the kids who wouldn't have a dad, the mom who would bury her son.

Screw them all. He had felt Lucy up, bound our wrists with zip ties, covered our mouths with tape, and was going to shoot us and leave us for the tide. It shouldn't have felt good to kill him. It did.

"You're wrong," I said, "I am a killer."

"That was a fucking accident," said Sal. "This won't be like that. You're gonna have to look him in the eye and say goodbye. You're not gonna be able to do it, and he'll kill you."

I said, "Believe me, I'll be able to do it."

"Are you sure it's him? Are you abso-fucking-lutely sure?"

"Yeah," I said. "I've got evidence that nails him. I'm going to show it to him and then kill him."

"Just show it to your FBI buddy. Let him do the work."

"No."

"Show it to me and I'll get Lyla to do it. This guy killed my aunt; Lyla would do it for free."

"No. I swore to God."

"You didn't even make Confirmation, now you're swearing to God?"

"Are you going to give me a gun?"

Sal reached into the car and fumbled around in the glove box. He produced a gun.

"Here. It's a fucking revolver; it's loaded. Just pull the trigger hard. You didn't get it from me."

"I know. Thanks," I said.

"You're gonna get fucking killed," said Sal.

"I'll be fine."

"Suit yourself," said Sal. He turned to climb into the car.

I ran around the car. "Hey, Sal."

He stood next to the driver's door, waiting.

I said, "Are we good?"

Sal grabbed me and pulled me into a bear hug. "Yeah, little cousin, we're good."

SEVENTY-SIX

My apartment door hung open. Crowbar bites ran down the door-frame, showing where someone had worked my door open. I stood at the door, revolver in hand, listening for someone in the apartment. My finger rested on the trigger. I moved it out along the side of the revolver. Never too late to implement gun safety.

Silence. Nobody was moving in my apartment. I considered calling Jael, but my cell phone was lying in a street somewhere, probably shattered. I placed my finger back on the trigger and pushed the door open with my foot. No sound. No movement.

I peeked through the doorway, looking down the hallway to my living room. My big black leather sofa was splashed across the living room, its cushions gutted. My flat panel TV lay on top of it. It had been ripped from the wall over the fireplace.

"That was unnecessary," I muttered.

I stepped into the condo, peering around the door. The mess got worse. Pans, spices, dishes, paper towels, bottles of Scotch, and the contents of the refrigerator were thrown across the floor. Bags of my mother's mail had been ripped open and spread everywhere. The countertop was covered with cereal boxes.

My thoughts turned to Click and Clack. I dug through the crap on the counter and found them under a torn plastic bag. They were unaffected by the maelstrom around them.

"Did you guys do this?"

They rested on their log.

"Because I told you no parties. I told you the tough kids would show up and ruin everything."

Their sponge was dry. I took it out of the terrarium, stepped across the former contents of my cabinets, turned on the water with my revolver hand, and wet the sponge. Tucked it back into the terrarium, sprinkled food on it, and replaced the lid.

"I don't know when I'll be seeing you guys," I said. "I'll make sure someone checks in on you."

The search had destroyed my office. All the drawers were pulled out, their contents dumped. The books had been ripped off the shelves and chucked onto the floor. My computer monitor had been smashed. That was just mean. You can't hide notebooks in an LCD computer monitor.

My bedroom had gotten the same treatment: shredded mattress, strewn clothes, posters torn off the walls. Clearly Talevi killing me would not have saved the person who trashed my apartment looking for notebooks full of damning evidence, evidence that should have been destroyed in my mother's house fire.

I had lied about having the notebooks. Jael had been right: you can't tell what will happen when you improvise. You can't even know whom to trust.

SEVENTY-SEVEN

IT WAS MIDNIGHT. I turned off the disposable cell phone I'd bought at Walmart and waited. This was all going to end in the next hour.

I sat at my father's desk, holding the revolver in my lap with one hand, flipping through the incriminating notebook with the other. The book contained all the evidence Bobby Miller and Lieutenant Lee would ever need. I probably should have called them, but I hadn't. I'd called my mother's killer instead.

My father had started a new notebook every six months. There were two per year, each a bound collection of green pages with a faint blue grid superimposed on them. These notebooks would have been useful if my father were getting a patent. Instead, they outlined the pressures that turned him into a spy and gave him an aneurysm.

My father had recorded his life in meticulous detail using tiny printed handwriting, always in pen, never in pencil. I flipped back through time, past meeting notes, past drawings, past phone numbers and org charts, circuits and flow diagrams, through phone call logs and maps and sketches.

My father made little distinction between work and home. A meeting with another engineer (whose name, like all names, had been highlighted with a yellow marker) was logged beside a shopping list that contained Twinkies, a snack that had never sullied my mother's kitchen.

My father had scored the '86 Red Sox playoff games in his notebook. I remember him doing it. It was a Saturday, and he was always home on Saturdays. I watched the game, scrunched up against him, my Red Sox cap crushed in my hands as I prepared to leap into the air. Afterward I cried. Dad told me not to be a baby.

Game 7 had been scheduled for Sunday, but it rained, and Dad traveled back to Pittsfield on Monday. I had watched Game 7 alone, my mother having long since gone to sleep.

I flipped further back in time to the note I had found before, the one that confirmed what I already knew because of what Talevi had told me:

Meeting with Mr. Talevi

I scanned down the page and found a number:

$500K for me

There it was. The price of my father's honor. Five hundred thousand dollars was enough to convince him to sell our country's secrets so he could support the babysitter he'd fucked and the son who resulted. Five hundred thousand dollars that paid for a house in Pittsfield, a diploma from UMass, and a few years of homemaking for Cathy. Five hundred thousand dollars that burned a hole in his conscience and blew out a blood vessel in his brain.

The note continued:

$500K for Walt.

"I see you found the notebooks," said Uncle Walt. He had padded through the doorway of the storage unit and stood in front of the desk.

I had called Walt an hour ago and told him I had the evidence. Told him to meet me here, in this deserted place, at this deserted time, or that I'd share the evidence with Bobby Miller in the morning.

I raised the revolver, finger along the side. "Throw away the gun, Walt."

Walt's eyes widened and he stepped back, raising his hands. He hadn't expected me to be armed. "Whoa. I don't have a gun. Watch where you point that."

"Don't fuck with me. Throw away the gun."

"I told you. I don't have a gun," he said.

"Let's try this, then. I shoot you in the chest, and then I look for the gun." I slid my finger under the trigger guard, reached up with my thumb, and cocked the hammer.

"Okay. Okay," said Walt. He reached behind his back and produced a black pistol, holding it between thumb and forefinger.

"Toss it behind the filing cabinet."

Walt hefted the gun toward the filing cabinet in an arc. It hit the top and rattled off onto the floor next to the wall. "You happy?"

"Is that the gun you used to kill JT?" I asked him.

"Yeah," said Walt, "it is."

"Why?"

"Why did I use that gun?"

"No, you son of a bitch. Why did you kill JT?"

"He was going to tell you about our deal with Talevi. Patterson had quit, we didn't have the password, and JT said that you would be able to break in. Turns out he was right about that part."

"I wouldn't have helped him," I said.

"I knew that, but JT wouldn't listen. That asshole thought you were some sort of bent Mafioso hacker, that you would jump at the chance at a million dollars."

"What million dollars?"

"My million dollars. Talevi was paying two million. JT was going to give you my million. Said I was useless now that he knew Talevi."

"So you killed him." Walt started to lower his hands. "Keep them up."

Walt raised his hands again. "Yeah. So I killed him."

"It was stupid to do it right in front of my house."

"I didn't know it was your house."

"And then Cathy Byrd, and then my mother."

"Just covering my tracks, Tucker. I was sorry about your mother. I just needed to destroy those notebooks."

Images flashed before me. I saw my mother, stumbling in the smoke, fighting her way down a flaming goat path.

"I'm going to kill you now, Walt. Just like I promised at her funeral."

Walt moved toward the desk, keeping his hands up. He stopped with the gun a foot from his heart. Then he dropped his hands and leaned on the desk, closing the gap.

Walt said, "You're not going to kill me."

I said, "I am."

"If you were going to kill me, you would have done it already."

"Wha—"

A spiking clang of pain speared my skull and tore at my balance. Walt had bashed me with my father's ashtray. The gun fired, but Walt wasn't standing in front of it anymore. I turned to shoot, but Walt brought the ashtray down again. Its torn edges exploded across my forehead.

I heard Walt say, "You always were a disappointment." Then I slipped into darkness.

SEVENTY-EIGHT

I awoke to the smell of lighter fluid. Flat on my back. My hands tied over my head. I pulled, but a length of rope ran from them to the leg of Dad's desk. Walt sat in the Barcalounger, watching me.

"Well, you finally woke up. I thought I was going to have to torch you without saying goodbye."

"Fuck you," I said.

"Yeah, I suppose I got that coming. Truth be told, I don't care about saying goodbye. I need to ask you a question. If you answer it, I'll shoot you and then burn your body. If you don't, I'll just burn you alive."

My head spun. I tugged at the rope, pushed myself toward the desk with my heels, and tried to lift the desk to slip the rope from under it.

Walt said, "That desk is a heavy fucker with all those notebooks on it. Your dad was almost as bad as your mother when it came to hoarding paper." Uncle Walt gestured to a pile of engineering notebooks on the desk. The pile stunk of lighter fluid. So did the desk.

Walt continued, "Did Talevi ever get the plans from you? He said that you called him."

I said nothing.

Walt rose and pulled out the filing cabinet drawers. He dumped all the papers on the floor into a pile.

Walt said, "I guess you figured out by now that I helped Talevi take Lucy. She didn't even see me shove her into the car."

He covered the pile of paper with lighter fluid and kept talking.

"I got to tell you, Tucker, there is nothing more exhilarating than the long con. JT was going to pay you a million dollars to break into Patterson's machine, and I got you to beg me to let you do it."

I tried again to lift the desk. But flat on my back I couldn't get leverage.

Walt said, "You didn't need to get Hugh to give me a beating, though. I was going to give in if you just crawled to me one more time. Then you even offered to pay off my gambling debts. You're so cute."

"You're gonna fry, Walt. You think I didn't tell people about the notebooks? Bobby's on his way here now."

"You know, Tucker, you are a shitty liar. I think you really believed you were going to murder me. You didn't tell anyone about the notebooks."

I spit on one hand and rubbed it onto my bound wrist. Tried to fold my hand and fit it through. The skin tore, but the rope held.

Walt said, "So anyway, to my question. Did you give the plans to Talevi? Did he get what he wanted?"

I said nothing. Let Walt find out about Talevi on his own.

"Last chance, Tucker. I'd like to get some money out of Talevi. Did you give him the plans?"

"You know what, Walt?"

"What?"

"You're not my fucking uncle."

Walt pursed his lips and sighed. "Ah, well, it figures. It's easy to see why JT was your father's favorite."

"You knew about JT?"

317

"Of course I knew about JT. I was his godfather, for Christ's sake. That's why I gave him a chance at the second deal with Talevi. Figured, like father like son, and I was right."

"Why not me?"

"You were always your mother's son, Tucker. A momma's boy and a straight arrow. JT was your father's son. Looked just like him; acted just like him. God, your father loved that kid." Walt moved toward the fluid-drenched pile of paper. "Time for me to torch this place and get rid of the Tuckers. Frankly, you've all been nothing but a pain in my ass."

Even with the blood, I couldn't slip free of the ropes. I glared at Walt. "Why?"

"Why what? Why am I going to burn all this? Isn't it obvious? It's the link from your dad back to me."

Walt lit a match.

I yelled, "Don't do this!"

"Bye-bye, Tucker." Walt threw the match onto the pile and the lighter fluid started to burn. The flames climbed the pile. Smoke wafted against the ceiling. Walt stepped out of the storage bin, turned, and watched.

A column of smoke and flame hid me from Walt. I tugged at the rope, trying to break it with brute force. The flames followed a line of lighter fluid along the floor and up the desk's other leg. Walt had not put the lighter fluid near me or the rope.

The notebooks on the top of the desk ignited with a *whoomp*. Smoke boiled toward the ceiling. The flames merged with the flames from the paper pile. Panic set in. I got to my knees, got my feet under me, and lifted the desk, flames dancing in front of my face. It rose an inch, but there was no way to slip the rope off. I coughed, dropped the desk, and fell back as the pile of notebooks slid off the desk and onto the floor.

The notebooks fanned open, burning brightly. I saw my chance. I pushed my wrists over the flame, fighting the reflexes that tried to pull my arms to safety. The rope tethering me to the desk caught fire. I gritted my teeth and kept my wrists in place to make sure the rope was burning, then I kicked back with both legs. The burning rope snapped and I fell toward the burning pile of paper.

I twisted my hips, planted a foot on the floor, and rushed through the flames, holding my seared and bound wrists in front of me. Black smoke enveloped my head as I coughed, ducked, and charged into the night.

Smoke had filled my eyes. Walt was on me before I could clear them. His shoulder rammed my gut and forced me back toward the flames. Panic worked for me now. I fell, caught myself with my bound hands, got to my feet, and bolted away from the heat.

I stopped running and turned, wiping my eyes clear. Walt was fumbling to get my revolver out of his jacket. I launched myself at him. He fired. Pain creased my side, but I had momentum. I plowed into Walt and he fell. I grabbed the gun barrel and its heat burned my scorched skin, but I held on and twisted. Walt grunted as his wrist bent. I took the gun, staggered away, and heaved it into the fire with both hands. I fell to one knee and coughed up black mucus.

Walt kicked me in the side. The pain from my burns screamed through me, blocking out the pain from the kick. I stood. Walt grabbed me and pushed. We both fell toward the flame. The heat tore into my body, making the cut in my side howl.

I couldn't fight anymore. I dropped, becoming dead weight and grabbing Walt as I fell. He fought to keep from going down. I kicked up, catching him in the midsection and slingshotting him over me into the inferno. He landed on the pile of engineering books. His flannel shirt blazed into flame. He screamed, rolled, stood, and ran blindly into the filing cabinet, ricocheted to the desk, and fell back onto the burning pile of engineering books. Walt scrambled to his feet, staggered toward the door, flames sheeting over his body. His skin blistered as he fell to his knees, pitched forward, and was still.

SEVENTY-NINE

THE EQUINOX SUN SHONE down on Boston as I surveyed the city from the Phillips 22 lounge in Mass General. I wished I had a smartphone. I still hadn't gotten a picture of this view.

I had stitches and a bandage where Walt's bullet had cut my side. The burns on my hands and arms had been morphined into submission earlier in the week, but now they were responding to a salve and more bandages. My cough had subsided. I was rested and ready to go.

"Hey, Tucker," Bobby Miller said. He had entered the lounge with Lee and Jael. "Jesus. Hell of a view."

"Let me use your phone," I said. Bobby handed me his phone and I snapped a picture.

Lee said, "The gun from the storage bin matched the bullets from JT and Cathy Byrd. You were right. Walt killed them both."

"I know," I said.

"There was another gun. A revolver with no serial number. Do you know where that came from?"

I looked off toward the North End. I said, "I have no idea. Probably belonged to my dad."

Lee said, "Because we just can't get the pieces to fit together."

I turned. "Lee, I'm done helping you fit the pieces together."

"Yes, but—"

"Done. I'm done."

Lee looked from Bobby to Jael to me. He held out his hand. "Of course. Thank you for your help, Tucker."

I shook it, wincing, having forgotten my burns. "You're welcome."

"May God be between you and me."

Lee pushed his way through the Phillips main entrance door and was gone.

I asked Jael, "What does that mean?"

Jael said, "It means that Lieutenant Lee likes you."

"Well that's good."

Bobby said, "The evidence that your dad sold those plans was rock solid."

"Okay."

"We're turning up more evidence of Walt Adams trying to recruit spies."

"And?"

"And GDS doesn't want to stir this up anymore. They've said, and I agree, that your visit to their facility the other day simply resulted in a misunderstanding. They're willing to forget about it. In fact, they're dying to forget about it."

"Good. So am I."

Bobby stuck out his hand. "I put you through hell, buddy. I'm sorry."

I waved my bandage and Bobby dropped his hand. I said, "It's not your fault that my dad was a scumbag, Bobby."

Bobby asked, "You heading out now?"

"In a while."

Bobby left Jael and me alone in the waiting room. We looked out the window across Boston.

I said, "I couldn't do it, Jael. I couldn't kill him."

Jael said, "I know. You should be proud. You could not kill him because you are a good person."

"I was weak. You would have been able to do it. Back when you worked at—you know."

"Good people do not murder," she said. "I am trying to be a good person now."

I said, "You are a good person."

"I will drive you home."

She turned and headed for the door. I took one last look at Boston, trying to imprint the panorama on my brain, then I turned from the view and followed Jael.

EIGHTY

A WEEK LATER, LUCY and I sat on my new couch. Lucy wore tight jeans and no shirt. So did I. We were smooching. As we kissed, my hand rubbed her breast in a clockwise rotation.

"Uh, honey," said Lucy, "you're wearing it out."

I stopped rubbing. "Oh. Jeez. I'm sorry."

We sat, side by side, partially disrobed but indifferent to our nudity. The week had been a long one, full of averted eyes and half-started comments. Lucy stood and retrieved her bra from the floor. She slipped her arms through it and latched the back. She picked up the Red Sox T-shirt I had recently removed, and slid it over her head. I didn't protest.

She sat next to me and extended her feet. She had recently taken to wearing socks and close-toed shoes. Talevi was right. She could walk, but that's not what disfigurement is about.

Lucy said, "It's broken."

"What's broken?"

"Us," she said. "Whatever it is that two people create when they come together. It's broken."

I said, "I'm sorry."

"It's not your fault. It was never your fault. You saved me, remember? You were willing to die for me, next to me. You were my hero. I'll never forget that."

"But."

"But, I'll never forget being taken either. I'll never forget the feeling of my toe when they put those bolt cutters on it. I'll never forget how afraid I was. I'll never forget it as long as we're together."

Guilt coursed through me. "I never should have lied about the notebooks."

"It had nothing to do with the notebooks, and you know it." Lucy squeezed my bicep. "Don't beat yourself up. It wasn't your fault. I don't blame you."

"Still, you can't be with me."

"I can't be with you." Lucy reached down and pulled on a pair of red Keds sneakers. Tied them and stood. I stood.

"You're a good man, Tucker. I'm sorry about us." She kissed me on the cheek. "Please don't be alone."

I blew out a sigh. "I'll do my best." We walked to the front door with its new doorjamb and heavier lock. She stepped into the hallway.

One more awkward peck on the cheek. "Goodbye."

"Bye." I closed the door behind her and turned to Click and Clack. "Easy come, easy go, right, boys?"

They clung to their log. I reached into the cabinet and took out my new bottle of Lagavulin. Cracked the seal, got some ice, and poured a glass. I toasted Click and Clack. "Here's to plenty of fish in the sea."

They stared at me.

"Right. You're land crabs."

The apartment creaked. Outside, a car started. I looked into my bedroom but knew what I'd find there: a perfectly made bed and plenty of nothing. I rattled the Scotch in my glass and looked at my new Droid. Considered a rousing game of Angry Birds. Perhaps watch the Sox on my new TV.

Click and Clack folded into their shells and slept. "What? Am I boring you?"

Nothing.

"I'm boring myself," I told them. A dog barked outside. Now there was a pet that could fill a room.

My eyes rested on a pair of Red Sox tickets on the counter. Tomorrow was the last game of the season. Lucy and I were going to go together, but now it looked like I'd have an empty seat next to me. I considered not going to the game. I wasn't certain that I could make it through a whole game alone.

Unless… A disused memory bubbled into my consciousness. I picked up my phone and dialed.

"Hey, happy birthday. Listen, are you free tomorrow?"

EIGHTY-ONE

THE GAME WAS MEANINGLESS. While I was chasing my father's ghost, the Red Sox had been losing their grip and were out of the playoffs. The Blue Jays had been out of it since August. A bunch of kids from the minors struggled to play major league ball so the managers could evaluate them. The play was sloppy, the players were lazy, and the season was over. Yet Fenway Park was as loud as ever.

I stood in the aisle, a beer in each hand, waiting for the inning to end. The late September sun was cool and bright. The blue sky beyond the Green Monster provided a backdrop to the CITGO sign.

I remembered my dad griping about the burned-out neon bulbs on that sign. He hated the idea of a broken landmark. It made no sense to him. In his world, there was working and there was broken. He hated broken things. Today the neon has been replaced with LEDs and there are still burned-out lights. I wondered if they had been intentionally disabled for the sake of tradition.

The Red Sox pitcher, a new kid just up from Pawtucket, laid into the Blue Jays. The speculation was that he might be The One. He had the chunky, leg-heavy look of Roger Clemens, a nasty fastball, and a diving splitter. The future looked bright for him as he struck out the last Blue Jay batter of the inning and the crowd roared its approval. I excuse-me'ed my way down the row, careful not to spill my Sam Adams or the Bud Light.

I reached my seats. Sal took his Bud Light and said, "Thanks for calling me, little cousin. How'd you know it was my birthday?"

I said, "I remember from when I was little. My mother took me to every birthday party."

Sal said, "These are fucking great seats." A mother in the row in front of us turned, scowled, and pointed to her son. Sal said, "Sorry."

I said, "Glad you like the seats. My dad did at least one thing right."

Sal raised his plastic cup. "Here's to having you back in the city." We toasted and drank.

I said, "Next year we'll go to a Yankee game."

"Fu—Eff yeah!"

We watched the Sox rookies batting. The first kid grounded out. The second flew out.

I said, "Sal, I want to apologize for the other day."

Sal reached over and patted my back. "Forget about it. I'm sorry I hit you. Sometimes I lose my temper."

The third rookie struck out and the teams changed sides.

Sal drank his beer. "Hey, what are you doing Sunday?"

"Nothing. Why?"

"You want to come over for Sunday dinner? My ma will be there. She's been asking about you. Also, Maria says that she misses her first cousin once removed. That's you, right?"

"I'd love to see Auntie Rosa and Maria."

"You know, it's nothing fancy. We're just having spaghetti and meatballs."

"Sounds good."

"My wife's gravy is almost as good as Ma's. Don't tell Ma I said that. She'll get all pissed off."

"I'll be there."

The Sox played on in the September sun. Autumn was here. It would bring with it another cycle of winter and holidays. Thanksgiving was coming. Christmas would follow. Sal and I sat shoulder to shoulder, sipping our beers, watching the season end.

THE END

© Lynn Wayne

ABOUT THE AUTHOR

Ray Daniel is the award-winning author of Boston-based crime fiction. His short story "Give Me a Dollar" won a 2014 Derringer Award for short fiction, and "Driving Miss Rachel" was chosen as a 2013 distinguished short story by Otto Penzler, editor of *The Best American Mystery Stories 2013*.

Daniel's work has been published in the Level Best Books anthologies *Thin Ice*, *Blood Moon*, and *Stone Cold*. *Corrupted Memory* is his second novel, sequel to *Terminated*.

For more information, visit him online at raydanielmystery.com and follow him on Twitter @raydanielmystry.